# COLD FEET

# COLD FEET

## KAREN PULLEN

**FIVE STAR**
*A part of Gale, Cengage Learning*

GALE
CENGAGE Learning

Detroit • New York • San Francisco • New Haven, Conn • Waterville, Maine • London

**GALE**
CENGAGE Learning®

**LIBRARY OF CONGRESS CATALOGING-IN-PUBLICATION DATA**

Pullen, Karen.
  Cold feet : a Stella Lavender mystery / Karen Pullen. — 1st ed.
    p. cm.
  ISBN 978-1-4328-2637-6 (hardcover) — ISBN 1-4328-2637-9 (hardcover)
  1. North Carolina. State Bureau of Investigation—Fiction. 2. Drug enforcement agents—Fiction. 3. Murder—Investigation—Fiction. 4. Secrets—Fiction. 5. Mystery fiction. I. Title.
PS3616.U46C65 2013
813'.6—dc23                                              2012032741

First Edition. First Printing: January 2013
Find us on Facebook– https://www.facebook.com/FiveStarCengage
Visit our website– http://www.gale.cengage.com/fivestar/
Contact Five Star™ Publishing at FiveStar@cengage.com

Printed in Mexico
1 2 3 4 5 6 7 17 16 15 14 13

To my creative, loving, compassionate daughters
Adrienne, Heather, and Melissa

# ACKNOWLEDGMENTS

This first novel has a team behind it. On my team were Stonecoast faculty members who asked questions that made my writing better: Clint McCown, Elizabeth Searle, Suzanne Strempek Shea, Julia Spencer-Fleming, and James Patrick Kelley. Ellen Neuborne and my writing group—Sam Brooks, Mary Bastin, Joanna Catherine Scott, Laurie Billman—read drafts and offered helpful critiques. John Bason of the NC Department of Justice provided complete answers to a lengthy list of my questions. Shirley Burch, retired undercover drug agent for the NC State Bureau of Investigation, allowed me to use her experiences and kept me from egregious mistakes. (Shirley and John are not responsible for the liberties I have taken with SBI protocol and procedures.) Elizabeth Trupin-Pulli's belief in the book was invaluable. My weeks as a writer-in-residence at the Weymouth Center in Southern Pines provided a distraction-free and beautiful space for writing. My family gave love and support. Thank you all.

# CHAPTER 1

*A Saturday in October*

I sagged onto a rocker on my grandmother Fern's porch and fanned myself with an old issue of *Police* magazine. My head ached and my joints creaked. Fern was sixty-two and I was twenty-six but you'd think it was the other way around, thanks to my perpetual adrenaline hangover. I'd been working nights, buying drugs undercover for the government.

Today promised to be a welcome distraction. Fern and I were going to an outdoor wedding. I was looking forward to mingling with people who weren't in the market for coke, crack, smack, ice, pot, or pills. Employed people, who paid taxes that eventually ended up in my bank account for a too-brief stay. I'd even left my SIG-Sauer P225 at home. A shoulder holster would have spoiled the look of my floaty rose-print dress with a sweetheart neckline.

The screen door squeaked open. "Hello, darling," Fern said, planting a lavender-fragrant kiss on my cheek. Her sundress, watermelon-pink like her lipstick, clung to her curves like green on grass. Fern is sexy, charming, and young at heart. It's hard to believe we share DNA.

"You look dazzling. Is that silk?" I asked.

"Polyester. Wal-Mart was having a sale so I bought a couple yards. You cleaned up nicely yourself, Stella."

We buckled up and set off along the gravel lane that wound through towering loblolly pines slowly being strangled by kudzu.

My Civic's air conditioning struggled mightily against the sweltering heat of a summer that had refused to tilt her sails and float away gracefully.

"Thanks for coming with me. You might even enjoy yourself," Fern said. "I was going to take Ricky but you're just as much fun."

I didn't bother to ask who Ricky was. Fern knew so many men that I'd given up keeping track. "You're the one who hates weddings," I said. "I'm fine with them. Dress up, free food, open bar. What's not to like?"

"You know."

I did. Eight months ago I'd been planning my own wedding. Until one night, while searching online for the perfect invitation paper, I discovered Hogan's cyber-chat with a stupid-dot-com *slut*. I returned the ring to Hogan and my dress to the store. It was okay. I didn't adore the sleeves.

"Anyway, marriage is a terrible idea," said Fern. "The state doesn't belong in your relationship."

"So why are we going to this wedding?" I waited for a Coke truck to pass, then pulled onto the highway, heading east toward Verwood.

"I have to schmooze. The groom's mother is a new client. Tricia Scott—do you know her? She wants me to illustrate a book cover for her."

Aha. I understood perfectly. Fern never had much money. She'd raised me with mostly bare cupboards, an near-empty propane tank, and school clothes from the thrift shop. A client was precious, and attendance at invited events was mandatory.

As for me, I had mixed feelings about going along as Fern's escort. My inner princess was fascinated by over-the-top weddings such as this was sure to be, at a faux Scottish castle in the middle of a tobacco field. My inner cynic wanted to avoid all weddings for the rest of my life.

"Who's getting married?" I asked.

Fern opened the invitation. "Tricia's son Mike Olmert is marrying Justine Bradley. Tricia's remarried so his last name is different from his mother's. Serial marriages, new names and all that. Not an issue for us Lavender girls, is it?"

"None have dared to change our name," I said, merging with traffic in the circle around the courthouse and heading north. Outside town limits, the highway expanded to four lanes and we zoomed into a rural landscape dotted with rolls of hay. After a few miles, a castle rose from the landscape like an apparition.

Rosscairn Castle Bed and Breakfast was a 1915 millionaire's folly, a sized-down replica of Bonny Prince Charlie's summer home, with gray stone walls, turrets, and battlements. Fern and I were greeted by a stout red-faced man in full Highland garb— white shirt, black jacket, black bowtie, plaid kilt exposing hairy knees, and a small purse dangling from his waist. A dagger was tucked into one knee sock. He smelled, appropriately, like Scotch. I expected a Scottish burr and was looking forward to being called a wee lassie garrrl. But Wyatt Craven—the innkeeper, according to his name tag—was from Kentucky, he informed us. "Come along, I'll seat y'all. You're late but it hasn't started yet," he said.

We followed his large personage as he trotted briskly along a brick path to a sweep of green lawn where a white tent sheltered about fifty wedding guests and a trio sawing at their violins, filling the air with baroque counterpoint. Under a second tent, tables set with dark red linens and bowls of white roses encircled a gushing fountain.

I sat down next to a woman about my age wearing a cornflower blue dress and a round straw hat trimmed with black ribbon. She had long straight flaxen hair, like Alice in Wonderland, and looked utterly fetching in the hat. I felt a pang of jealousy—that hat on my mane would resemble a pot lid on a volcano. Ignoring me, she twisted in her seat and clicked away on a camera.

"Who do you know?" I whispered to Fern.

"First row, big brown hat? My client, Tricia Scott. She's a—what do you call it—life coach? She has a lot of business gigs." Tricia was thin and elegant, with a spray-hardened bundle of dark hair. Fern pointed to three tuxedoed men standing together in front, next to a man in the black robes of a minister. "Fellow in the middle is the groom, Mike Olmert, Tricia's son. Her husband is the minister. Scoop Scott."

All four men had similar serious expressions, as if they'd eaten something indigestible. Perhaps they were uncomfortable in their formal outfits, or impressed by the solemnity of the occasion, or hung over. Mike Olmert had thinning blond hair and the bulk that comes from hours of weight-lifting. One of the groomsmen wore a white cervical collar that immobilized his neck; he'd left his shirt and bow tie loosely open around it.

Above his black robes, Scoop's complexion was the deep red of high blood pressure and a wicked temper. He gnawed on an unlit cigar. My boss Richard smokes cigars, and my theory is it's to balance out his handsomeness and fashion-plate attire with something wet and stinky. However, Scoop wasn't handsome. Maybe he just liked wet stinky things in his mouth.

"Tricia said he has a cyber-church. You know, a website. That's where they sell her books, too." Fern pulled out the invitation. "This says one o'clock. They're running behind. It's one-thirty."

I turned to my neighbor in the straw hat. "Fashionably tardy, isn't it?" I asked.

"Never would be soon enough for me." Despite her smile, tension lined her face.

"Never? Are you going to speak up?"

"Hold my peace, I guess. It's too late, isn't it?" She seemed serious. She stood abruptly and snapped a picture of the four waiting men.

"I'm Stella Lavender." I held out my hand and she gripped it firmly.

"Gia Mabe. I'm an old family friend."

"Which family, his or hers?"

"Oh, his, of course. *She* has no friends."

A young woman, a bride, with no friends? Gia had to be exaggerating and I was about to ask her why when a young woman in a strapless red dress came flying off the Castle's back porch. She was rectangular all over, with a Christopher Robin haircut, boxy shoulders, and a flat chest. Even her dark-rimmed glasses had ninety-degree angles. She stopped at the last row, whispered to the innkeeper urgently, then tugged at him until he got up from his seat and followed her back into the inn.

"That's Ingrid, the maid of horror," Gia said.

Besides that curious comment, something felt wrong. The ceremony was more than thirty minutes late, and a distressed-looking bridesmaid had just dragged the innkeeper inside in a flurry.

"I'm going to find the ladies' room," I whispered to Fern.

"The wedding is about to start."

"I'll be right back." I nudged past her.

In the back hall of the Castle, slouched against a doorway to the kitchen, a teenaged boy in a stained apron smoked a cigarette and thumbed a phone. He wore earbuds and twitched to music only he could hear. Except for the scythe-wielding ghoul on his tee-shirt, he was a cuddly-looking fellow with brown curls and pink fuzzy cheeks.

"Excuse me," I said. He pulled out one earbud and raised an eyebrow, the one that wasn't sporting a silver stud. "Where did Wyatt go?"

He pointed up and went back to his texting. I walked through the hall and started up the stairs. Black Watch plaid carpet, inky green wallpaper, dark wood molding. Swords hung everywhere, some rusty, others shiny and ceremonial. The overall effect was formal, aggressive, and gloomy. Agitated voices came from a room at the end of the hall, the Falkirk room, according to the brass plaque on the door.

The door was unlatched, so I pushed it open and slipped inside.

# CHAPTER 2

*Saturday Early Afternoon*

"Dead" and "bride" don't belong in the same sentence, but this bride was dead.

She lay on the floor, impossibly contorted. Her head nearly touched her heels. Some lethal agent had drawn her head back, arched her spine, clamped her jaws shut, and pulled her facial muscles into a grin. Her skin was a mottled bluish-gray, a horrible contrast with her creamy satin dress and the pearl beads elaborately woven into her dark hair.

The bridesmaid Ingrid was crouched by the body, tugging on her shoulders, ineffectually trying to straighten her. Wyatt stood over them, hands on hips, his face beet-purple.

I took a deep breath. "Did you call an ambulance?" I knelt and felt the bride's neck for a pulse. Her skin felt clammy and her hazel eyes stared fixedly, sightless. I had no doubt that she was dead.

"Of course," said Wyatt. "Get out. We don't need gawkers." His imposing bulk moved toward me but I didn't budge.

"I'm police. State Bureau of Investigation." I pulled out my ID.

"SBI? It gets worse by the minute." His eyes were bloodshot and the smell of alcohol stronger than before.

"I'll try CPR," Ingrid said. Trembling, she leaned toward Justine's frothy grin to puff into her mouth.

15

I reached out to stop her. "No. You don't know what's caused this."

She pressed on the satin bodice. "I can't get her mouth to open. I can't straighten her out either. It's like she's frozen." Her voice rose in a near-shriek. "What should I do?"

I turned to Wyatt. "Go find the minister and tell him that Justine's ill. Keep everyone outside." Something in my tone, or perhaps it was the twisted body on the floor, convinced the innkeeper that he should do as I said, and he left.

"You found her like this?" I asked.

"Yes. I could hear her moaning but the door was locked. I had to get him to open it." Ingrid's eyes were magnified behind the harsh black frames of her glasses. Mascara mixed with tears ran down her cheeks.

"Come. Sit up here." I led Ingrid to a chair, away from the body. I thought about all the drugs I knew of—legal and il-legal—and couldn't recall any that would cause sustained muscle contractions like these. I pulled out my cell and dialed. The dispatcher said she'd send someone from the county sheriff's department. If Justine's death was a homicide, it would be their case to solve, because this property was in an unincor-porated area.

"You're a friend of hers?" I asked.

"Her best friend. I've known her since elementary school. We did our nurse's training together. We work together." She stared at the grotesque twisted body of her friend. "Can I cover her? She looks horrible."

"Sorry, no." I looked around. The room was a pleasant space with yellow-painted walls, a hand-carved cherry wood dresser, and a four-poster bed canopied with lace. Plaid curtains and pillows added a Scottish touch. On the bedside table was a glass half-full of water, and I leaned over to sniff it. It smelled like water.

The bathroom floor was strewn with damp towels. Jumbled on the counter were a half-eaten scone, hair gel, makeup, jewelry, an electric kettle, a small carton of soymilk. A nearly empty mug smelled chemical and bitter.

Ingrid came into the bathroom. "I need to wash my hands," she said. She had calmed down.

"No. Don't touch anything in here." I put my hand up to the kettle—it was warm. Next to it was an open box with Chinese writing containing teabags and the bitter smell again. "Phew."

"I know. It's some special cleansing tea," Ingrid said. "She drinks it all day long. She had some around noon when I was fixing her hair. Do you think it made her sick?"

"Well, did it? Did she complain after drinking it?"

Ingrid shook her head. "She didn't say anything. She seemed fine."

I shivered. On the surface I'd slipped into my professional self with a job to do. But some perversion had taken Justine's life, minutes before her marriage ceremony. She'd died in a cloud of J Lo and sweat. It didn't help that her eyes were wide open. It must have been an agonizing death.

The wail of a siren grew louder then abruptly stopped as the ambulance rolled along the Castle's long driveway. Two EMTs rushed into the room, and I went downstairs to find Justine's family. As I passed by the arched opening to the parlor, a young woman stopped me. She had pale blue eyes and aquiline features, softened by wispy blond hair and a trio of tiny black moles on one cheek. A dark-red strapless gown, a bridesmaid's dress like Ingrid's, showed off her strong neck and shoulders.

Bridesmaids are either family or a close friend. "I need to talk to you," I said, motioning her back into the parlor, trying to appear calm, though inside I ached for her, for what she didn't yet know. I showed her my ID.

"You're with the police? I'm Kate Olmert, Mike's sister."

17

Kate rolled her shoulders and flexed her fingers, as if preparing for a typing contest. "What's going on?"

"The ambulance is for Justine."

"Does Mike know? Is the wedding postponed? Oh, dear. I didn't mean that was important. But all those people . . ." She stood and turned around slowly several times, her billowing dress nearly knocking a couple of stuffed Scotties off the table. "I'll talk to Mike and my parents. They'll decide what to do." She paused. "What's the matter with Justine? Tell me what's going on."

I shook my head, unable to think of any euphemism that would soften the truth. "Are her parents here?"

"No." She grabbed my arm with a hand like a vise. "Is it bad?"

"It's bad." I gently unpeeled her grip. "I think she's dead."

The color drained from her face and the three tiny moles looked like ink dots. "What happened?"

"I don't know. Would you go and help the innkeeper guard the back door? No one is to enter this building."

Kate danced on her toes for a bit, then went into the hall to the back door, pushing past Wyatt and raising her arm to get the guests' attention.

Someone rapped on the front door and I opened it to a man in slacks and sports coat carrying a notebook. A detective. I automatically sized him up—mid-forties, six feet, a fat-free one-sixty pounds. He wore wire-rim glasses and his hair was cut short, peppered with a premature gray.

"Lieutenant Anselmo Morales," he said, with a hint of an Hispanic accent. I identified myself and told him briefly what to expect upstairs in Justine's bedroom. I offered to help.

"We'll talk later." He started up the stairs.

I decided to check on the crowd control. I had almost reached the back door when it flew open and Mike Olmert barreled

18

through. For an instant I thought to stop and warn him, but he was too wild, pushing past me and charging up the stairs only a minute behind Morales.

In back of the inn, bedlam reigned as the guests milled about, buzzing with speculation. The musicians continued to play seventeenth-century dance tunes but the chatter nearly drowned them out. Wyatt and Kate stood guard at the door. "Did you make an announcement?" I asked.

"I told them Justine was ill and there'd be no ceremony," Kate said. "My stepdad told the waiters to start serving champagne. They're going to put the food out too."

Sweat beaded on Wyatt's flushed face. "Wait till the papers get this. I'll be ruined. Ruined!"

I pushed past him into the crowd, looking for familiar faces. I wasn't a bit surprised to see Fern talking with a new man who seemed entranced by her smile. She accumulates them like some people collect state quarters. Despite a vicious scar running from hairline to chin, partly covered by a patch over his left eye, he was handsome in a tough-guy way, olive skinned with a spare build. I whispered in her ear that she should take my car, that I'd get a ride since I'd be very late, and handed her my car key.

Then, to my utter shock, I saw Hogan Leith, my ex-fiancé, looking equally surprised at the sight of me. Until eight months ago, I'd lived with Hogan. For four years, I scrambled his eggs. Cheered on his softball team. Washed his boxers with my briefs. Until the evening I found him having cyber-sex with a teenager. Okay, she was twenty, but still. He loved her, he said, so I packed up and moved out. Seeing Hogan usually stirred up unwelcome feelings of anger, humiliation, and loneliness, a big problem since I had to work with him. He was an SBI researcher, and such a good one that I couldn't dismiss him entirely from my life. But it took all my self-control to act professional around him. Sometimes I had to let a little something out. I crooked my finger and beckoned him to me.

"What are you doing here?" I asked, keeping my voice low.

"Mike's a fraternity brother, a good friend." He grinned. "You look amazing, by the way."

I might have known they were both Pi Kappa Alpha. Hogan's entire social circle is comprised of Pikes from NC State. "There's a dead woman upstairs, the Falkirk room," I said. "Can you help with perimeter control?"

His grin faded. "Someone died? Who?" He took hold of my arm and leaned close. I felt a brief stab of confusion as his familiar smell and the feel of his hand on my arm mixed with irritation and sorrow, and no, I still wasn't over Hogan.

"Justine Bradley. The bride. She's dead. I don't know what happened but you could be useful right now."

The back door opened and Mike Olmert came outside, pushing his way past Wyatt and Kate to face the crowd of guests. He'd taken off his tuxedo jacket and bowtie, and rolled up his shirt sleeves to expose gym-hardened forearms. His face looked carved from ice. "Folks, I have terrible news." He bowed his head and ran his hands through his hair, and the crowd grew quiet, waiting. He took a deep breath, then, his voice low, said, "Justine is dead." He covered his face with his hands. Kate wrapped her arm around her brother's thick shoulders and pulled him to her.

Only a few people heard him. Murmurs grew—*What? What did he say? She's dead? Justine is dead? What happened?* Shocked, unbelieving looks spread through the crowd as they shifted gears from a tardy bride to a dead one. A buzz of chatter surrounded Mike as people lined up to express sympathy.

In the food tent, wait-staff had spread long banquet tables with a lavish buffet. It looked like the party would go on, though it was more like a wake at this point. My stomach growled and as I thought about food, I realized the obvious—Justine had probably been poisoned. Should people be eating here?

I corralled the caterer, a sprightly woman wearing a chef's coat. "No one has tasted the food yet," she said. "It didn't come from the inn, it's been in my van until a half-hour ago."

"Do you know the bride? You sure she didn't sample something?"

"Of course I know her but I haven't seen her in a week. My food is amazing, the best. Here, have a plate and see for yourself." Unfortunately I now felt officially on duty, more than a wedding guest, so I couldn't very well pick up a plate and load it from the seafood station, an ice sculpture filled with shrimp, crab claws, and oysters. Or sample the canapés. Or taste-test the spring rolls and beef medallions. I reluctantly passed, but allowed her wait-staff to begin serving guests.

Anselmo Morales was responsible for solving this murder, if indeed it was murder, and I hoped he'd resolve it as soon as possible, in days. Surely not months, nor years, if ever. I felt a chill, reminded of my mother's disappearance long ago— eventually a presumed homicide, never solved. A cold case. Grace Lavender was only twenty-three when she vanished. She'd gone into a gas station to pay, leaving me in the car, and apparently interrupted a robbery. A college student tending the cash register was murdered, my mother Grace presumably abducted. The cops found me clutching my Talking Beans doll, scared by the flashing lights of the ambulance and the crowd of uniforms. A gentle young policewoman took me under her wing and bought me a soft-serve ice cream cone and a teddy bear with a red hat.

The bear is still around, in Fern's attic—it pops up in her paintings now and then.

Four years ago, right after joining the SBI, I scrolled through the dusty microfiche of my mother's case file to see what I could learn. But there had been no witnesses to the robbery or shooting; the only physical evidence, two spent thirty-eight bullets and casings. Barring a deathbed confession or the gun popping up in another crime, the case was as cold as Antarctica in July.

A familiar tension crawled up my spine to my neck, then down my arms. I dug my nails into my hands.

"Call me Anselmo," he said. His voice was gravelly and gentle. "She didn't die of natural causes."

"Whatever it was, it developed quickly," I said. "According to the bridesmaid, she was fine at noon, calling out just after one, and dead a few minutes later."

Anselmo surveyed the wedding guests wandering into the food tent, carrying champagne flutes. "We won't know for certain for at least a couple of days," he said. "Meanwhile, I've sealed off the entire inn until the evidence team is finished. I could use assistance with today's interviews. I want to start with the innkeeper. I also want the identity of everyone else on the premises."

"There's an SBI researcher here. He'll be glad to help, I'm sure." I pointed to Hogan, still guarding the back door. Screening was the ideal job for him, a perfectionist with neat handwriting and a compulsion for detail.

He studied Hogan, seeming to size up his lean physique and plentiful brown hair. "Your date?"

I shook my head. "No, he's a friend of the groom," but my face warmed. I turned away before my blush was obvious. "I'll get us a room to work in."

Anselmo picked up a knife and clanged it against a wineglass. I cringed—didn't he know that was the traditional signal for the bride and groom to kiss? But it got the crowd's attention, and they hushed and turned to listen with expressions of alarm, curiosity, and sympathy. They'd been told there was to be no ceremony, and why.

Now they'd be told that one of them may have committed murder.

# CHAPTER 3

*Saturday Mid-Afternoon*

Afternoon light poured through arched windows into the cavernous dining room, bounced off the chandelier crystals, then vanished into muddy green walls. Fraying tapestries captured scenes of medieval mayhem—kilt-clad warriors clubbing each other, a pack of greyhounds chasing a rabbit. Dreary, brutal, and dim. No wonder they invented Scotch.

"I'm done for. Finished." Wyatt Craven's eyes were closed, his lashes damp, his expression twisted as he bubbled those tearful words of defeat. He had gargled mouthwash recently and smelled like a mint julep. "Suspicious death at my inn. The cancellations will pour in. They've been trying for months to shut me down and now they've succeeded." He sat back abruptly and wiped his nose. "But I'll rise again! Like a phoenix from the ashes!" He raised a dented pewter tankard like a salute and took a large slurp.

"You think this death is an attempt to close you down?" Anselmo sounded astonished.

"The final straw."

Hardly a straw, I thought. Not that I was buying his hypothesis, but if there was an ongoing conflict with this innkeeper, perhaps it had gotten out of hand.

"It's war, and it's being going on for months. My business is being sabotaged right into the ground. First the health department inspector shows up—without warning—on the same day

24

someone's put ammonia in the water softener. Not a co-incidence! And last month it's a hundred degrees and the air conditioner dies. We find maple syrup in the compressor. I lose a dozen bookings. They want me to quit! To give up my dream!"

"Who does?" Anselmo asked.

"Don't know. Maybe you can find out?" He looked at us with hopeful bleary eyes.

"It's not our first priority today, Mr. Craven. Tell us who stayed at the inn last night."

"You're missing the point. It wasn't a guest, I know it!" He lurched into his office, a small space that also functioned as a coat closet, clicked on his keyboard a few times, and pulled a sheet of paper from the printer. He slid it across the table. "Last night's occupancy chart. Dates down the left, room names across the top, guest names filled in."

The inn had been full, all five rooms occupied. I recognized the names of the occupants of two of the rooms—Justine in the Falkirk room and in the Balliol room, Tricia and Scoop Scott, Mike's mother and her minister husband.

"The Canmore room. Webster and Delia Scott. Any relation?" I asked.

"He's Scoop Scott's brother." Wyatt pointed to the names Evan and Lottie Ember in the Stirling room. "This couple have a child, a little girl in a wheelchair. Sad." He took a sip out of his tankard and I caught a whiff of coffee and the alcohol he'd spiked it with. The drink also smelled like hazelnuts, very pleasant all together. "Gregor McMahon is in Dunkeld, by himself. The best man, I think. All wedding guests. They'll all be here tonight, too. That is, if you ever let them back in."

Not so, I thought. Tonight, one room will be empty.

"Give us whatever you have on these guests—phone numbers, addresses," Anselmo said.

Wyatt sighed, then went back to his computer and tap-tapped

for a minute. The printer spit out more paper.

Anselmo put the pages in his notebook. "Tell me about your staff."

Wyatt's chuckle turned into choking laughter. "That's funny. Staff."

"I saw a boy by the kitchen door. Looked like he worked here," I said.

"That's Blue Stone. He does odd jobs, whatever I need. And Liesle comes in every morning to help with breakfast and cleaning."

I thought about the timing. If Ingrid's account was to be believed, just after noon she'd helped Justine with her hair and veil, leaving her dressed for her wedding. An hour later, Ingrid heard Justine's dying moans. In that hour did someone enter Justine's room and administer a lethal substance? Or was it planted earlier in the morning, or even days before? The time window was crucial. "Did everyone show up for breakfast?" I asked.

"Breakfast was at nine, and no, they didn't all show up. The groom's parents slept in. So did Delia Scott. I think she gets her nutrition somewhere else." He raised his tankard and grinned. "Scotch nut coffee. Want some?"

"No, thanks," Anselmo and I said together.

Deep green velvet curtains, frosted with dust, swathed the tall dining room windows. Past them I could see the tented dining area where Hogan was interviewing the wedding guests. They waited in clumps, seated at the tables. The men had removed their jackets; some of the women were barefoot.

I imagined the goings-on after breakfast. People taking showers, shaving, talking, listening to the news, going up and down the stairs to fetch things from their cars. Lots of traffic, in and out of rooms. "Are all five bedrooms upstairs?" I asked.

"Stirling and Dunkeld are downstairs, off the parlor. Gregor

McMahon and the Embers were in those rooms."

"The best man, and the couple with a child in a wheelchair," I said. "And the guests upstairs were Justine; Mike's mother and her husband; Mike's step-uncle and his wife."

"Sounds right. You're good!" Wyatt took another generous sip of his nut coffee.

It's not that hard if you're sober, I thought. So Mike's sister Kate and the bridesmaid Ingrid had not been staying at the B&B. And none of these people were Justine's family or friends. Kate had told me that Justine had no parents. So far, no siblings or other relatives had identified themselves.

"Find these people for me, please," Anselmo said, handing Wyatt the list of inn guests. "And file a report with the sheriff about those sabotage allegations."

"Yeah, yeah." He pushed himself up from the table and left the room.

"Knees that hairy should be covered up," Anselmo said.

"Who's first?" I asked.

"In a murder, always start with the one called sweetheart," he said.

"Did you see her?" Mike Olmert spat out the question. He'd taken off his tuxedo jacket and bow tie. His face was blotchy and knotted in a grimace. "It's a horror show. What would do that? Do you know? You better tell me if you know anything."

Was he bluffing? Mike could know more than we did. Though, to poison your girlfriend just before the ceremony? Surely it's easier to stay home, or hop on a plane, or go to a football game. She would get the message.

"We'll know in a couple of days," Anselmo said. "Right now it's a suspicious death."

"So what do you want from me?" Olmert rotated his white-knuckled fists in a jerky motion. It must be some sort of family tic, this business of odd gestures.

"Just background, Mr. Olmert. Start with where and when you two met."

Mike took a deep breath and blew it out. "I met Justine about a year ago, at a party at my sister's house. She was a gentle soul—an angel—and we hit it off right away. I thought we had a wonderful life ahead of us." He wiped his eyes and I handed him a tissue. His grief seemed genuine but that meant little. Grief takes many forms, ranging from catatonic silence to hair-tearing and wailing. Just like guilt.

"When did you see her last?" Anselmo asked.

"Last night. We had a small dinner here. I said good-night to her around eleven. She seemed fine, excited about today." He took another shaky breath. "This morning I talked with her twice. She called me around ten, to make sure I was up." He croaked out a chuckle. "Firefighters are on twenty-four-hour shifts. So I'm good at sleeping, and she knew I could oversleep."

"And the second time?"

"I called her about twelve-forty because my mother was look-ing for her corsage. I remember being nervous, thinking it was about to start. Not because I was getting married, just nervous that everything would go right, that Justine would be happy."

So Justine was alive and well at twelve-forty. Was Mike reli-able? So far he didn't seem to be hiding anything. But we didn't know what we were looking for, yet.

"I wasn't the last person to talk to her," Mike said. "Someone knocked on her door while we were talking. I don't know who it was. Once she was sure I knew how to find the flowers, she hung up."

Was "someone" the last person to see her alive? "Did she have problems with anyone recently?" I asked.

"Everyone liked her. Except Gia Mabe. Gia and I were engaged once. When I broke it off, she took it hard."

"But you asked Gia to your wedding." I remembered the young woman in the straw hat in the seat next to mine. That she was once engaged to Mike explained her snarky comments.

Mike shook his head. "She wasn't invited. But I wasn't surprised that she crashed it. She still pesters me, I guess you'd say. Calls me, follows me around, writes emails. I wish she'd stop."

"How far would she take that?" Anselmo asked. "Any incidents or threats?"

Mike frowned. "When Justine and I were first dating, Gia got a little crazy. She followed us to Justine's apartment and tried to break in. I stopped her, and after that she left Justine alone, far as I know." He paused and looked away. "I have a request. Find the person who did this. Then step aside." He smacked his thick fist into his other hand.

Anselmo and I shared a glance. His eyes were flecked with green, not as black as I'd first thought. "That's all we need right now. If you think of anything?" He handed Mike his business card.

Mike left through the French doors that led onto the patio and sank onto a chair. His mother leaned down to him, her hand on his shoulder, her big brown hat hiding their faces.

I turned back to Anselmo. "Was he telling the truth?"

"A good actor, if he wasn't."

There were seven inn guests still to question. Anselmo told the Embers—the couple with the little girl in a wheelchair—that they could leave, and they'd be interviewed another time. Tricia and Scoop Scott, Mike's mother and her husband, were also allowed to depart as they had to prepare for a conference in Colorado where Tricia was speaking. They agreed to be accessible by phone, and to be interviewed as soon as they returned on Thursday.

The evidence team wanted time with Anselmo, so I left them

and sat down in the parlor to talk with Mike's step-uncle and his wife. Webster and Delia Scott came into the parlor, Delia all a-wobble, glass in hand, Webster gripping her upper arm firmly. They fell back onto a black and blue plaid loveseat.

Web Scott was about six feet tall, like his brother Scoop, but better looking. For one thing, Web had no hair, which sounds like a negative until you saw Scoop's comb-over. Web's head appeared to be shaved, and he wore a high-maintenance goatee, a precision stripe of beard that outlined his chin. Delia had the physical symptoms of a lush—a pretty face spoiled by puffiness and dry reddish skin, swollen liver pushing out above her waistline, a tic-like pursing of her lips.

I asked Delia how well she knew the bride. She leaned close and grabbed my arm. "Well enough, my dear." Her breath was richly foul. She leaned further and I held her up. "Did you know, I nearly killed her once?"

Before I could ask how, when, and why, Webster eased her back into the sofa. "Please excuse Delia, she overdoes it a little now and then," he said, showing me a mouth full of big shiny white teeth. "How do you do, I'm Webster Scott, the groom's uncle. I hear you're a famous investigator." He took my outstretched hand in both of his and leaned so close I could smell him. He smelled like gin.

I twisted free of his grasp and flashed my ID at him. "Not famous. Actually I'm an SBI Agent, out of the Raleigh Field Office."

"Any openings for financial officers?" He laughed as if he were joking.

"We're unemployed," said Delia. She upended her glass and drained it, then shook it, tinkling the ice cubes. "Booted out. Golden parachute and all that." Webster gave his wife a look but she wasn't noticing. She went on, "We live in Southport now. S'okay, we play a lot of golf."

"And we love it there, Agent Lavender," Webster said, absorbed in a study of my sweetheart neckline.

Not to be dragged off-topic, I asked, "Mrs. Scott, you said you nearly killed her once?"

"A bad moment," Delia said. "Never mind me." She met my gaze with bleary eyes. She shook her head in a conspiratorial way. Web continued to shine his teeth at me in a way that must have made his face hurt. I had the impression Delia would prefer to speak to me privately.

I asked them to tell me about Mike and Justine's relationship.

Webster's smile dimmed by a few lumens. "That boy was sure smitten! You couldn't get him off her with a crowbar. He was obsessed. She had this little purry whisper . . ." He shook his head, seeming to express sadness at the loss of her purr.

Delia slowly leaned back and turned her head to look at her husband. " 'Bewitching' is the word you used, darlin'." She put her glass down and nodded. "S'empty."

The ball was in Webster's court. His smile vanished. "Charming young lady. Such a tragedy. What else can we help you with?"

Hmmm. I couldn't wait to get Delia alone. Maybe I could buy her a drink, soon. I dismissed them, and asked Wyatt to bring me the best man, Gregor McMahon.

Gregor McMahon was furry. He had thick black hair, a mustache, and a mat of hair covering his hands. Eyebrows crawled like caterpillars across his brow, tufts sprouted from his ears, and a few stray wisps grew on the bridge of his nose. He wore a thick white cervical collar, yet still his head was tilted, his shoulders rigid.

Gregor McMahon, unlike Webster Scott, made no effort to be charming. He was stern and officious, reminding me of my eleventh-grade chemistry teacher. In a blink I was smelling chalk dust. On a hunch, I asked, "Are you a teacher, Mr. Mc-Mahon?"

He nodded by jerking his torso up and down. "I teach part-time at Gardner University," he said. "I'm an economic analyst."

"What does an economic analyst do?" I knew the words but not the meaning. To me, "economic analysis" meant figuring how much I could afford to pay each month on my credit card bill. Never enough, on a state salary.

He pursed his lips and frowned at me as if assessing my intelligence. A tsunami of high school déjà vu swept over me. "Cost benefit, risk analysis, decision support," he said. "Aren't we here to talk about Justine?"

"How long have you known her?"

"I met her only once, six months ago, on the worst day of my life." His face grew somber and he closed his eyes. "The day my wife died."

His wife died on the day he met Justine? A coincidence? I don't believe in them. Though it was nearly six o'clock, and I was famished, I leaned back. I had plenty of time to hear about his dead wife.

"It was a fraternity alum get-together at Lake Crabtree. Emma didn't really want to go. She had severe allergies and needed to avoid bug bites and even too much sun. Well, to make it short, something—an insect bite or sting—triggered a deadly attack. Her throat closed up and she suffocated within minutes." He sounded matter-of-fact but his face was blotchy-red and his hands gripped the chair arms so hard his fingers were white. "It was my fault."

"Your fault?"

"She always carried epinephrine in the car. But the car was locked and I couldn't find my keys. I should have broken into the car faster but I didn't know she was so ill. The reaction was so severe, so quick."

Gregor's face was stony, his voice strangled and flat. I almost forgave him for his fur and arrogance. This man was hurting, now and forever.

"I never met Justine again, until last night. Mike tried to get us together but I haven't been very social since Emma died. What actually happened to Justine, do you know?" He raised his woolly eyebrows. "You're a cop, right? You wouldn't be talking to me if she died of natural causes."

"I don't know. The medical examiner will have to tell us."

"Do you have a suspect? Be sure you look at Mike's stepdad." Gregor didn't even smile. "He wants you to think he's so righteous."

My turn to raise eyebrows.

He shrugged. "Hearsay. I'm just saying . . . I know how you people work. It's a suggestion. You can follow up."

I wanted to snarl back at him, "you people?" I wrote down his contact information and let him go. In spite of the sympathy I felt, the pompous man grated on me. He was wound tighter than a Slinky. He harbored secrets, I'd bet my dog on it.

By eight o'clock, the evidence team and most of the guests were gone. A few diehards remained under the dining tent, prolonging the drama. Kate urged us to eat, so Anselmo, Hogan, and I each put together a plate of leftovers from the buffet. Hogan's was piled with salad, Anselmo's with beef and pasta. I had a bit of everything. Carefully I carried my heaping plate to the inn's dining room where the three of us were going to meet.

"Hungry, Stella?" Hogan said. He was an obsessively cautious eater, a food-label reader, a fat-gram counter. I, on the other hand, considered dieting only when I couldn't zip my jeans. Since I dumped him (as I prefer to think of our breakup) he hadn't been cooking for me anymore, and yes, I'd put on a few pounds. Nothing you would notice unless you saw me trying to zip up.

I dipped half a spring roll into a sweet-and-sour sauce. As we munched in silence, I thought about Anselmo's investigation. As soon as the toxicologist and medical examiner gave him something to work with, he could start. Until then, we could only surmise. Between bites, I asked, "Why kill a bride just before the wedding?"

"An ex-boyfriend," said Anselmo.

"Or girlfriend," I said, thinking of Gia in the straw hat.

"But someone else might want to stop it," said Hogan. "A family member."

"There would be plenty of time to do that, long before the wedding day," Anselmo said.

I tore a piece of rosemary focaccia and dipped it into olive oil. "Unless the killer didn't have an opportunity. Maybe he or she was from out of town."

"Or," said Anselmo, "something happened at the last minute."

"What could that be?" I said. "No one's mentioned anything unusual. Family dinner last night, this morning everyone's getting ready."

"Something from her past, maybe," Hogan said. He'd finished every scrap of salad and eyed my two remaining spring rolls. I forked one onto his plate. "Thanks," he said. "What about the inn staff? They'd have opportunity."

"The innkeeper Wyatt was worried about sabotage," I said. "He said this death was an attempt to close him down."

"It could have been an accident," said Anselmo. "Perhaps she was not the intended victim. We'll know more in a day or two."

I thought about the bitter-smelling tea in Justine's mug. And the timing—right before the ceremony—seemed choreographed for maximum effect. But Anselmo was right, we didn't know enough.

Hogan looked at his list. "So what's next? Background? Work?

Old boyfriends?"

Anselmo looked at me. "I don't know. We can't say for sure it's a homicide until we get the ME's report. Probably Monday."

"Any useful evidence?" I asked.

He shook his head. "They took a lot of fingerprints from her room. Stella, are you available? We'll have to talk to quite a few people."

I chased a bit of basilly pasta around my plate. "You'll have to ask my boss. I'm a drug agent these days." My requests to work homicides had been turned down by Ricardo. His reason—I was too valuable to undercover drug operations around the state. But I wanted to help Anselmo, wanted to be in on it. If Justine had been murdered, the killer was probably someone who'd come to the Castle B&B for her wedding. A finite pool of suspects, each with secret fears, secret desires, somehow tied to the dead bride or her grieving groom. It wouldn't be easy to identify the killer in that well-dressed, well-lawyered pool, but people talked. The tipsy Delia Scott and Mike Olmert's ex-girlfriend, Gia Mabe—they would be at the top of my list.

I waited while Hogan removed and carefully folded his Porsche's cover. He rolled down the gravel driveway slowly, so no stray pebble would ding its shiny red paint. When he pulled onto the highway, he was at seventy in a minute. "Mind if I hurry?" he said. "Got plans."

No doubt he had a date with what's-her-name and had to get rid of me quickly. A throbbing began behind my eyes and I pressed my lips together so no swear words would slip out. "Where is Candy, anyway?"

"She didn't want to come. She doesn't like to eat in front of other people."

Weird. "You could've skipped the dinner."

"She's afraid of having her picture taken, and lots of people at weddings carry cameras."

Oh wow. Candy was a quivering neurotic mess. Oddly, I felt a little better as I mentally took a step away from Hogan and his new gal. "Tell me about Mike Olmert."

"He's a Canes fan. An outdoors type—likes hiking, mountain climbing."

Hogan wasn't the most perceptive of men but I tried anyway. "Is he controlling? Is he critical or romantic or private? Can you trust him with a secret?"

"Whoa, Stella. One at a time. He's not controlling. The opposite. He's good at calming down a situation. Critical? Sometimes, in a subtle way. He's very principled, did he tell you? He usually mentions it. He has high standards and most people disappoint him. What else?"

"Do you know Gia Mabe? She sat next to me while we were waiting for the wedding to begin."

"Yeah. She's a little—" he pointed at his head and twirled his finger.

"How so?"

"She and Mike dated for a year. They were always together, then he broke it off. She was too needy or something. I don't really remember. Anyway, she just harassed the hell out of him for a while. It's odd she was at the wedding." He slipped the Porsche around a slow-moving truck loaded with pine tree trunks, casualties of the latest McMansion building spree, and we flew down the highway into Verwood.

I remembered what I had to ask Hogan. "Gregor McMahon was telling me about the day his wife died. Were you there? A picnic at Lake Crabtree, six months ago?"

"It was a nightmare. An insect sting, they thought. She went into shock so quickly."

"And Justine, you met her too?"

36

"For the first time. Did he tell you Mike proposed to Justine that day? They went for a canoe ride and she came back with this huge rock on her hand. They were both over the top, until Emma died. Man, a day like that you can't forget. Horrible day to get engaged."

"What was Justine like?" I wanted to replace the image of a convulsed corpse with something more human.

He grinned. "Hot. Too gorgeous to be real. Like a super-model."

I was taken aback. "Really?"

"Candy told me Justine was pretty fake. She'd had implants and fake nails and hair extensions. I guess women can spot that kind of thing. Me, I just thought 'Wow.' All the guys thought Mike was lucky."

So. Justine was so fake that even Candy, Hogan's uber-slut, recognized it, but he just didn't care. This exchange did little to enhance my opinion of Hogan, so easily swayed by silicone and batting eyelashes.

He stopped his Porsche in front of my house. "Can I come in, say hello to the pup?" He wanted to visit Merle, a yellow hound of the mutt breed, subject of a bitter custody dispute. Hogan had finally settled for the forty-two-inch plasma-screen TV and the promise of visitation.

"Sure," I said. "Just don't take him with you. I need something warm at night."

My neighbor Saffron looked up from her weeding and waved at the two of us. I waved back and scooted inside before she could trap me for another weepy episode of her divorce saga. Merle greeted us at the front door, tail a-wagging, whimpering ecstatically at the sight of Hogan.

I slipped my shoes off and went in my bedroom to change into running clothes. I had stripped to my underpants and was searching for a sports bra when my bedroom door opened and I heard Hogan say, "I've missed this view." I turned around to see him leaning in the doorway watching me.

"You should knock." I pulled on a tee-shirt. "What, Candy doesn't have tits?"

"She's, uh, more athletic."

"You get to choose. Curves or muscles. Fat or flat."

"You're not fat, Stella."

"I thought you had plans?" I was confused and more than a little angry. He should have known I was hurting. Did he want me back? Did I want him back? Did I want to dig around in his email trash and obsess over his Internet history?

"I'll cancel them if you say so."

He stepped toward me and slipped a hand under my tee-shirt, gently touching the small of my back. The heat of his hand started a meltdown. He kissed me and, surprised, I let him. When I came up for air, I removed his hands from my waist and looked into his eyes. "What's this about?"

"The way you looked in that dress, Stella. I couldn't help it. I've missed our chemistry."

"How sweet. But you're a serial cheater, remember? Next time, ask permission."

"Let's be polite for Merle's sake. He shouldn't see us fighting."

I pushed him to the door. "Don't call me," I said. "I don't want to hear from you tomorrow."

"I'll call if I feel like it." He got into the Porsche.

I picked up Merle's paw and waved it. "Say good-bye to Daddy." Merle whimpered. The Porsche began a rumbly purr, carrying Hogan back to his life with Candy.

Well, that was interesting. He'd stirred up some feelings, surely, but the ripples would die down eventually. Better a placid serenity than the whirlpool he'd created when he left. I didn't want to go through that again.

I knelt and let Merle slobber my face. "You're much better than any old boyfriend," I told him. "Trainable. Not afraid of commitment. Wanna go for a run?"

I loved my tiny house, a rented refuge where the neighbors were law-abiding. I wished I could afford to buy it but real estate values in Verwood had crept above the buying power of a state employee's paycheck. The rooms were cozy—or cramped, depending on your point of view—and furnished with thrift-shop finds covered with sheets so Merle could sleep anywhere he wanted to. Fern's paintings enlivened the sterile white walls. She painted what she loved—cows grazing, ducks on a pond, the roses climbing her front porch. Her paintings compensated for the dust bunny conclaves. There wasn't much point in cleaning for myself, when myself was never there.

Not bothering to stretch, I grabbed my headphones and jogged a half-mile to the high school track. I huffed and I puffed, Merle ran circles around me, and we called it done after eight revolutions, ten songs starting with Hootie and the Blowfish and ending with Squirrel Nut Zippers.

Walking home, I took off the headphones and thought about the next few days. Either tomorrow or Monday, the coroner would autopsy Justine's body and take samples from blood, urine, stomach, brain, liver, kidney, hair. The toxicologists would fire up their machines, prepare their solutions, add and subtract, dunk and extract. And give Anselmo Morales an answer. If he wanted my help, he'd call the SBI on Tuesday, perhaps. I'd have to wait two days, maybe three.

I wiped the sweat off my face and filled Merle's water bowl. It was Saturday night, ten o'clock, party time. I added seltzer to a half-glass of wine, drank it, poured another, and stuck *The Big Sleep* in the DVD player. Perhaps the wine, Bogie and Bacall, an incomprehensible plot, and some racy talk about horses would erase the image that kept floating into my consciousness, the image of a twisted corpse in a beaded satin wedding gown.

# CHAPTER 4

*Sunday Late Morning*

"You'd think at my age I wouldn't *feel* so much," Fern muttered as she forked hay into the donkey pen. Hillary and Bill, her inseparable jack and jenny, gently nosed her with their white muzzles. She rubbed their foreheads, their coarse hair. She didn't want to work, couldn't stand to look at the half-done painting on her easel, a field of tulips, all yellow except for one stray red one. So blurry and boring she couldn't face it.

"It's the death of that girl," Fern whispered into Bill's white ear. "Same age as Grace was, you know." She steeled herself for the familiar wash of grief that still, after twenty-two years, dragged her under an ugly gray quilt of sadness. "Can't you guys help me think about something else?" Busywork would lift her mind, or at least tire her out. She should take the screens down and put up the storm windows. She should wash the rocking chairs, still coated with summer's drab yellow pollen. She could bake—Ricky had asked her over for dinner tomorrow and he loved her bread. The appeal of should and could was weak, though, and when she saw her answering machine blinking she felt grateful for the distraction. She pushed "play."

The first message was from Tricia Scott.

A week earlier, Fern had met Tricia at the art gallery where Fern showed her paintings. They'd hit it off despite their surface differences: Fern, an impoverished feminist, and Tricia the well-off evangelist. But Fern recognized a spark in Tricia, a certain

41

twinkle that said appearances weren't everything and she didn't take herself too seriously. Furthermore, Fern didn't judge people based on their bank account. She bartered paintings for dental services, sewed her own clothes, and charmed her many men friends into performing maintenance and repairs, a recurring need at her hundred-year-old farmhouse, a tin-roofed frame building with knob-and-tube wiring and antique plumbing. When Stella had once suggested Fern might sell her farmhouse and sixty acres right on a state highway, in order to create a nest egg so she could move into a cute little apartment in town, Fern had told her, "I have all I want. Poor is wanting more than you have." Then she'd turned away so she wouldn't have to watch Stella roll her eyes.

But Fern wasn't immune to the lure of cash. The point of her gallery show had been to sell her work, attract new students, and contract for commissions. Meeting Tricia Scott had been the frosting on the gallery sales cake. Tricia looked affluent. Though her dyed-black helmet hair was dreadful, she was dressed like no one Fern knew could ever dress, in a lime-green silk suit with a thick silver coil necklace. Tricia bought a painting of a sunset casting a farmhouse shadow across a field of mown hay, declaring that it reminded her of her grandmother's house. She asked if Fern ever painted people, and Fern showed her photographs of portraits she'd worked on. And on the spot, Tricia had commissioned her to illustrate the cover of her new book. "It's one of those books for executives. In this case, Christian executives."

Fern had wondered, but did not ask, what the difference was between a Christian executive and any other executive. Perhaps the book would spell that out. "I'd be delighted and honored to illustrate the cover. I'd need to read the book."

"My son's getting married on Saturday, and your farmhouse painting will be my gift. Can you come, bring a guest? One o'clock, Rosscairn Castle B&B. I'll see you there and give you a copy of my book." Then Tricia had dashed out of the gallery and into a blazing red convertible driven by a man with an unfortunate comb-over. Their shellacked hair was wrong for a convertible, Fern mused.

Yesterday she had gone to the wedding with Stella, and it ended so hideously that she couldn't approach Tricia about the book or the commission. But in her message today Tricia's voice sounded calm and controlled, explaining she was going out of town for a few days and wanted to make sure Fern had a copy of the book. She'd stop by soon.

The second message was from Jax Covas, the delightful one-eyed man she'd met yesterday. "Buenos días señorita! Do you remember me, the pirate from Guatemala? And chicken-coop builder? I am coming this afternoon to measure. Ciao!" Fern laughed softly. Jax would cheer her up, and planning the chicken coop would be fun.

Message three was from Stella, saying she'd be over later and would make dinner for them both. Fern's heart beat a little faster with a burst of joy at the sound of her voice. She loathed everything about her granddaughter's work: the stupidity and paranoia of the people Stella associated with, the guns they so idly flaunted. She went to bed every night praying for Stella's safety to any gods that might be listening.

Better get ready for visitors, Fern thought. She headed upstairs for a shower.


Tricia Scott stood in the doorway, holding a large black binder. Fern scanned her face, looking for the imprint of the tragedy but seeing only a shadowing beneath her new friend's eyes, a bit of tension around her mouth. "Come on in," Fern said, biting back an apology for the shabbiness of her home. Tricia looked so expensive, in tailored navy slacks, yellow sweater, and colorful silk scarf, surely not purchased at the thrift shop. She was thin and pale, and her hard black hair aged her.

"How are you? And your son?" Fern asked.

"My son is distraught of course. My daughter is with him today. I'd be there but we have speaking engagements in Colorado and are flying out this afternoon." Tricia's voice was controlled, her expression deadpan. Botox, Fern thought, her forehead's smooth as glass. But how does she feel, or not feel— perhaps there's a trick to keeping grief at bay. Fern encouraged her to sit at the kitchen table and gave her a glass of tea.

Glancing at her watch, Tricia accepted the drink. She tapped the binder, labeled JESUS ON THE JOB. "Unfortunately, I have a deadline. How quickly can you work?"

"What are you thinking of for the cover?" Fern asked.

"The Lord Himself."

"The Lord being . . ." Fern did not want to have to paint a portrait of God. Michelangelo had been there, done that.

"The Lord Jesus, of course."

When you make your living as a visual artist, and your living is so scant you're dependent on your men friends for dinner invitations, you don't turn down a commission. As she leafed through the binder, not for an instant did Fern think she might not want her name attached to the cover illustration of *Jesus on the Job*. The book exhorted employers to start the day with morning prayer, conduct Bible study in the lunchroom and insert Christian goals in the mission statement. Fern did flinch a little at the more activist paragraphs but suppressed any flicker of doubt, even though there was a clear disconnect between her view of Jesus' message and Tricia's interpretation:

Make your views known. Boycott businesses that market to, or are run by, gays. Don't let your tax dollars support schools that hire gays, or libraries that have books about them. You won't be liked by all. You might lose a few customers. But those are worldly desires, not the Lord's service. You must sacrifice for the moral recovery of our nation! Christ is coming to earth with a sword. Onward, Christian soldiers!

Fern turned the pages and found more of the same, aimed at alcohol, divorce, juvenile delinquency, abortion, immorality. "Intolerance as a virtue? What happened to love and forgiveness?" she asked.

"Tolerance is weakness and compromise," Tricia said flatly.

Fern nodded, studying Tricia's thin face, every mascara'd eyelash perfectly separated, wondering how such tribal notions had ever lodged themselves in her brain. Then she moved on. What did Tricia want? You had to please the client. "I can do this," Fern said. "You see Jesus as a leader, almost like a general."

"Exactly! Surrounded by his troops."

"I usually paint portraits from life, or a photograph. I'll have to do a little research."

"Use your imagination. You're a very creative person, I can tell." Tricia waved her arm to encompass Fern's living room, dominated by a boxy kerosene space heater. The walls displayed Fern's paintings as well as the works of her artist friends, an eclectic grouping: realistic paintings of ducks and fields and hydrangeas mingled with collages, Pollack-like acrylic drips, and cubistic abstracts. "I like old houses."

"My great-grandparents built this house, in 1903, when their son—my grandpa—was a baby. Six generations have lived in this house." When she said it like that, Fern forgot about the termites and peeling paint and felt proud of her inheritance.

"Not to be nosy but do you have a son? You brought your granddaughter yesterday, didn't you? The SBI agent, Stella Lavender. She has your last name."

Fern shrugged. "I never married. And my daughter Grace

never married. And that was fine with me." She knew she sounded defensive, but she didn't want Tricia to think she was ashamed.

"Sounds brilliant." Tricia made a wry face. "I've been married twice. My first husband was Mike's father. He was a pillar of the community, a church deacon. We practically lived at the church. And that was the problem."

"How so?"

"It was a hothouse of suppressed emotions. The preacher constantly reminding us of sin, sin, sin, until it's all we thought about. You know, like how diets backfire? All you can think about is fried chicken."

"Did someone eat some fried chicken?"

Tricia sniffed. "You might say. My husband fell in love with the church secretary. It happened really fast. He moved out, the church secretary left her husband, I took my babies and moved back home with my parents."

"That must have been tough."

"I should have done like you, moved into my own place. But I thought I needed a man. Along came Scoop and here we are. He's just like my first."

"Ah, you see," Fern said, "marriage is unnatural, in my opinion."

"I'm like, 'la-la-la-la-la, I won't ask, you don't tell.' I'm too tired to divorce him at this point. I bet the men are all over you, aren't they?"

Fern laughed. "The older ones are. I like men. I love men, actually. I just don't want to be owned by one."

"Here comes one now," Tricia said. They could see a white Lexus rolling into view outside.

"Jax Covas. I just met him yesterday."

"Oh yeah, Jax. He's some pal of Scoop's. Well, I have to skedaddle. Thank you so much."

Fern watched Tricia pick her way carefully down the porch steps—those steps really should be roped off, they were so bouncy—and thought about what Tricia had revealed: stuck in her comfort zone, writing books to make money, miserably married. What Fern wanted to know, and hadn't a clue about: what did Tricia feel about Justine's death?

She watched Jax Covas speak briefly to Tricia then stride across the driveway. He had to be one of the most attractive men ever to knock on her front door. He was trim—no paunch or sag—and his smooth olive skin contrasted with his white hair, cut very short. Trickling down his face was a thin white scar, partly covered by the black patch over his left eye. He looked like a pirate, a respectful and courtly pirate, as he presented her with a dozen yellow roses just barely open and delicately fragrant.

"You are lovely today," he said, kissing her hand. "Alas, I have only an hour. My phone stays in the car and I am yours. Where shall we begin?"

The dance of courtship? Or measuring for a chicken coop? Fern decided on the latter, though the former was definitely on her radar. They walked over to her shed, a ramshackle structure of weathered boards.

"We have chickens in Guatemala, when I was a child. I know about chickens. Along there we put a vine arbor for shade." He pointed to the long wall of the shed. "A fence around it all, to keep chickens in, foxes out. Inside, nesting boxes. You will have eggs by the dozen."

"I can sell them."

"I repair the roof. And I will dig a garden space in that corner. The chickens will eat the bugs and fertilize the vegetables. Organically."

"You'll do all that?" Fern was thrilled. She imagined her eyesore of a shed transformed by a flowering vine arbor, a lush garden of peas, tomatoes, and squash vines. She expressed her appreciation the best way she knew: she moved into his arms and playfully kissed him on the mouth. He seemed unsurprised, as though women threw themselves at him every day. He pulled her closer, fitting his hands onto her hips. *So it begins,* she thought, humming as she looked into his one carbon-black eye.

"You trade kisses for promises," Jax said, "I expect a very nice reward when I finish building."

They were startled apart by the sound of a car rolling up the graveled drive, squeaking as it bounced in the ruts. Fern peered around the corner of the shed and saw Stella's Civic. "It's my granddaughter," she whispered. She leaned against him, absorbing his warmth, breathing in his faintly cinnamon smell. She heard the donkeys greet Stella with their "haw haw," and the screen door bang as Stella went into the house to look for her.

"I will get to work," Jax said. "Fern's chickens will live here very happily."

As he made measurements and took notes, they talked. Jax told her he'd moved here recently for his business; he was delighted at the opportunity because he got to see his grand-daughters who were being cared for by his ex-wife. He pulled out his wallet and showed her a picture of six-year-old twins with identical gap-toothed smiles. Fern exclaimed she'd raised her granddaughter, too. It seemed they had more and more in common.

He made a sketch in his notebook and she approved it, offering to pay for the materials. He waved his hand. "We discuss after." They walked to his car. Seeing Stella through the screen door, Fern introduced them. Stella nodded hello but Fern knew she wasn't much interested—Jax was just another man lured into Fern's sticky web.

"I will be back with materials," Jax said, kissing her cheek.

His phone begin to chime. "You see, it is ridiculous, my business."

As his car lurched down the ruts of her drive, Fern realized she didn't know what his business was. It didn't matter. He was going to build her chicken coop, and then, well, they would see.

Stella was sweeping in the kitchen. "This flooring was here when you were born, I bet."

"I think you're right," Fern said. The pink-specked linoleum wore like concrete. "It's older than the stove"—two of the burners didn't work—"and the fridge," which chose that moment to cycle off with a great shudder.

Stella bent down with the dustpan. "Someday I'll replace them."

Fern felt a surge of affection for Stella and held out her arms for a hug. "You okay? Any word on what happened to Justine?"

"We won't hear for a few days. Who was that guy? You met him yesterday, right?"

"He's going to build me a chicken coop."

Stella gave her a look. "Chickens?"

"He has to fix the roof first."

"I do like a man with a tape measure."

"Who knows how to use it," Fern giggled.

"You hungry? I brought some bread and I'm going to make soup." Stella took celery and carrots out of the fridge and began to chop onions.

"That detective yesterday. Did you know him?" Fern asked.

"Anselmo Morales? No."

"He has nice shoulders."

Stella slid the onions and celery into a pan to brown in olive oil, then added water and kidney beans. "You have any potatoes?"

"Where they've always been." Fern pointed to the closet. "He's eye candy."

"He's smart and ambitious."

"You like him?"

"What's not to like? He's very good at his job." The water was boiling and Stella turned down the heat. "I know where you're going with this conversation. You wonder why I don't have a dozen boyfriends like you do, or even just one. Well, I wonder, too, sometimes, when I have a minute to think about it."

"You know what I mean. Do you *like* him."

"Do I *like* him. I haven't given it much thought, Fern, since I just met him. I didn't inherit your talents. I can't paint like you do and I can't attract men like you do."

"You attract them, they just don't stick."

"I want to give you a really hard pinch right now." Stella tasted the soup and added salt. "What else can I do?"

"Sit down and tell me about your work. Are you being careful, darling?" Violence had taken Fern's only child and she was consumed with worry about Stella's safety.

"My work isn't that dangerous. It's not really different from a roadside produce market. They're selling drugs and I'm buying. We exchange a few words and some merchandise for cash."

"They're high. Aren't they crazy? Hopped up?"

"Usually they would like to be hopped up. They aren't, that's why they are selling, to get money."

"Do you make arrests?" Fern knew arrests were more dangerous.

"No. I'm undercover." Stella didn't go into the details but Fern knew arrests of low-level dealers would turn some of them into informants, drilling a tunnel to the big dogs.

Stella ladled the soup into faded, chipped Fiestaware bowls. Fern couldn't look at them without thinking of her mother, who had bought the dishes piece by piece in the fifties, the only "bought new" items in the decade. Lavenders were scroungers.

Flea market, garage sale, thrift shop customers. Shabby before it was chic. She took a bite of sourdough bread, chewy and yeasty.

When they finished, Fern stacked the dishes and took them to the sink, a single porcelain basin with double sideboards, as old as the house. "Want some dessert? I've got ice cream, Cherry Garcia."

"I always have time for my dear friends Ben and Jerry."

"Tricia Scott was here earlier."

"The day after Justine's death, and she's visiting?"

Holding the ice cream scoop, Fern paused. "I know. I couldn't read her. She left her book for me." She pointed at JESUS ON THE JOB. "What do you think?"

Stella opened the binder. "Kind of uncomfortable if you don't share the boss's faith."

"You're right. And it's not all benign. There's a message of activism."

Stella turned the pages. "Onward, Christian soldiers? This book will offend some people. Are you sure you want to do the cover?"

"It's a commission." Fern cleared the table and slid the dishes into a tub of sudsy water.

"Did Tricia talk about Justine?" Stella asked.

"Tricia said her son was distraught."

"Did she get along with Justine?"

Fern shrugged, momentarily entranced by the dots of color dancing around the room, a magical effect caused by the setting sun passing through the beveled glass panes in the back door. The rainbow flickering across Stella's shining dark hair kindled a memory of Grace, Stella's mother, sitting in the same place, turning the pages of a book. Fern had to say something. "You've always had your mother's hair and eyes, but these days, when I look at you, it's almost like I see her. Same eyes, shoulders, straight back. When you talk, you sound exactly like her."

Stella kissed Fern's cheek. "You know, someday I will find out what happened to her. For both of us. And now I have to go to work."

# CHAPTER 5

*Sunday Early Evening*

The pink-gold setting sun gleamed in slivers through an eggplant storm cloud. Gusts of wind rocked the truck and rain splatted on the windshield. I pulled my hood up so I wouldn't have to watch Fredricks eating, and tried to psych myself up to buy drugs.

The State Bureau of Investigation had been teaming with the Essex County Sheriff's Department for months. The team divided into two groups. One group knew the neighborhoods and the networks; they traced money, recruited informants, and set up wiretaps. The addicts and dealers recognized them. The other group worked undercover, making drug buys to gather evidence so arrests could be made. I'd been assigned to undercover because, as my boss put it, "You don't look like a cop." I was five-three and even wearing a gun holster barely tipped the scales at one-twenty. I could dress like a high school tramplet and easily look ten years younger. In a room full of undercover cops, I was always the only young white female. Gosh, was I special.

"When you're ready," my boss Richard had said, after each of the three times I'd formally requested a transfer to homicide. "I hear good things, Stella. Keep it up."

Easy for him to say. He didn't have to hand over perfectly good taxpayer money to criminals and pretend they were doing him a big favor. Night after night, I'd been buying drugs in all kinds of neighborhoods—convenience stores, low-rent streets, bars, high-rise apartments, fast-food places, health clubs, gated communities. Every single town in North Carolina had its share of dealers, most of them carrying a weapon and as ready to pop it as spit.

Anselmo hadn't called, leaving me to wonder about Justine Bradley's death. Probably the medical examiner didn't work on Sundays. Or someone had confessed. Or the sheriff didn't want SBI help. A lack of information, the feeling of being left out, made me edgy and agitated, and I didn't want to leave the truck. It was a confiscated pickup the SBI had kept for drug stings, shabby, dented, a plausible vehicle for a drug addict. I liked it. It was peppy and unpretentious. Cozy even.

I hugged my arms and looked out the window at the lights of the apartments. Inside, people were watching TV and washing dishes and rocking babies to sleep, normal things people do even in a crappy complex like Evergreen Place. "Evergreen" must refer to the crabgrass, now drinking the rain and preparing for tomorrow's growth spurt.

"We're gonna make four buys tonight. Don't worry, sweetheart, you'll be fine," Fredricks said through a mouthful of grilled mahi-mahi sandwich. Fredricks was my partner, my mentor, protector, guide to the underworld.

I'm not your flipping sweetheart, I thought, gritting my teeth. No way, not ever. "How do you like my outfit?" I wore a frayed denim skirt, green hoodie, lace-up boots. I'd penciled eyeliner on thick like a raccoon, and attached fake eyelashes. My hair hung loose and tangled.

"It's good, real good. You don't look anything like a cop."

"But do I look like a customer?"

"Everyone looks like a customer. Now remember, lay on a thick drawl. Slouch. Cuss. Make faces." He illustrated, chewing on the inside of his cheek, pursing his lips. "Hide your self-esteem. You're a despicable addict."

"And I don't care."

"That's right. You just want to get high. Let your eyes wander like you can't focus. Time to go, sweetheart."

I opened the truck door. Through the rain I could make out two folks lurking under a lighted mail shelter. They weren't waiting for the mailman—only one reason they were outside on a night like this. I trotted over there.

The man and woman were gaunt and pale, shivering in the chilly weather and smoking cigarettes. "What's up?" I asked, slouching and chewing on my cheek.

"Whatcha need?" He coughed wetly from the exertion of speaking. His arms were heavily tattooed with red-and-black swirls.

"Rock," I said, "a fifty," and the woman vanished down the sidewalk.

He took my money. "You from around here?"

I nodded. "Verwood."

"I have a buddy in Verwood. You know Loren Baird?" Like we were meeting at a barbeque. Soon we'd be sharing our favorite movies, restaurants, and investment tips.

"No, I don't." I wondered how old he was. He looked at least forty except for dark plentiful hair. Addicts wear out real fast, so maybe he was in his twenties. Mrs. Crack Seller appeared out of the mist and handed me a small plastic bag. We were under the light, the rain had let up some, and I knew Fredricks was getting decent video, if he'd finished his dinner.

"Thanks," I said. No reason not to be polite. They smiled. She was missing quite a few teeth. They'd be easy to pick out in the photo books. "I'm looking to buy coke, a key. Can you hook me up?" I'd been instructed to use these street sellers to reach up the chain for bigger buys.

The woman's all-black eyes scanned my face. "Who are you?"

She had the cheekbones of a famine victim.

I laughed to cover my nervousness. "I'm Stacy." My cover name.

"You don't look like no dealer, Stacy."

"I came into some money. Wanna make more, you know?" I wiped my nose on my sleeve and sniffed loudly.

"And jail wouldn't work for Mo and me right now." She opened her parka to show me a sizeable baby bump. Whoa, lady. Add Child Protective Services to the list of state agencies interested in your habits.

"I'll cut you in. Five percent." I wrote my cell phone number—the state phone I used for drug agent work—on a piece of paper and gave it to them. They now knew my face and if he had a cocaine connection, I might hear from him. He would soon have family responsibilities and a thousand bucks could buy a lot of diapers, if he didn't spend it all on meth.

I trotted back to the truck, put the rock in a baggie, and recorded the date, time, and location. "Did you get the buy?" I asked, cleaning my hands with a baby-wipe.

Fredricks had finished the sandwich and was sucking up a mocha latte. "Sure 'nuff. Want to look?"

The camera screen showed the couple clearly; they'd been nearly facing the truck, standing under the light. My face was hidden by my hood. Excellent.

"Good job," Fredricks said.

"I forgot to cuss. Where to next?"

He started up the truck. "Downtown." Squeak, squeak went the wipers, and I heard a distant rumble of thunder. The night was murky, like my mood.

"Gotta shop after this. I'm making a special dinner for my wine club Saturday," Fredricks said. He was driving slowly because of the rain.

"What are you having?" I was curious. I'd been to one of his special dinners, a five-hour-long event. Too much wine, too much food, too much pretentious conversation about wine and food. He took pictures of each dish for his scrapbook. I'd avoided his house ever since.

He got a dreamy look. "A fall feast. Wild mushroom bruschetta. Roasted winter squash purée. Cornish game hens stuffed with wild rice."

I didn't like Cornish game hens. They looked like roasted babies. The bruschetta sounded good though. "Dessert?"

"Rosemary apple galette."

"What's a galette?"

"Like a pie, but not in a pie pan."

"A pizza?"

He chuckled. "Yup." He began a drone about wines. Peeno chard pooly fussy mumbo jumbo. Shut up shut up shut up. I felt really cranky. Was it the prospect of another week with Fredricks? The bench seat pulled all the way forward so his short legs could reach the gas pedal? His shirt stretched tight across his bursting belly?

Fredricks parked across the street from a twenty-four-hour convenience store and gas station. Unhappily for the immigrant families who invest all their money and eighteen hours a day in them, convenience stores are hubs for street sales. I rolled down my window and surveyed the scene through the drizzle. A couple of kids were hanging out in front, each with one hand gripping a cell phone, the other shoved into a pocket. Handling dope? A wad of cash? A gun? I began to worry, to feel hot. I sunk into my seat and pulled my hoodie neck up to my ears and took a deep breath of my own smell, not too bad yet.

"A special agent doesn't care if it's raining," Fredricks said.

"It's not rain I'm worried about." I opened the truck door and scampered across the street, watching the boys' eyes follow me, watching their hands in their pockets. "Hey," I said.

"You new," said the darker boy. He had a wanna-be mustache and a complicated corn-row hairstyle.

"Whatcha got?" I blinked and unfocused my eyes.

"Name it," the other one said. He had a shaved head shaped like a bullet.

"Got any grass?" I showed them a fifty-dollar bill.

They looked at each other. Baby Mustache said, "Maybe," and took the money. He sauntered to the corner of the building and around, out of sight.

Bullet Head looked me over. "You a working girl? For the dope?"

Ah, that's what I love about this job, I thought, the scintillating conversation. "My old man's waiting in the truck," I said, tipping my head toward Fredricks.

"He a big guy."

"You said it." We waited. I studied the litter in the parking lot: foam cups, broken glass, bottle caps, a dead pigeon.

Baby Mustache returned. "Nothing but blow, baby. You want it?"

"How much?" I had a budget.

"One-fifty for an eight-ball."

"Sure." I would have bought whatever they were selling, but tonight's special was blow. I handed him the extra money and took the eight-ball of coke, pushing the baggie into the sleeve of my hoodie. I thanked them politely and memorized their young faces. From the heavens came an explosion of thunder and lightning, and I dashed for the truck. I don't like lightning. Even Fredricks was preferable to lightning.

Fredricks pulled a praline from his pocket and began to work on a corner of the wrapper with his teeth. He spit a piece of it aside and peeled the wrapper off. He broke it into pieces and offered me one. "No thanks," I said. His snacks were the kind that stick to my hips.

We drove a couple more blocks to a cinder-block house on East Waters. Fredricks parked in the yard, strewn with bottles and fast food trash. "This place is a squat for addicts," he said. "Stay in the truck, let them come to you." He adjusted the mini-cam between our seats.

The door opened and a tall heavy woman with frizzed beige hair and hollow eyes emerged and walked to our truck. She smelled of tobacco and piney air freshener. It was impossible to estimate her age. She looked us over, seemingly unimpressed by Fredricks's physique and my eyelashes. "Whatcha want?"

"Ice," I said, "a gram." She went back into the house.

"She has a record," Fredricks said. "Her name's Dana De-Grasso. Try and set something up with her." In a few minutes she came back. It was raining harder than ever and she stood there getting soaked. I pushed my umbrella out the window to her and she popped it open.

"Thanks," she said.

"Keep it," I said. I gave her fifty dollars. "Any chance of getting more?"

"Another paper?"

"No, like a kilo."

"Honey, you want a serious party. We don't have that here."

"Know where I can get it?"

"Yeah, maybe. I can ask around." I left Dana my cell phone number. If she could set up a bigger deal soon, she'd stay out of jail.

Fredricks was working his way through a pack of raspberry licorice sticks. He was a steady, methodical chewer, and the gluey sound was more than I could take. I hummed under my breath, oh my God I'm going to kill you, kill you, kill you.

"Huh? Want one, sweetheart?"

"Gosh no, I just brushed."

He consulted his notebook. "Let's pick up oxys, what you

say?" Ten minutes later we were in a newish golf-course development called Victory Ridge. The oxy lady lived in a neighborhood of traditional colonial-style houses, each on its own quarter-acre. To look less hookerish, I wiped off the eye makeup and put on a raincoat to cover the frayed miniskirt.

Her shiny black door was bracketed by a pair of rosemary topiaries. I clacked a gleaming brass knocker. A dog began to bark, reflexively, like Merle does. Sort of a "who's there and did you bring treats?" bark, not threatening.

The oxy lady opened the door. I'd bought from her twice before. Lynn had very short dyed-red hair and a wide smile. She wore a white linen pants suit, the kind that wrinkles the instant you sit down in it. Apparently she had been standing since she put it on.

"Come in, come in! It's Stacy, right? Good to see you again." She motioned me into the kitchen where there was more light, and studied me closely. I studied her right back, noticing her necklace, a custom-made gold pendant in an abstract design, studded with colorful gems. Her dog, a black Lab, nosed me sweetly until she told him to stop.

"What a lovely necklace. Are those emeralds?" I asked, pointing to the little green stones.

"Oh no, honey. They're green diamonds. And this"—she pointed to the larger blue-green stone in the middle—"is an opal. These pink ones are sapphires."

"I've never heard of green diamonds, or pink sapphires."

"They are rare, yes." As in pricey. Well, that must be what she spent her profits on. According to Fredricks, her markup was around four hundred percent. "So, what do you want tonight?"

"Oxys? Whatever you have."

She left the room and I patted the dog until he went to his bed in a corner and collapsed creakily. The kitchen had pickled oak cabinets, granite countertops and a six-burner two-oven stove. Fredricks would be jealous of this kitchen. A double-door stainless steel fridge was plastered with snapshots of little girls riding bikes, swimming, digging into a birthday cake as they grinned into the camera.

She came back and handed me a small bottle of tablets, forty-milligram oxycodone. "There's a dozen in there."

"How much?" I said.

"Five hundred."

I pulled the money out of my jacket pocket. "Thanks. Listen, this is getting expensive. Any way I could sell for you?"

Her twinkle dimmed a bit. "For a cut?"

"Increase your volume."

"No. Just find your own source. It's not that difficult."

"You mean the Internet?"

"No. Get prescriptions, fill them. All legitimate."

"Not easy though, not in quantity."

She winked. "Depends on who you know, right? Like everything."

"Doctors, you mean. Who writes yours?" I asked.

A frown creased her face. "You ask a lot of questions, Stacy. Find your own."

I laughed. "I've tried. I can't get more than a few pills. And it costs to see a doctor."

"Well, this is my business. I've worked hard to develop my sources and I'm not going to give them away."

She sounded like she ran a tea room. I decided to back off. "No problem." There were other options. The task force could tail her to see what pharmacies she visited, then subpoena the pharmacies for her prescriptions to get names of the doctors signing them. Or, arrest her, turn her. She would cooperate for a reduction in charges or jail time.

Maybe she'd trust me after a few more visits. Trust, to be repaid with betrayal.

"Homeward, Fredricks," I said, climbing back into the truck clutching my bottle of pills. Home to wait for the call, an invitation to the prom, the request to investigate Justine Bradley's death. I wanted out of the feathery eyelashes, away from this truck and the smelly pretentious food and thwack-thwacking wipers and stricken looks on gaunt faces.

Fredricks drove slowly on the rain-slicked pavement. Outside, street lights quavered like a mirage in the darkness and drizzle.

# CHAPTER 6

*Monday Very Early Morning*

A phone call woke me from a disturbing dream—I was lost in a cave, squeezing through damp tunnels of rock, hardly able to breathe, as my headlamp dimmed and flickered. I didn't have time to think what the dream might mean as I groped for the phone.

"Darling," Fern said. "I'm researching what Jesus looked like for Tricia Scott's book cover. He was definitely dark-skinned."

"Not to be rude, Fern, but what's your point?" I slid out of bed and headed to the kitchen to start coffee. Merle was on my heels. I checked the clock—six-twelve. Jesus, indeed.

"And he might have been gay."

"Oh, Fern."

"Well, no one knows for sure. But he hung out with guys. He wasn't real macho."

"Surely it doesn't matter."

"That's my point. It shouldn't matter to anyone."

"It might matter to Tricia Scott." It was too early in the morning for a Sunday School lesson from Fern.

"I'm going to paint him as I see him," she said.

"As you should. That's why Tricia hired you."

"Did you hear any more about what happened to Justine Bradley? You know, the bride?"

"I didn't. Maybe I will today."

"Well, I hope you get to work on it."

Priceless words of support, coming from Fern. No liberal-thinking right-brained artist wants her grandchild to carry a gun, and my decision to join the SBI had been the subject of many loud, fierce, and wounding disagreements between us.

"Thanks, Fern. I'll keep you posted." I filled Merle's bowl with chow. He gobbled it all in seconds, following up with an enthusiastic slurping that managed to splash water in every direction. I opened the back door and let him into the yard. The night's rain had left the air soft and cool. High in the pines, a couple of fish crows held a raucous conversation.

I took a coffee mug outside to my small deck. My body ached from the hours spent in the truck. I sipped the wake-up potion, pushing away thoughts of the day to come—paperwork followed by more drug buys. Merle nosed around, looking for the perfect chew stick. My neighbor Saffron's yard looked lovely, with flower beds, shrubbery borders, and bright green grass. I aimed for a more natural look. Pine needles, pine cones, pine seedlings. Sticks for Merle. I did pick up his poop. It wasn't that natural.

I had just started a second case file—the two kids at the convenience store—when my boss Richard walked into my cubicle. Today he wore a charcoal-gray pin-striped suit, a crisp shirt of pale blue, and a paisley tie in swirls of blue and gray. A cigar stub offset his dimples and *GQ* menswear. "By-name request for you from Essex County? A dead bride?"

Normally "dead bride" isn't a cheery phrase, but it certainly lightened my mood, which had been in the doldrums all morning. Richard wouldn't be talking about it if he intended to keep me off the case. I told him what happened Saturday at Rosscairn Castle B&B.

"Morales said she was poisoned," he said.

Definitely murder, then. "It's an interesting case," I said. I didn't want to sound too excited about it. Four years of working for Richard had taught me he didn't like to be pressured by my enthusiasms.

"What else is going on?" he asked.

"There's that terrorism grant meeting."

He sucked on his cigar. "And?"

"Midge left me with a list of reports to finish." My coworker Midge had taken maternity leave. Her "list" meant paperwork, a week of staring at a computer screen while the sands of my life passed in an unceasing stream through the hourglass of my cubicle.

"Anything else?"

"You know, the drug stings. With Fredricks."

There was a pause. He knew—I'd told him enough times—how I'd appreciate a change from drugs. "Sorry, Stella. You're needed there. You're an excellent drug agent, because you don't look like a cop."

"What *do* I look like?" I wondered what he'd say. A butcher, a baker, a candlestick maker? I was a twenty-six-year-old girl with hips and uncontrollably curly hair.

"You're not middle-aged, muscled-up, or male. You're not threatening."

I didn't want to beg so I didn't say anything. Neither of us did, for a moment.

"How about this. I'll get someone else to cover the grant meeting and Midge's paperwork. You can help Morales on this case. It's not often I get to make a sheriff happy. But you'll have to go on supporting the drug work. They need you, and you're really good at it."

"Thank you," I breathed. It was true, then, that underneath his Sea Island cotton shirt and handmade silk tie, a real heart beat. Humming cheerfully, I dialed Anselmo's number and left him the message that I was available to help with the investigation. I turned back to my computer with fresh energy, finishing my reports by noon.

Now I was free to think about a homicide. I called the medical examiner's office and reached a technician. I identified myself, and asked him to fax me a copy of Justine Bradley's autopsy report.

"Hold on," he said, but returned quickly. "Not yet available."

"Was there a preliminary workup?"

"There's a toxicology report here. We analyzed blood and urine samples this morning. What's your fax number?"

The fax arrived a minute later. I scanned the page. There it was.

Strychnine.

A nasty poison, mostly used to get rid of gophers. I went on-line, Googled "strychnine," and found a pithy Wikipedia article on the stuff: alkaloid, very bitter, soluble in water. Rapidly absorbed into the intestines. Muscles spasms ten to twenty minutes after exposure, convulsions, back arches, death from asphyxiation caused by paralysis or exhaustion.

Yep. That explained the horrible contortions. Mike talked to her at twelve-forty, and Ingrid heard her moaning about one-oh-five. So Justine must have ingested the strychnine sometime between twelve-thirty and twelve-fifty. Right now it seemed the inn guests and staff, and possibly even the wedding guests, all had opportunity.

But why? Motive was absent. A lovely young woman, an "angel," who should be on a plane to Cozumel, hand-in-hand with her new husband. Poison was so premeditated it seemed someone wanted to prevent the marriage.

I needed information, so I decided to visit Hogan. He could search all the criminal and civilian databases. He could tell me what you bought your brother for Christmas three years ago and whether your cat was up-to-date on her vaccines. He knew how to get phone, bank, and credit card records. With a subpoena, of course.

He was hunched over his keyboard, staring at the screen. He looked miserable, or perhaps I was just projecting my own vile attitude toward life in a cubicle. "Psst," I whispered.

He turned around. "Stella." In his face I saw the heat and embarrassment of our encounter in my bedroom.

"Are we friends?" I asked.

"Hey, I'm a moron," he said, trying on his "I am irresistible" smile. It didn't work.

"Classic. You don't get it at all."

He sighed. "Let's start over. What do you want?"

"I need a favor. Justine Bradley's death looks like a homicide. I'm going to help with the case."

He pushed a chair toward me. "What do you need?"

"Anything you can dig up on her. Credit cards, transcripts, job history. Can you have it for me tomorrow morning?"

"Absolutely."

"And I need to talk with Gia Mabe. She's not in the phone book."

"No problem."

"You look tired."

He grinned. "I'm fine."

"Not enough sleep?"

"None of your business."

He was right, of course. Like crunchy cheese snacks or late night TV, caring about him was a bad habit I needed to break.

The Rosscairn Castle B&B parking lot was nearly empty, except for Anselmo's county car and a beat-up black truck. I knocked on the castle's front door and Wyatt opened it.

"You again? Whatcha want?" Today he was wearing standard American clothes—khaki twills and a faded red polo shirt that matched his complexion. He stood aside and motioned me in.

"There's a cop in the sun room and a deputy wandering the grounds. I'm expecting the health department any minute—there's something wrong with our water, again. And guests are due in two hours. I don't need this aggravation."

In the sun room, a mildewy enclosed porch furnished with black wicker and Black Watch plaid cushions, Anselmo stood by a window overlooking corn fields, listening on his phone. I used the moment to study him. I didn't know him but he seemed self-possessed and serious. Certainly he was ambitious, to have made lieutenant at his age.

He looked up from his phone call and smiled hello. His smile was crooked but nice. I smiled back. "The housekeeper's upstairs," he said. "Can you talk with her?"

I headed toward the sound of running water, into Falkirk, Justine's room. In the bathroom, a woman was upended over the bathtub, scrubbing and muttering to herself. I cleared my throat and she bounced up. Liesle Harvey was a frazzled-looking blond, about forty, I guessed. A blurry tattoo half-hid in her cleavage—was it a rabbit? A rabbit wielding a sword? I tried not to stare at it as I introduced myself.

"Sorry, mind if I keep working? Guests coming in here soon. I couldn't clean the room until you guys were finished with it." She sprayed the toilet seat and squirted blue cleanser into the bowl. Swipe, wipe, swish. The sink got a spray and a rinse.

"You're an expert. Really fast. Guess I don't do it enough to get good at it."

"I'm sure you're good at other things, like shooting at targets and chasing suspects." She slid towels and washcloths onto the bars, and lined up toiletries on a tray sitting on the toilet tank.

I didn't want to tell her I was good at buying crack so I just chuckled. "How's the water? Wyatt said there was something wrong with it."

"It's got a smell, I don't know. It's okay to clean with." She

68

moved into the bedroom and pulled the sheets off the bed. "I can talk while I do this. What do you want to know?"

"Perhaps you've thought about this past weekend? Anything come to mind that might help with the investigation?"

"I wish. That was a terrible thing. But I don't remember anything except working like a dog all weekend. Dinner for eleven Friday night, just the two of us with Blue helping. Full house in the morning for breakfast."

"And then?"

"Why? Am I a suspect?" She smiled as if to show she was joking. "I was outside nearly all morning, setting up for the ceremony. The caterers always need something." She tucked the bedspread around the pillows and patted them. "Wyatt made us some lunch around eleven-thirty."

"Did you see anyone who wasn't staying here go upstairs?"

She frowned. "I don't remember seeing anyone who wasn't an inn guest. Wait. The two bridesmaids were running around. They weren't guests. Are we done? I have to vacuum. I've got about twenty more things to do."

"No problem," I said. She switched on the vacuum cleaner and I wandered back downstairs to find Anselmo still on the phone, so I went into the kitchen where Blue Stone was slowly sweeping the floor, swaying with the hip-hop I could hear spitting from his earbuds. I gestured that he should remove them. He complied, smiling tightly over a mouth full of braces.

Blue said he was sixteen, which I could have guessed from the awkwardness that comes from a recent growth spurt. His eyes shifted like a puppy's, meeting mine for an instant, then darting off. He had a red bumpy rash on both arms, from his wrists to the sleeves of his tee-shirt.

"You and Liesle are the only two employees, right?"

"Yes, ma'am."

Oh, I liked that. The ghoulish shirt and ripped jeans were a uniform, not an attitude. In a couple of years he might be a punk, but right now he was a large nervous child talking to police. He twitched and wriggled. "And what's your job?"

"Mow grass, wash windows. Whatever Wyatt wants me to do." He scratched his arms.

"Lots of work this past weekend?"

"Friday night there was, with the dinner. I set up the table with dishes and all. Then I cleaned up after."

"You be my eyes and ears," I said. "Were there arguments during the dinner? Did you overhear a conversation?"

"I stayed in the kitchen." He paused. "They were taking video. Maybe you could watch the video?"

"Very good." I made a note to ask Wyatt who had a video camera. "How about the next morning, before the wedding—what did you do then?"

"Liesle told me to fluff up. You know, make the beds, empty the trash. Replace towels." He scratched his arms and smiled again, this time showing the metal. He was a sweet boy and once the braces came off and he felt more comfortable in his body, he would be a handsome man.

"Did you see anything at all while you were, uh, fluffing up? Anything that might be related to the woman's death?"

"Nope," he said, too quickly. I stared at him and let him twitch. He rolled his shoulders and peered out the window at the fascinating cornfield.

"One last thing you can help me with," I said. "Is the barn open?"

"No, locked. Why?"

"I love old barns," I said. "Did the sheriff's deputy look in there?"

He shrugged. "I dunno."

"Who's got the key?"

He dug in his pockets and pulled out a key. "Bring it back,

okay? Wyatt'll kill me if I lose it."

I walked to the barn, an outbuilding of weathered splintered boards and a rusty tin roof. Its door was a simple wooden plank secured with a padlock. I went back to my car and found a pair of latex gloves. I unlocked the padlock with Blue's key, opened the door, and pulled the chain dangling from a light fixture. Overhead, a harsh fluorescent bulb flickered on.

With my next breath, I nearly gagged from the damp stink of mildew and decomposition. I pinched my nose shut and fought the urge to retreat into the sunshine, to slam the door on this dirty, chaotic, jumbled mess. Tetanus-bearing rusty nails poked out of a pile of wood scraps. Every square inch of wall surface was covered with tools, ropes, plastic containers. Sagging shelves held miscellaneous jars, boxes, trash bags. Bags of peat moss, fertilizer, and lime lined one wall. In the back, paint cans were stacked, partly covered by a jumble of tarps, and overhead, stored on the rafters, was more lumber—four-by-fours, boards, old doors. Broken windows and torn screens leaned against the back wall.

Where was the smell coming from? I remembered Wyatt's claim that something was wrong with his water. Poking around behind the broken windows, I found a cabinet containing a water softener, a big blue tank, and a PVC pipe—sealed. Was that the pipe to the B&B's well? It looked impenetrable, which made sense—a well shouldn't be open to every little creature that wants to hop in.

I breathed shallowly through my mouth as I examined the pipe. In the back of it, out of sight, someone had carved a hole about two inches in diameter. I couldn't bring myself to sniff at that opening. I had to do it. I had to. I knelt and un-pinched my nose at the hole in the pipe. My stomach heaved and I stag-gered to the door for fresher air. Yes, there was some critter dead and rotting, down inside that pipe.

But right now, my concern wasn't the water supply, but Wyatt's gardening chemicals stacked on the crude shelves. Lawn fertilizer, lime, aluminum sulfate, herbicide. Half-open bags, unlabeled jars. Ant killer, fungus control, mice traps, roach powder. I noticed an old bottle of deer repellent, "a unique formula derived from animal by-products." Fern might need to know about that when she got her garden going. Slowly I studied each container and pushed it aside, until I found what I was looking for—a grimy plastic jug, smudged with fingerprints. A faded label said Restricted Use. The active ingredient in Gopher-Get-Away? Strychnine. I left the jug where it was and locked the barn behind me.

Possibly that jug contained the poisonous crystals that killed Justine. The fact that it was in a normally locked barn pointed to someone with access to a key—Wyatt, or one of the employees, Blue or Liesle. Would an inn employee have left the jug there? Even though it was very simple to get rid of it? Did a guest find the poison and borrow a spoonful? How did he or she get into the barn? Lift the key? Had the barn been deliberately left open?

I went looking for the deputy and after a good ten minutes found him hiding in the woods sneaking a cigarette. They're not supposed to smoke in uniform. He stomped on the butt and made his way to me.

"Look out for the poison ivy," I said.

"Yeah. What's up?" He eyeballed me up and down. He was about my age, a hard-body with a shaved head. His posture conveyed Marine Corps.

"I'm Stella Lavender, SBI."

"Howdy do, ma'am. Dave Alston."

I hid my pain as he crushed my hand. "I found what you're looking for. In the barn," I said, handing him the key. "Give this back to the kid in the kitchen."

"Yes, ma'am," he said and I felt quite elderly even though that's how a Marine addresses every female over the age of twelve.

"I'm glad you're here," Anselmo said. "Let's strategize." I followed him to the front of the Castle B&B, onto the stone veranda strewn with rocking chairs. He took out his notebook and ruffled its edges. "I have a problem. Have you worked on a homicide recently?"

"Uh, no." A more accurate answer would have been "never." I didn't want him to know how green I was.

"Do you mind if I talk philosophically about murder? I promise to get to the point eventually." His dark eyes crinkled—he knew I was green. This would be part of my education.

"Please, go ahead." I liked listening to his gravelly voice with just a hint of an accent, enough to let you know he could easily make his way in Miami or Peru.

"In San Antonio, where I started out, most of the cases were drug-related. Those murders were solved with the help of witnesses. Or the killers told someone. Murder committed in the course of a robbery is sometimes difficult but surprisingly often it's a neighbor or someone already suspected in other crimes and there are fingerprints. Then there's the domestic cases— obvious and easy. You know all of this, of course." He paused. "Then, rarely, we couldn't close the case." He spoke softly and somberly and I realized he could know my history. Richard might have told him.

"One-third of homicides are never solved," I said.

"Yes. And this case particularly concerns me. It's bizarre."

We were interrupted by the deputy carrying the grimy jug of gopher bait in an evidence bag. He showed the jug to Anselmo. "Found this in the barn, sir. Contains strychnine. Actually, she found it." He pointed to me. "I'm going to take this to the lab, sir." He marched off, holding the bag away from his body.

"That illustrates why I asked for your help," Anselmo said. "Good work."

I demurred modestly. He consulted his notebook. "Other than the victim, there were seven adult guests staying at the B&B. Three staff. Forty-one wedding guests."

"Are the wedding guests part of the pool of suspects?"

"Good question. Far as we know, none of them went inside the B&B. But they may have seen something. I'm going to have my investigators talk to them. Problem is, most of these folks are neighbors or cousins or buddies with someone in our department, and that could prejudice the investigation. Even me—my wife's sister-in-law was the caterer. I need an impartial investigator."

His wife. Of course he has a wife, why wouldn't he? My Anselmo-fantasy balloon fizzled limply to the floor and I ground it beneath my shoe.

"When the autopsy's done, I'll see you get a copy," he said. "We already know what killed her, so I doubt we'll learn anything else useful."

# CHAPTER 7

*Monday Late Afternoon*

Hogan called as I was pulling away from Rosscairn Castle B&B. He not only had Gia Mabe's home address, he told me where she worked—at a biotech startup named Psylex. "They specialize in drugs that cross the blood-brain barrier. She's the comptroller."

So Gia, the smart, obsessed, spurned girlfriend, worked at a company that made nervous system drugs. "Can you find out more about what they do? See if anyone mentions strychnine," I asked. Hogan could find anything. The man was born to perform research. Too bad he'd applied those talents so wrongly, so effectively, in his search for a soul mate.

I checked my watch. Gia should be at work.


The walnut walls and marble floors of Psylex Corporation's lobby had been designed to impress. Through a mile-high window the afternoon sun flooded onto a purpley-blue orchid on the receptionist's desk. I felt out of place in my black leather jacket, loose enough to hide my holstered SIG. My hair was being particularly obstreperous. I'd run out of frizz control cream and had wrestled it into a braid of sorts. I looked different from the other women passing through the lobby in their tailored suits, neat hair, and comfortable shoes. My ankle boots were awesome but the receptionist couldn't see them from where she sat.

"Ms. Mabe's in a meeting," she said. "Is she expecting you?" Not exactly. "I'll just wait," I said.

She frowned as though she couldn't think of a tactful way to get me out of her lobby. "Our workday ends in a few minutes."

"Mine ends around midnight," I said, making small talk.

"Oh, really? What do you do?"

Okay, smart mouth, think of something. Something not a lie. Searching, searching . . . "I work for the state."

She raised an eyebrow and turned to her monitor. I leafed through the magazines stacked on a table next to me. Pharma, medical, packaging, test, bioprocess, chemical. Finally, at the bottom, a readable publication, *Scientific American*. I was deep into an article about smallpox and bioterrorism when I heard a hiss.

"What are you doing here?" Gia's face matched her attitude—pissed. She wore a black suit, almost nondescript until you noticed the exquisite black beading around the collar and cuffs. Her blond-streaked hair slithered silkily around her face.

"Oh good, you remember me then. Can we talk?"

"Whatever are you thinking, coming to my workplace?"

"It seemed the quickest way to reach you." I said this softly.

She sniffed, and turned toward the elevator. "Follow me," she said. To the receptionist, "It's okay, Rachel. We'll be in my office."

She punched a button and the glass box rose, lifting us above the lobby all the way to the top floor. I followed her down a long hall to a corner office nearly as big as my entire house. It was furnished with a soft wool carpet, leather sofas, and shelves filled with binders.

"What do you want? I have very little time for this." Impatiently, she jiggled her foot, clad in a pleated-toe ballerina flat.

I opened my notebook and leafed through each page. I was

practicing the studied pause, a stretched-out wait, to imply that time is required, lots of time, if a murder was to be discussed. "I understand you had a relationship with Mike Olmert at one time."

"He's the love of my life. There will never be anyone else." Her slightly crossed blue eyes stared into mine, not really seeing me, looking somewhere else—into her virtual reality, the only place this star-crossed love currently existed, according to Mike.

I decided to go along. "How long have you two been—you know, a couple?"

"Years. Here, I'll show you." She tugged open her briefcase and hauled out a black leather photo album. "Go ahead, look through it. Take your time."

The album was really a scrapbook. The first part contained memorabilia from their dating period—a pressed corsage, movie ticket stubs, a photo of the two of them dressed up for a big evening. A florist's card with "To my funny Valentine, from Mike." Not much, after all. Then pages and pages containing many photos of Mike, alone, interspersed with odd bits—the corner of a pizza box, soda pull-tabs, discarded envelopes with his name on them. Stuff she'd apparently pulled out of his garbage. She'd scored a few pictures of the two of them together, and even an email from him, asking her to leave him alone, decorated with little heart stickers.

She'd scrapbooked her stalking.

"Gia, we met at Mike and Justine's wedding. Doesn't that mean he loved her?"

Gia's perky nose wrinkled with distaste. "Oh, he had to marry her. She was blackmailing him."

"Enlighten me, would you?"

With that brief prompt, Gia launched an explanation as convoluted and twisted as her thinking. She practically spit out the words—Mike had a criminal past, he spent time in jail, he lied about it on the firefighter's application, Justine found out and if she told on him, he'd lose the job he loved, he was a reformed man, the only way to shut Justine up was to marry her.

Or kill her? The glint in Gia's eyes, the way she gazed into the distance as she recited her venomous story, convinced me this woman was losing it, maybe already *had* lost it.

"Now that Justine's dead, will he marry you?" I asked.

"He's lying low right now. He has to pretend to grieve," she said gravely.

"Are you in touch with him?"

She shrugged. "We text some but don't see each other. Not yet. He has to let time pass, to protect my reputation." She dimpled up at this thought. "Here, help yourself." She pushed a bowl of M&Ms toward me.

"Justine was murdered." I tilted my head to get her attention.

"You think I did it?" Her eyes roamed the room. She popped a green candy into her mouth, and her foot resumed its jiggle.

"You just told me why you might have."

She frowned. "You don't understand."

An understatement. "What time did you arrive at the Castle B&B on Saturday?"

"A bit early. I wanted to get pictures." She opened her handbag, took out a camera, and fiddled with it. "Here, look."

She had taken at least twenty pictures of Mike, from different angles. He didn't appear to be posing or smiling for the camera; they were long shots with a telephoto lens. In a couple he held up his hand, like he was shielding himself from her. The pictures were time-stamped, beginning at twelve twenty-three, and every minute or so thereafter. If the time hadn't been reset on the camera, her camera had been under the tent for the crucial half-hour before the wedding was due to begin. Who else had been there? Or not been there? The pictures might hold a clue.

"Those are great. Can I get copies? Email them to me?"

"No. He's mine." She frowned and clutched the camera to her chest. "Find your own boyfriend."

"He's so handsome, Gia. You are very lucky. Just let me look one more time?"

She held out the camera but didn't let go of it. She peered into the tiny screen along with me, advancing it with her thumb. I felt her breath and a strand of silken hair brushing against my cheek, smelled the chocolate candy. Pretty Gia, locked in a metallic cage of high-functioning insanity. I wondered if anyone ever cracked her reality.

Together we watched. Some pictures had been taken through a window—Mike helping Kate attach her corsage to her wrist. Kate inserting his boutonnière into a buttonhole. Mike speaking to a little girl lying back in a wheelchair, the child of Evan and Lottie Ember. Talking with his stepfather, the minister Scoop. Sitting next to his mother, his face half-hidden by her brown straw hat. Kissing Delia's cheek, shaking Webster's hand. Mike on the phone, arms folded across his pleated shirt. Evan Ember standing next to him, in a despondent slump. That one was almost artistic, the two men framed by the scarlet fall-blooming camellias. She took six in a row of Evan and Mike, ending at 1:05. Then came the picture taken when I was sitting next to her—Mike, his two groomsmen, and Scoop Scott ready to play minister, all looking past the camera, down the aisle, waiting for Justine. These pictures provided a decent alibi for her, since I was there too and could vouch that they were correctly time-stamped.

Since the wedding day, Saturday, Gia had taken three more pictures of Mike. One, a photo of Mike beside a car, was time-stamped this morning. "You took this today?" I asked. "Where?"

"I take one every day, either at his apartment or where he works. Sometimes at the gym. He's amazing, isn't he? I bought him that red shirt." Her face lit up with a shining smile. "Everything is working out for us."

"Gia, were you actually *invited* to this wedding?"

She grabbed the scrapbook and camera and backed away. "What are you implying? He wanted me there."

"Convenient of Justine to get herself murdered."

"I didn't do it! Nobody liked her—she was a control freak! He despised her! She drove him crazy!" By this time she was shrieking, and her assistant opened the door to see what was wrong. Gia waved her arms, shooing us out of the room. The assistant scuttled backward, and I followed.

So she didn't want to be friends. The feeling was mutual.

# CHAPTER 8

*Tuesday Mid-Morning*

I hated paperwork but it wasn't difficult. No need to be creative or even particularly grammatical, just type fast. I had three reports to write after last night's rounds with Fredricks. We started at a pizza place where the manager had a little side business in pot. Then Fredricks had a tip on an out-of-the-way barbeque joint selling some unique items not on their menu, where I picked up a chocolate milkshake and an assortment of pills of unknown formulation. Finally, we went into a bar and grill where I traded a hundred-dollar bill for a packet of crystal and two lemonades. Enriching the local economy, one tax-free transaction at a time.

Mid-morning, Anselmo called to tell me that the medical examiner had completed the autopsy of Justine's body. "He wants to show us something."

"Huh? Something about the body?"

"He won't say. Says we have to see it. Meet me there in an hour."

Curious.

I made a quick call to Wyatt and asked him who took video during the weekend. He remembered that Kate Olmert, Mike's sister, had used a video camera at the rehearsal dinner. I called her and left a message, then headed out.

It was time to visit a corpse.

★ ★ ★ ★ ★

Anselmo was already in the lobby when I entered the brick
building housing the Office of the Chief Medical Examiner. We
got into the elevator. "Ten," he said, and I pushed the button.
He was rubbing his hands together, shifting his shoulders, taking deep breaths.

"You're antsy," I said.

"It's nothing."

"Autopsies bother you?"

"Maybe, a little. The smells, mostly." He put his hands in his
pockets, took them out. Loosened and straightened his tie. His
face was putty-colored. I hoped he'd last through whatever the
medical examiner wanted to show us.

"Bite your tongue, hard," I said. "It will keep you from thinking too much."

"Thanks," Anselmo said. "Good advice. I'm fine, really."

I knew the ME, Allen O'Brien, from his appearances in court.
He was often called to testify in a homicide trial, and recently
North Carolina had had a couple of sensational ones. He was
around sixty, bald, with rimless glasses and a red bow tie, and I
swear he clicked his heels when he shook my hand. He handed
us gloves, gowns, and masks, and after we were suited up, he
led us down the hall. On the way, we passed a room full of
students crowded around a gurney. The sound of a saw made
me wince. Anselmo looked greenish; I hoped it was the lighting.

A wall of windows brightened the general autopsy room,
empty except for equipment. I expected Dr. O'Brien to bring
Justine's body out on a gurney but he pulled two chairs together
and motioned that we should sit.

"You'll get a full report, of course," he said. "But I've never
seen a case like this. That's why I asked you to come, because it
might have a bearing on your investigation."

I couldn't imagine what it could be. I thought about

abnormalities that might show up on autopsy. Something upside down or inside out? Duplicate organs? Certainly medically interesting, but not pertinent to the investigation. We already knew about the poisoning, so it wasn't that.

"Related to the cause of death?" Anselmo asked.

"No. Let me explain." He stood and clasped his hands behind him as though addressing a class of medical students instead of two impatient cops. "Have you ever attended an autopsy?"

We both nodded yes but he told us anyway. "I remove all the trunk organs in a single block. Then one by one, I isolate individual organs, remove and dissect them. The esophagus, the lungs, the heart, larynx, thyroid. Then I turn the block over, and take out the liver, spleen, intestines. Stomach, pancreas. The last organs I look at are urogenital—kidneys, bladder, uterus and ovaries in females, testes in males."

He bounced up and down on his toes. "I stopped halfway through with this one. After removing the upper organs, I turned the block over. I examined the viscera carefully, to get a mental picture before I started cutting. And do you know what? Something was missing. Let me show you. Wait here."

Dr. O'Brien left the room. I looked at Anselmo. The suspense and the smells emitting from the nearby sink were doing him no good. "He's enjoying this," Anselmo said. "He's showing off."

I was about to agree when O'Brien returned pushing a metal two-tiered gurney. On the top shelf, a body; on the shelf below, a large tray. Both were covered with white plastic sheeting. He leaned down, lifted the tray and slid it onto a dissection table.

"These are the abdominal organs of your poisoning victim." He pulled the sheet aside.

The pile of innards was messy, red with blood and white with fat, slick and slimy, but they didn't look human the way the outer body does. Psychologically they were perhaps easier to look at than a cracked-open corpse. The smells weren't bad—

like disinfectant, though slightly sweet, and musky. I peeked at Anselmo. His face was still pale, but he was hanging in there. I couldn't tell whether he was chewing on his tongue.

"What's missing? Anyone? Anyone?" O'Brien chuckled at his little joke.

I peered closely at the pile of viscera. The liver was obvious, a dark red slab. The kidneys were easy since they were kidney-shaped. Anselmo pointed to a pinkish thing. "What's that?"

"Gall bladder. And there's the pancreas, and the spleen. All this below is intestines."

And that was all that was below. "Where are the girl parts?" I said.

"Bingo!" said the doctor. "She hasn't any. No ovaries, no uterus, no fallopian tubes."

"Surgically removed?" I asked.

"Nope." His eyes crinkled as he grinned under the mask. "Never had any. She's a he. Well, she used to be, anyway."

I was speechless.

Anselmo wasn't. "You sure? How do you know?"

"This gal's had surgery, vaginoplasty. A surgically created vagina. It's anchored to this ligament." We both looked where he pointed. "Once I discovered that, I examined the body for other modifications. Breast implants, of course, but I also believe she'd had facial recontouring. See this?"

He turned around to the gurney and folded the sheet back to expose Justine's head and neck. Her muscles had relaxed into a flat softness. Her face was still and doll-like, with perfectly sculpted features. Someone had removed the pearl beads from her hair. Dr. O'Brien gently tipped her chin and ran his gloved finger along a thread-like scar.

"Okay," I said, "got it." I needed to process this revelation. Justine was transsexual. It hit me, how much her gender colored my thinking about her. I'd had an unvoiced connection with her. We were single American women, about the same age. Now I didn't know what to think. I knew nothing about her. Nothing.

"He became a she in every way," Dr. O'Brien said. "Whoever did this surgery knew what they were doing. In my opinion, no one would know without a DNA test." He handed us each a copy of the autopsy. "She was a healthy person. She would have lived another sixty years."

I thanked Dr. O'Brien profusely. He seemed happy, his day had been interesting, he'd surprised us with medical sleuthing.

In the elevator, Anselmo looked less queasy now that the lesson was over and he didn't have to stare at innards. We had a lot to talk about. The implications were huge, weren't they? Was Justine's gender change related to her murder?

We sat in his cruiser. "Whew," said Anselmo, rolling down his window and taking a deep breath.

"That was a bit much," I said. "He could have spared us the show and tell."

"Puts a new light on the case, though."

"She clearly presented as female. No one has said anything about this, right?"

"Yeah. Two really important questions. Who knew? When did they know? Starting with Mike Olmert."

"Right. If Justine had kept it a secret, he might be very angry to find out," I said.

"It's not something it's okay to keep to yourself. She wasn't biologically like other women. She couldn't have children."

"And if he found out, at the last minute, is it a reason to murder?"

Anselmo shook his head. "He could always just call the wedding off. Doesn't seem enough, to me, to kill her."

"Not to you or me. But gender change is hard to accept. It's stigmatized." I thought about Tricia Scott's book, her homophobic rant. Did she really deep-down believe what she wrote, or was she parroting rhetoric? How would she react to this information about her future daughter-in-law? Screams and hysterics? Pleading with her son, weeping? Or taking up a soldier's sword to set the world right?

"Let's find Mike Olmert," Anselmo said. He pulled out his notebook and his cell. His color was back to normal, and he was his usual cool relaxed self. He smiled the crooked smile I liked, and I also liked being out of that cold facility with its smells of chemicals and fluids. The only smells in Anselmo's cruiser were the leather of the seats and his faintly spicy scent. A bit of plastic from the protective gown still clung to his shoulder and I plucked it off, my hand lingering a half-second longer than necessary. He was warm, alive, male, everything Justine Bradley was not.

Despite his parents' conservative beliefs, despite his cultural conditioning, despite the ribbing he'd get from other firefighters, had Mike Olmert knowingly asked a transsexual woman to marry him? It was hard to believe and we needed to hear it from him in person. He agreed to meet us at a gym where he worked as a personal trainer on his days off.

A knotty-muscled woman in purple Lycra guarded the Lakeway Fitness Center. She gave Anselmo a friendly wink but eyed me up and down, as if assessing whether she could lift me overhead. When I told her we were there to meet Mike, she said he'd be out in a few minutes, and offered to give us a tour. After passing through an acre of body-building equipment, she showed us the rooms for spinning, yoga, aerobics and childcare, and a lap pool with adjacent steam room. Overlooking it all was a balcony of treadmills, bikes, and elliptical trainers aimed at a bank of televisions. The place was nearly deserted except for a few diehard weight lifters and a toning class full of women struggling to perform crunches on huge rubber balls. I've been in those classes. The real exercise comes from trying to stay balanced on the ball until it gets away and bounces rudely into a ninety-pounder in a red yoga bra who shoots you a dirty look that says *Can't you even control your ball?*

"Hey, guys." Mike emerged from the men's locker room. His tee-shirt said, "Train hard, win easy," and his body was a walking advertisement for the benefits of regular workouts—muscle definition, flat stomach, pecs you could balance a wine glass on.

Anselmo asked him to find us a room where we could talk privately. Mike led us into the deserted spinning room, full of one-wheeled bikes on bright blue iron frames. When he turned on the light, a disco ball started to revolve, sending rainbow flashes around the room. I studied him as the light danced across his face. His face was stony, his eyes shrouded in dark. We sat down on the instructor's platform.

Anselmo didn't sidestep the issue. "When did Justine have the surgery?"

"What are you talking about?"

We waited.

"Breast implants you mean? I knew about those but why does it matter?" He folded his thick arms across his bulky chest.

"Mike, we know," Anselmo said.

He sighed. "Come on. What do you want?"

I moved closer to him, willing him to open up. "The truth, Mike. It's liberating."

He shook his head. "Honest to God, I don't have the patience for this."

No more futzing around, I decided. "Did she tell you she'd had a sex change?"

His eyes met mine and he began to laugh. "What the hell are you talking about?"

"It was revealed in the autopsy. Justine was born male. She

took hormones and had surgery to change her sex. Are you saying you didn't know?" I asked.

"You are completely nuts. There's no way." He hopped onto a bike and started to pedal slowly, mechanically. He turned the knob to increase resistance, and pumped harder, as if trying to ride away from us.

I shared a glance with Anselmo, and he took over. "Mike, either you're lying or deliberately twisting things. Perhaps we should go downtown for a formal interview, start at the beginning and go over every single moment of your relationship with her." His graveled voice held little compassion.

"And you need to do your job, not harass me."

"Did your family know?" I asked.

Mike shrugged. "The subject didn't come up since it's complete nonsense."

"I'm sure they accepted Justine as a woman," I said.

"She *was* a woman. This is really stupid." He looked at his watch, stopped pedaling and eased off the bike. "Sorry, I've got to go. The funeral is this afternoon."

Anselmo planted himself in the doorway. "When did you know, Mike?"

"I didn't know and I don't know and won't ever know. It's the most ridiculous thing I've ever heard. Find out who killed her." He turned off the flashing disco light, leaving us in serene darkness. He walked us to the door. "Look, I don't want to be difficult," he said. "It's just not that complicated. She was my girlfriend. About to become my wife. What you're saying makes no sense to me."

"Of course," I said. "But the autopsy revealed she'd had sex-reassignment surgery."

"Doctors aren't perfect. In this case they are wrong." His eyes filled and he blinked. "It's funny how much I miss her. We talked about everything."

"Not funny. A terrible loss," I said. And apparently they didn't "talk about everything." I put my hand on Mike's shoulder—his body was hard, bulky, and unyielding. My touch must have helped, because as we walked away he called out his thanks. I looked back and waved. He must have been thanking us for working the case. He surely didn't mean thanks for the revelation.

Anselmo pulled out of the parking lot. "What do you think?" he asked.

"He didn't believe us."

"He could have been lying."

I shrugged. I was wondering that myself.

# CHAPTER 9

*Tuesday Early Evening*

When I walked in the door, Merle gave my shoes extra attention, fascinated by the molecules I'd picked up in the ME's facility. I took him for a run. Out, damned smells! Be gone, visions of viscera! After forty minutes of pain, I felt better.

I was in the shower when I heard Merle's tinny woof—the ring tone for my drug agent cell phone. I turned off the water and grabbed a towel. "Hello?"

"Stacy?" A man's voice.

"Who's this?"

"Evergreen Place? Sunday night?"

The gaunt guy with the pregnant woman. "What was your name again?"

"Mo. Listen, I can hook you up. For the key. You still want it?"

A rush of adrenaline sent tingles to my toes. I wrapped the towel a little tighter and tried to sound calm. "Yeah, sure. What's the deal?"

"Twenty-two."

"When and where?"

"I'll have to take you there. How's about tonight, around midnight? Meet me at Evergreen."

"Can do." I looked at my watch; it was six-thirty. Fredricks would have to help me and I didn't know how long it would take to get everything together.

"Yeah, great. Don't worry, Stacy, it'll go down like ice cream."
He sounded excited. Mo was seeing his chance to broker a deal
and pull in some cash, a promotion in his drug-selling career.

And a promotion for me, of sorts.

I met Fredricks at the office. I had called ahead to alert him
and he asked me to pick up Mexican take-out. He started working his way through the Combo Magnifico. I had a chicken
enchilada—too salty, I threw it away—with a side of guacamole.

He was excited. He put his fork down, stood up, pumped his
arms in the air, and popped a button. "Good job, Stella. Tonight
is perfect. I'll line up surveillance. And ride along."

"What for? Mo doesn't know you."

"You'll tell him I'm your muscle, because you're carrying all
that money and want protection."

"No way he'll believe that."

"You can't go alone. You know the rules. What's to stop them
from bumping you off and taking the money?"

I thought about it. "It's not good business?" I dipped a chip
into the guac. "Want some?"

"Funny." He took a scoopful.

"I'll pat him down first."

"And when you get there? No, Stella. And it's not because
you're female. We wouldn't let Batman go alone."

"Robin's on the payroll?"

"You haven't seen my moves."

"Moves?"

Fredricks stood and grabbed my arm. Quicker than a cat, he
had me facing the wall with both hands behind my back. He
leaned his bulk into me and I was trapped. "Like this," he said,
breathing a little cloud of garlic into my ear.

"Let go of me! How did you do that?"

He backed off. "Brazilian jiujitsu. It's all in the leverage."

"There's so much about you I don't know. What else?"

"I speak Spanish. I won't let on unless I have to." He sat down and resumed eating.

"You think they're Latino?"

"Maybe. And we'll both be armed."

"No." He and I had talked about this before. I didn't like carrying a gun when I bought drugs. A weapon made me look more like a cop, less like a street buyer. And, I had a fear of being shot with my own gun. It happens.

Fredricks put down his fork, a sign he had something really important to say. "Stella, it's protocol. And they'll expect you to be carrying because of the money. Surveillance will follow us, two guys. They'll keep an eye but they can't move in, you understand, unless we summon them. And at midnight, someplace strange—if something goes wrong they might not even know until it's too late. You'll feel better with a gun."

If something goes wrong . . . too late . . . Fredricks was trying to scare me with his jiujitsu and gun talk. I was more of a glass-half-full type. I hoped we'd have a short drive, meet some guy, exchange cash for goods, and leave. No one, including the guy, wanted it to go any differently. I said as much.

Fredricks nodded. "Sweetheart, that's what we all want. No drama, everyone behaves. We determine who they are and what they've got and inform the local authorities so they can prepare warrants. Then they'll raid the place and get the taxpayers' money back." He popped open a ginger ale and took a swig. "Probably at four o'clock some morning when everyone's asleep."

"Whatcha gonna do with the key, Stacy?"

In my opinion, Bebe, Mo's pregnant girlfriend, should have been in bed asleep, not leaning on a dented blue station wagon at midnight blowing cigarette smoke into my face, quizzing me about my narcotics business plan. The full moon reflected enough light to read by, casting deep purpley-black shadows to hide in. We were at the mail kiosk at Evergreen Place, waiting for Mo.

I had invented a story just in case. Fredricks had said they wouldn't really care, they wouldn't believe me because they all lie and expect lies, but I'd better have a story. "I'm in school at State," I said. "I'm going to sell it over there, for school money."

"Good idea," she said. "Someone fronting you the cash?"

"It's mine. My dad died. It's an insurance settlement."

"Oh, I'm sorry. You miss him?"

"Not really. He wasn't in my life much."

"Honey, I can relate to that. Now Mo, he's a good daddy."

"Where is Mo, anyway?" When Fredricks and I arrived at Evergreen Place, Mo and Bebe had been loitering under the kiosk. Fredricks stayed in the SBI truck and Mo disappeared right away, leaving us women to make small talk.

"He's getting directions. Here he is. Christ, would you look at him."

Mo bounded up, his pupils like black nickels. He wore a red-and-black plaid shirt that coordinated perfectly with the swirling tattoos on his arms. "I'm good," he said. "Let's go." He bounced on his toes. "Get this show moving."

"We'll follow you," I said. No way was I getting into a car driven by this tripwire.

"Who's we? Just Stacy with the money. The honey with the money."

"I brought a friend. See him, in the truck?" I pointed to Fredricks, who saw me and waved to the three of us. "We'll follow you, okay?"

"Not okay. Not one bit. Not him. No following."

Bebe stepped in to negotiate. "The reason Mo doesn't want you to follow is, the location is secret."

"And the reason I need my friend along is, I'm nervous about carrying all this money god-knows-where by myself. Plus I'm not riding in a car with you driving all coked up."

"Aw, fuck," said Mo. He ran his hands through his hair and tugged his head back and forth. "You're gonna mess this up."

Bebe took his arm. "Listen, we can work it out. Let her bring her friend, I'll drive all of us. How's that, Stacy?"

"It's okay, I guess," I said. The surveillance team would follow in their car, and if anything went wrong, Fredricks and I wouldn't be trapped, we'd be able to call them.

"I gotta ask. Be right back." Mo bounded back into the shadows.

"Sorry," said Bebe. "He's just nervous."

"And high."

"Well, yeah. He's always high."

"You too?"

"No, I'm pregnant. I quit."

"Rehab?"

"Nope. Just quit on my own."

"Good for you." I wanted to believe her though Fredricks's cynical warning—"they all lie"—made me skeptical.

Summer had finally sailed south and the temperature was in the low fifties. I shivered in the chill, wishing I'd worn a warmer coat. I'd dressed up for this transaction in a black skirt and turtleneck with a belted suede jacket, a gold necklace for bling. Fredricks had won the gun argument and I had tucked a sweet little pistol, a Seecamp LWS 32, into a thigh band holster.

Mo returned. "Okay. Here's the plan. Bebe drives, your friend can come. But you have to cover your eyes." He produced two calico bandannas from a pocket.

I motioned Fredricks over. As Mo and Bebe studied him, I was thankful Fredricks didn't look like a cop any more than I did. He wore jeans and a frayed sweatshirt with a hood, measured five feet six on his tiptoes and many flabby pounds over the weight limit for agents. We had split the money; we each carried eleven thousand dollars in hundreds in a waist stash.

Before Mo put the blindfolds on us, ensuring we couldn't see, I peeked at my watch—12:23. Bebe didn't seem to drive very fast, which was good; the surveillance car would be able to stay back and still follow without being spotted. She didn't say anything about being followed, and Mo seemed more focused on telling Bebe where to turn. I tried to memorize his directions, along with the time delay between turns, but I was disoriented right away as Bebe made two lefts, then a right, then another left. She then drove straight for twenty minutes, but I couldn't tell which point on the compass we were aiming at. The radio played eighties oldies, accompanied by Mo's percussive whistling when he wasn't directing Bebe.

I didn't talk; it seemed too strange to make small talk through a red calico bandanna. Fredricks sat so still I thought he might be asleep. I envied his ability to relax. Despite my earlier positive thinking, my optimistic dream that the cocaine buy would be a simple exchange of money for drugs, as the car sped along I felt increasingly anxious, unable to see or control the inevitable. My fingers had developed a tremor and I pressed my hands together to stop it. Mo began crooning and I longed for silence.

A right turn, a drive of another two minutes, a right turn and an immediate left. Gravel road, couple of bumps, roll to a halt. Homicidally barking dog.

"Wait here," Mo said, and got out of the car. I pulled the blindfold off, checked my eyelashes, and looked at my watch. Forty-one minutes had elapsed. I glanced out the back window—no headlights. It would have been impossible to drive undetected on the gravel road. The guys would have parked on the paved road, and followed the drive on foot. They were out there somewhere.

Bebe had parked close to a building—a house, I thought—though it had become very dark due to cloud cover and I couldn't see much. She rolled down her window and lit a cigarette. The door opened, and Mo went inside. The smoke from Bebe's cigarette stung my eyes and I tasted sour guacamole as my stomach churned. The barking continued, containing threats that froze my spine.

Mo came back to the car and opened my door. "Just you," he said to me. "Bring the cash."

Fredricks got out of the car anyway. "No, no," said Mo. "Come on, man."

"She's not going in there alone," said Fredricks. I looked at him gratefully, for once delighted to have the company of this squat menacing man.

"Man, just go with the program, okay?" Mo pulled his skull cap off and stuffed it into his pocket. He took my arm and pulled. "Come on, Stacy."

Furious at being handled, I unpeeled his fingers from my arm and twisted from his grip. "He comes along or the deal's off."

"How about he holds the money, she gets the kilo, brings it back out to him, gets the money, takes it in?" Bebe asked, ever the negotiator.

Fredricks looked at me and I nodded. "I'll wait by the door," he said. I unbuckled my waist stash and handed it to him. Overhead the clouds suddenly parted and moonlight poured through, lighting up the scene. I took a mental picture. Woods pressing in close, overgrown shrubbery. A second story with dormers, shingle roof, red door with a knocker. Mildewy siding, cobwebby eaves. A German shepherd, on a lead tied to a stake in the ground, growled anxiously. I knew just how it felt.

Mo took a minute to process Bebe's suggestion. "Okay." He motioned me along with his arm. "Come on."

On either side of the door, planters held long-dead vegetation. Fredricks wedged himself up against the door jamb to wait. Moonlight reflected off his bald head. As I passed him, he winked at me. I followed Mo inside.

Oh, the smells. Heavenly smells. Someone was cooking, reminding me I was once again starving. I smelled roasting chicken and coconut and lemon, heard sizzling Latin jazz. We had entered into a center hallway. The room to the left contained leather sectionals and a huge flat-screen TV on a thick multi-colored Persian rug. The room to the right was empty except for a pile of flattened cardboard boxes.

"Wait here," Mo said, pointing to the room with the TV. He didn't tell me to sit so I stood, hearing the party sounds, smelling the party food, feeling utterly unwelcome, hyperaware of the gun mashed against my thigh. Minutes passed.

"Ah, Stacy, welcome to my humble abode." A smiling man advanced toward me, hand outstretched for a shake. "I am Jax. I am sorry you had to wait."

I froze, shocked. A spurt of adrenaline flooded my body. Did he recognize me? Was I blown? I flipped my hair forward to hide more of my face as I shook the hand of my grandmother's latest acquisition. Jax, the chicken-house-builder. Jax with the vicious scar. At least he'd be easy to pick out in a lineup, if I lived long enough to reach that point. He wore an embroidered white cotton shirt, linen trousers, and sandals. He turned to Mo. "You didn't tell me she was so attractive. I would have lowered my price. What is a pretty girl doing with all these drugs?"

Ah, patronizing sexism, how charming. It seemed he didn't recognize me. Fredricks had assured me no one would, and I hadn't thought I cared but it now seemed terribly important. I tried to breathe normally. "A lower price sounds good," I said in my best southern-cracker accent. "Ah'm a starving student."

He smiled, crinkling up his eyes. The left one wasn't real. "Then how about something to eat instead? Join us in the kitchen? We can talk, develop a trust."

My hunger had vanished, leaving cement in my gut. Behind him, Mo was shaking his head no no no. I thought of Fredricks by the door and Bebe waiting in the truck, wanting me to buy the coke and get out of there. "It smells wonderful. Maybe next time, Jax. It's late and my mom will wonder where I am."

He burst into laughter. "*Encantadora!* Certainly I understand. One minute." Jax left the room and Mo rolled his eyes. I dug my nails into my hands to prevent trembling. I thought about meeting Jax at Fern's. I'd been standing in the doorway while he was thirty feet away next to his car. I'd been wearing jeans, a Haw River Festival tee-shirt, no makeup. My hair had been bunched behind my ears with a couple of retro plastic flowers. I looked really different tonight, didn't I? Didn't I?

I thought he'd come back with the drugs but when Jax returned, a woman followed him. Another face I knew. A familiar atmosphere of air freshener enveloped Dana DeGrasso of the squat on East Waters, who'd sold me an envelope of ice Sunday night. Small world, I thought, wondering what to make of the coincidence. Mo knows Jax knows Dana. And everyone knows me. I wondered if she still had my umbrella.

Dana was dressed up tonight, in a soft drapey blouse, tight black pants, and four shades of eye shadow. She towered over me in four-inch wedge heels made entirely of clear plastic, and outweighed me by a good hundred pounds. Jax motioned toward her. "Just do as she says," he said. I frowned at Mo but he shrugged, clueless.

Dana led me into the kitchen where a dark-haired woman was stirring something fragrant in a saucepan. "Hi," I said, and the woman muttered "Hola," as she studied me with big black eyes. A cake on the counter looked like German chocolate, its milk chocolate frosting lumpy with coconut and pecans. Dana issued a command in Spanish, and the woman turned off a burner and left the room.

"I remember you," Dana said. "How ya doing? Someone hooked you up with Jax, I see. Show me some ID." I pulled out my wallet and showed her Stacy's driver's license, everything about it fake except the photo. "Give it to me."

"No problem." Dana couldn't kill me with a piece of plastic.

She carefully copied every item of data from the license, including Stacy's organ donor status (yes). "Okay, sweetheart, I'm going to pat you down."

Her hands moved down my back, over my hips, down my legs, until I had to stop her. I took hold of her wrists. "I'm carrying a gun. For protection, that's all," I said.

"You don't trust us, darling?" She twisted back but I didn't let go. "You want to wrestle?"

That was the last thing I wanted, my nerves were screaming to get out of there, but I couldn't let her touch the Seecamp. Too bad for me. She shoved me into the wall, raised a knee to pin me there, and forced my right arm over my head while she blocked my left with her weight and fished for the gun strapped to my inside thigh. We banged elbows and I kicked her good a few times, but I twisted like a hooked trout, caught by her hundred-pound advantage. When I knocked my head into her windpipe she grabbed my hair and pulled, stepping back, holding my gun in one hand. I dove for the gun and she stiff-armed me. I fell back, side-swiping the chocolate cake and bringing it to the floor.

With shaking hands she raised the gun and pointed it at me. "Aghck," she said, clutching her throat. I must have bruised her esophagus—good. The only thing good at that moment. I lay on the floor in cake and hurt. Fredricks was outside, probably napping. Mo and Jax? Not on my side.

"You can have it," I said. "Just don't aim it at me, okay?"

"Get up," she said. "You shouldn't have brought a weapon into this house." She took hold of my arm—she had hands like steel claws—and pushed me into the other room. She conversed with Jax in rapid Spanish. I wished Fredricks were there to translate, but the gist of the discussion was clear enough.

Jax took the Seecamp from Dana and held it midair, loosely. "Students do not carry guns in leg holsters."

I wanted to scream *Fredricks! Get your jiujitsu moves in here!* at the top of my lungs. "I came into some money and wanted to make more. Just like you," I said. I threw a glance at Mo. He had eased himself out of the room, into the hallway, and had one hand on the doorknob. He was watching Jax like a mouse watches the cat.

Jax stared at me. His good eye was as cold and emotionless as the glass one. "Stacy, if I find you are lying to me, you will pay with your life."

"I'm not lying. I'm just trying to buy some coke. If you don't want my business, I'll leave." It wasn't an idle threat. I was sweaty with fear, sticky with coconut frosting, and ready to be anywhere else.

"Release her." Jax left the room, taking my gun with him. Dana let go of me and I pulled away from her, out of arms' reach. I heard him go up the stairs. After a while I leaned back against the wall and took deep slow breaths to calm my pounding heart. Dana went into the kitchen and fixed herself a plate from the saucepan on the stove—chicken and rice, it looked like—topped it up with some sour cream, came back into the living room carrying the plate, sat down in a chair, crossed her legs, and began to eat. She didn't offer me any, not that I could've eaten anything. My stomach was clenched in a tight spasm.

Jax returned with a plastic-wrapped package and a digital scale. He set the scale on the floor and weighed the package in front of me, exactly two point two pounds. "So you know you are not being cheated. Do you want to try some?"

I shuddered. "I don't. What's the purity?"

"Eighty percent. Very good product."

"I believe you, Jax. Part of that trust between us." I couldn't wait to get out of there.

"So get your money now, chica." He held out an empty manila envelope.

I pushed past Mo and opened the front door to find Fredricks leaning against the planter, rubbing the German shepherd's head. He handed me his cash and my waist stash. I unzipped it, pulled out my half—a hundred hundreds and twenty fifties— and put all the money in the envelope.

It made me sick to exchange twenty-two thousand dollars for a plastic-wrapped block of white powder but I put on a happy face and gave it to Jax. He handed me my gun and I slid it into my pocket. At that moment I decided to go so far undercover even a bulldozer couldn't unearth me. It was time for wigs, brown contacts, aging creams and powders, padded clothing.

Like that, the deal was done. Now it was up to the surveillance team, the sheriff's department, and the DEA to organize a raid, and send Jax and Dana to jail for a long time. I wanted never to see his scarred face or smell her sickening toilet water again.

Fredricks and I were back in our blindfolds, Mo was humming along with a hip-hop ditty. I took deep breaths and every so often I trembled, a peculiar aftereffect of adrenaline. It was almost over.

"So how'd it go?" Bebe asked, once she'd pulled onto the highway.

"They didn't like that she was carrying," Mo said. "Gave her a bit of trouble about it."

"I fell on top of a cake," I said. "Ruined it."

Bebe chortled. "What kind? Did you bring us some?"

"Chocolate."

"Stacy? You okay?" Fredricks asked.

"Sure, fine." What I had to say couldn't be said, yet.

No one else seemed to want to talk much for the rest of the ride. When we reached the Evergreen Apartments, Mo removed the blindfolds. I stretched, twisted right then left, looked behind. A block away, headlights. My watch said 2:17. Bebe pulled into the parking lot.

Mo turned in his seat to look at us. "I'll take my payment now."

"Good job, my man." Fredricks reached inside his sweatshirt and pulled out an envelope. Mo extended his swirly-tattooed arm and took it.

Bebe grabbed the envelope from him. "Give me that."

"No, it's my seed money. Gotta spend money to make money."

"You can keep a hundred." She handed him some bills and he stuck his hand out again. "More," he said.

"Uh, we're gonna get going here," I said. Their bickering was fraying my last nerve. I wanted to throw the boots, these clothes, into a trash can. I needed a long shower to wash away air freshener and coconut frosting and cocaine powder. I nudged Fredricks with an elbow and he opened the car door.

"Bye, honey," Bebe said to me.

Mo shook Fredricks's hand. "Take it easy, man," Mo said.

Lovely evening, thank you so much.

★　★　★　★　★

"What happened back there?" Fredricks asked. We were in the truck, driving to the lab with the package of coke.

"That woman, Dana. Remember her, from the squat on East Waters?"

He nodded. "Sure. Big gal, rode hard and put up wet."

"That's the one. She was there. She patted me down and tried to take my gun. We tussled. Then the guy didn't believe I was a student since I had a gun."

"But you convinced him."

"I guess so. And here's the kicker. I recognized him. He was at the wedding I went to Saturday, the one where the bride died. He goes by Jax." I'd decided not to mention the budding friendship between Jax and Fern. He would be behind bars in twenty-four hours and I didn't want to drag her into this. I described him to Fredricks.

He shook his head. "I don't know him. Did he recognize you?"

"I don't think so."

Fredricks studied me. "A scary guy, huh?"

I nodded. "Very." The tremors had stopped, but the real damage didn't show. My body felt bruised and disrespected. First Fredricks, then Mo, then Dana had pulled, shoved, and handled me roughly. Possibly, Brazilian jiujitsu was in my future.

But first, it was imperative—Fern needed to be warned. Before Jax figured out who I was.

# CHAPTER 10

*Wednesday Morning*

We disbanded around five. Aching, exhausted, I managed to get about two hours of restless sleep, clutching my phone in one hand and dangling the other over the bed to rest on Merle's smooth fur.

At eight, I handed the Seecamp to an evidence tech who pulled a good print off the barrel and told me to come back in two hours. I hoped it would help to identify Jax for the raiding team.

My boss Richard wanted a debriefing. He was *GQ*-ready as usual, in a tailor-made charcoal suit over a pale pink shirt of a fabric woven so tight it would repel water, French cuffs, gold knot cufflinks, and a solid burgundy silk tie. He set the fashion bar high for the rest of the agency, too high. Many had quit trying, like Fredricks in his extender-waist Dockers.

I stood in his office doorway listening to the familiar screech of his coffee grinder. Richard roasted his own beans. If he lived within eight degrees of the equator, he probably would've grown them. But he didn't share. Only the director got a cup of Richard's brew.

The coffee maker huffed and trickled. I took a big sniff and told the part where Dana had lifted my gun. I wasn't proud of that.

"You did well not to get killed," he said, as close as Richard would get to a compliment. He held out his left arm and adjusted the shirt cuff to a perfect inch. "And where was Fredricks?" He gazed over my head at his wall of awards and pictures of himself protecting visiting dignitaries. George H. W. Bush, King Abdullah of Saudi Arabia. Glory days, until he was promoted to managing the likes of me.

"They insisted he wait outside." The memory of the wrestling match with Dana made me shiver. "I didn't want to wear the gun in the first place. Next time I'm not wearing a gun. There's an advantage to being nonthreatening." I wanted him to agree with me.

"It's your choice." His intercom buzzed and he picked up the phone. "Yes?" He listened then hung up. "A warrant is being prepared. They'll put the house under surveillance and go in sometime tonight to make arrests." He stood and picked up the coffeepot, my cue to leave. "Good job, Stella."

A pat on the head didn't quite cut it. I wouldn't relax until Jax and Dana were locked into new living quarters.

I set two turkey club sandwiches and a pint of Chunky Monkey on the table. Between a vase of daisies and the salt shaker I slipped a manila folder containing a single-page printout of the criminal record of Juan Xerxes Covas, aka Jax Covas, to be discussed after eating.

Fern greeted me with a cautious hug. "Careful—I've got paint on me." She led me into her painting room and gestured at a canvas. Hillary and Bill's sweet donkey faces peered at me. They looked so real I could almost hear them. Actually I could hear them—they were outside hee-hawing at Merle, who was in the field sniffing, digging, pouncing as another vole went to rodent heaven.

"Let's eat," I said.

"Thanks, darling." She took a big bite. "Mmm, good sandwich. The turkey's really juicy."

"I can only stay a little while," I said. How much to tell her? Not much. While supportive of me personally, she was ambivalent about government agencies. "I had occasion to become reacquainted with Jax. He's not what you think." Though I didn't know what she thought, actually, other than he was good with a tape measure. "He's a drug dealer."

Fern sat up straight and sipped her tea. "Don't be ridiculous."

I opened the file and extracted his booking photo. "He was arrested fifteen years ago for obstruction of justice, witness tampering, and four counts of distribution of a controlled substance. He went to prison for six years."

She studied the picture with a puzzled expression. Jax's flat scarred face, even fifteen years younger, was unmistakable. "Yes, that's Jax. But so what? It was years ago. People make mistakes."

"But he's still dealing, Fern, I know. You have to distance yourself."

A pause. She folded her arms. "How do you know?" Though the words were challenging, her voice was gentle.

I didn't say anything. We looked at each other for a long moment, Fern's gaze drilling into my eyes as if she were trying to read my mind. "You can't tell me."

"That's right." I spooned some ice cream into a bowl and handed it to her. "I don't usually interfere with your relationships, do I?"

"Not exactly. But I always know what you're thinking, darling. You are transparent to me."

"Really?" I wanted to stump her. "Which one did I like the best?"

"Oh, too easy. The Irishmen."

I smiled, remembering. "They were wonderful." When I was in school at NC State, studying criminal justice and working three part-time jobs, too busy to call her, let alone come home, Fern had two entertaining suitors from Ireland, unrelated but alike in their love of football, dry stout, and her. She'd met them at a kiln opening—they were potters. Ted from Wexford liked music and horse racing, and Arlo from Dingle appreciated dirty jokes and dancing. When she was with either one of them, Fern never stopped laughing.

"Okay, maybe they were the best," I said. "How about the worst?"

I didn't think she'd offer up a name. Then, "Ben Parsons. Remember him?"

"The psychologist with the convertible? He was okay. Why do you pick him?"

"You were going through that bad patch your senior year of high school. When you disappeared with that guy. Ben said I was negligent and you were tired of parenting me and that's why you ran away." She looked sad, and I took her hand.

"Fern, please. We both know I just wanted to have sex. And I was only gone a week. Hey, you raised me good." The police had found us. They weren't after me, the runaway, but Chuck, who'd picked me up at the State Fair and was wanted for a list of crimes, starting with failure to pay child support. "Ben Parsons wasn't the worst. This one's the worst, by far." I tapped Jax's photo. "Stay away from him."

She shook her head. "It's too bad. He was going to build a chicken house. You sure you don't have him mixed up with someone else?" She pulled out her knitting. "I'm making him a scarf, see?" The scarf was striped in Carolina blue and white, with matching fringe.

"He isn't someone you should associate with." I rinsed our bowls in the sink, and cleared the sandwich wrappings from the table. "I mean it, Fern. He's very bad news."

"If you say so," she said, though I detected a note of regret.

★  ★  ★  ★  ★

I dropped into Lottie Ember's chocolate store, Cacao Café, for an informal interview. Lottie's husband, Evan, had been one of the groomsman at the wedding, and they had been guests at the B&B. The smell of chocolate instantly dunked me into a vat of trufflely anticipation.

Next to the cash register, their child lay on her back in an overlarge stroller, her twisted torso restrained by a quilted harness. She aimed brown eyes right at me in an unwavering stare. She wore a red knit dress patterned with hearts and butterflies; her hair was a froth of black curls. Slowly, slowly she raised a hand in a wave and moaned something like "hello."

"Hi there," I said. I patted the child's foot and she frowned, twisting her neck to catch her mother's eye.

"Don't touch her," said Lottie sharply. "Do you like it when strangers touch you?" Lottie had a heart-shaped face and a fashionably spiky haircut. She got away with it. That haircut on me? People would avert their eyes in horror.

"What's her name?"

"She can talk. Ask her."

"I'm Stella," I said to the child. "What's your name?"

"Aah-ess," she said.

"Alice?" I guessed. Lottie nodded. "How old are you, Alice?" She held out her hand to me and I almost took it until I remembered Lottie's injunction. Her thumb was folded under. "You're four?"

"That's right," said Lottie. "Alice had a birthday yesterday. We had a party, didn't we, sweetie?"

"Cake," Alice said so distinctly I smiled. Then she said something else I didn't get.

"Presents," said Lottie. "She got books and a dollhouse. She loves books. Alice can read."

"Just turned four, and she can read? Impressive."

Lottie ignored the compliment. "I remember you from the wedding. You're the SBI agent."

I nodded. "And I need a few minutes of your time."

"Do you want to talk to Evan, too? He's here, in the office."

"Sure." I knew Evan was a lawyer—maybe he was here to help Lottie out with her business.

Lottie went down a hallway and poked her head in an open door. I inhaled the store's intoxicating smells—chocolate, yeast, cinnamon, coffee. She came back, followed by Evan. He was a heavy guy, unshaven, with a dead expression. He didn't look at me, but sat at a tiny table and stared at his feet.

Lottie wheeled Alice around to face a small TV behind the cash register, and started a movie for her. "Would you like a cappuccino? Or hot chocolate?" she asked me.

I scrutinized the pastry display. "Can I have some of that?" I had spied a three-layer cake labeled Chocolate High that looked dense as fudge. "Just a tiny sliver. As a customer, of course."

She cut a piece the size of a dozen slivers and slid it onto a doily-covered plate, motioning for me to sit next to Evan. "We're waiting for my salesclerk to get here," she said, "so I can take Alice swimming. What do you want from us?"

"I'm following up with the wedding guests who stayed at the inn." I took a bite of the cake. Oh my. Velvety as only cocoa butter can be, not too sweet, with a hint of raspberry.

"Ingrid told me Justine was poisoned." Lottie stared at me with her vibrant brown eyes. "How are we supposed to help?"

"Do you remember anything unusual about the morning? Anything said, arguments, that sort of thing." I took another, larger bite.

"We all had breakfast together, except for Mike's parents, and his aunt Delia. She wasn't feeling well. It was buffet style and we all ate the same things. The breakfast was pleasant, a treat for me. Alice enjoys being around people." Lottie spoke with energy, glancing at her husband now and then. He sat expressionless, contributing nothing, his dull gaze fastened on the pastry cooler.

"And afterward?"

"Evan and I took her outside. We walked around for a bit with the stroller, then we found some chairs on the porch and read. It was nice to relax. Around noon we came in to get ready for the wedding. I gave Alice a snack but we didn't eat because there was going to be plenty of food after the ceremony."

"How about traffic up and down stairs, after noon?"

"Our door was shut most of the time. Excuse me a minute." She went over to a customer in the back of the room who wanted to pay.

While she was busy, I tried to get a word out of Evan. "You hang out much with Mike Olmert?"

He shook his head, staring at the floor between his feet.

"How well did you know Justine?"

Evan raised his gaze from the floor and stared at me for a long moment, then shook his head. Lottie got a bottle of water and sat back down. She took her husband's hand and squeezed it but he didn't respond. "Evan's a little depressed," she said gently. "He lost his job a few weeks ago."

"There's a lot of that these days. Cutbacks and layoffs," I said.

"Evan was fired for cause." She said it like he wasn't listening, and indeed, he appeared not to be. "He is clinically depressed."

"I'm so sorry," I said, trying to sound sympathetic. But to be honest, I wouldn't have hired him for traffic court.

"He tried to hide it. That's the irony. If he'd come right out and told them, he would have gotten treatment and a disability check. Instead he didn't say anything, just got less productive until clients complained. Isn't that right, sweetie?"

Evan blinked.

"How did you know Justine?" I asked.

"Evan's known Mike Olmert for about ten years. They were in the same fraternity at NC State. A bunch of them and their families got together a few months ago for a picnic. Mike brought Justine, in fact he proposed to her that day. They went for a canoe ride and when they came back Justine was wearing a gorgeous ring. But then a terrible thing happened—this woman died. Did anyone tell you about it?"

"Emma McMahon, you mean?"

Lottie nodded. "Her death is the main thing I remember about that day. I'll never forget it. Emma was eating at the picnic table with the rest of us, then she got this panicky look and started gasping. Her husband was frantic, trying to get medicine out of the car, but it was locked and he couldn't find his keys. Within minutes she was dead." She shook her head as if to dispel the image. "Mike tried CPR for a long time but apparently her airway was closed. It was awful."

"An allergic reaction, was it?"

"She came up in hives all over and her husband said she was probably stung. Poor girl. But you want to know about Justine."

"What was she like?"

Lottie paused. "Well, she was nice enough." She looked over at Alice, who was singing along with the movie, musically and on-key, but the words were indecipherable. "Pleasant. Very, very attractive. Some of the women were annoyed about it. You know, she didn't have to wear such tight clothes. Oh, and she was an amazing cook. She brought a big pot of chili that could have won awards, in my opinion."

"Did you talk to her?"

"She and I had a brief conversation about Alice, actually a disagreement about obstetrics. Probably I started the argument. She was a midwife. I told her I wished we'd had a real doctor

111

when Alice was born. Right, sweetie?" She turned to Evan, touched his arm. He stared ahead as though lost in his thoughts.

I was taking notes and my mouth was full of cake or I'd have said something. Instead I raised my eyebrows and nodded encouragingly.

"Instead of the incompetents at the stupid birthing center." She looked at her daughter, who was rocking her head side to side along with the beat of the music. "I try not to be bitter. Just deal with it. It's too easy to be angry, but I have to be careful—Alice knows what I'm feeling. She's quite sensitive."

I didn't know quite how to ask what was wrong. "Was she born with this condition?"

"No one can say. The birth was routine but Alice had seizures almost immediately. She stopped breathing. God save me, I wish I'd been in a hospital." She looked over at her daughter. "When you have a baby, you know your life will change. But not like this."

I put down my fork. It felt rude to be shoveling in cake at that moment, and besides, my arteries were clamping shut. I murmured something about how difficult it must be.

"Don't get me wrong, I don't resent what I have to do. I'm her mother, it's a pleasure. I resent on her behalf. For her limitations." She looked out the window. "There's our salesclerk. Say 'good-bye,' Alice."

"Goo-eye, Aah-ess," the girl groaned, thrashing her body on the stroller to look at me.

Lottie and I laughed. "A comedienne, too," I said. "See you later, gater."

Alice smiled. " 'Ay-ter, 'ay-ter." Outside, Lottie talked briefly with her salesclerk, then together they lifted Alice's stroller into the van. I put money on the table. What had I learned? Alice was smart, Lottie was a saint, Evan was depressed. Justine wore tight clothes. No one unusual had been seen going upstairs in the B&B. Though Chocolate High had added to my hips, none of this added up to murder.

Kate's rocketing return of serve drew the man to center court and he returned the ball with an overhead smash. She lunged and caught the ball on the tip of her racquet, flipping it just over the net. He rushed up and tapped it back. She killed it with a drive down the sideline. "Love-thirty," he called, and retrieved the ball. Kate bounced from foot to foot and spun her racquet, as focused as a predator on the incoming serve.

Watching from the sidelines was a woman I recognized as rectangular Ingrid, the maid of honor who'd first heard Justine's cries through the locked door of the Falkirk room. Today Ingrid was preppy in khaki slacks and a pink polo shirt.

"She's an amazing tennis player," I said to her. I had arranged to meet Kate, Mike Olmert's sister, at this tennis club where she was the pro, to pick up a copy of her video taken during the rehearsal dinner.

"She's retired," Ingrid said.

"Yeah, right." Kate looked about thirty.

"From competition. She still coaches. This guy's paying two hundred an hour to play her."

"Will she win?"

Ingrid grinned at me. "She will. She'll let him take a few games, to keep his hopes up." She sneezed. "Pardon. Allergies. Here's the video." Ingrid handed me a DVD case. "How's the investigation coming?"

"It's a tough one." That was an understatement. We didn't have a single suspect, not even a person of interest.

With a final thwack Kate cemented her win and shook hands with her client. She trotted over to us and Ingrid handed her a bottle of water and a towel. Kate patted her face and neck, then drained the bottle.

"How's your brother doing?" I asked her.

"He's devastated," Kate said. "He could hardly bear to go back to their townhouse but he had to take care of Justine's cat and fish."

So Mike and Justine had been living together. Sleeping together. There was much I didn't know. "Got a minute for a few questions?"

Kate looked at Ingrid, who shrugged her square shoulders. "Yeah, I guess. What do you need?"

"Somewhere we can sit?"

Kate led the way, through the clubhouse, furnished like an English drawing room with fat chairs dressed in faded chintz and walls of salmon pink and willow green, out the other side to a swimming pool. We sat down at a wrought iron table. A couple of diehard swimmers performed slow laps in the clear blue-green water. It was sweater weather, and the breezes were laden with pollen. A few yellow leaves floated on the pool surface.

"Kate, how well did you know Justine?"

Her elbows flew up and she ran her fingers through her hair. "I wasn't close to her if that's what you mean. We were different as night and day. I like to be outside, hiking or climbing or skiing. She was always inside perfecting her eye shadow or shopping for lingerie. Nothing in common." Kate rotated her torso left and right, then rolled her shoulders. She raised both her legs straight in front of her and flexed her feet, then pointed her toes. Flex, point, flex, point.

I asked her when she first met Justine.

"A year ago, when Ingrid and I moved in together." She nodded toward Ingrid. "We had a party, and Ingrid invited her. They were old friends."

"You two are roommates?"

"We're partners," Ingrid said, smiling at Kate and squeezing her hand.

Aha. I spent a second trying to put this revelation together with her mother's homophobia and Justine's gender change, and gave up. "And Mike came too, right? He said he met Justine at your place."

"We invited everyone," said Ingrid. "Our families, our friends, everyone. Remember the quail eggs, Kate? And the tiny chocolate cupcakes?"

"You did a wonderful job with the food."

"I wanted them to like me." Ingrid looked wistful.

Kate frowned. "Geez, Ingrid. Screw them."

"I wished they'd given me a chance."

"Who are you talking about?" I asked.

"My parents," Kate said. "They've never approved of our relationship."

"No matter what I do, how hard I try," Ingrid said. Tears filled her eyes and she looked away.

Kate patted her hand. "Sweetie, it isn't you. They're horrible bigots."

Ingrid sighed. "I know. I just keep hoping . . ."

"Mike met Justine there?"

"He fell hard," Ingrid said. "He wouldn't talk to anyone else. Remember?"

Kate nodded. "Well, she was absolutely beautiful. You'll see, on the video I took."

I wanted to know what Justine had looked like in better times. She'd not been beautiful on Saturday, or yesterday on a rolling cart. "The morning of the wedding, do you remember anything unusual? Any arguments?"

"I was the last person to see her alive," Kate said. She rolled her shoulders with an audible crack.

"What?" Kate surely had an astonishing way of putting things.

"After I put on that awful dress—remember, the red taffeta?—I went in her room to get help with makeup. She had insisted, because she knew I lacked that gene."

"What time?"

"Around twelve-thirty. She put some stuff on my face, not much, because I wasn't used to it. I didn't like the way I looked, all painted up, and I wiped some of it off. Geez, I feel bad now, because she was disappointed."

"You looked fine, Kate," Ingrid said. "Natural."

But nature sometimes needs assistance. Mascara had been invented for blond eyelashes like Kate's. "Did Justine say anything, do anything, that in retrospect . . . ?"

"Provides a clue? No." Kate raised her arms overhead in a giant stretch. Ingrid watched her, seeming to wonder what she would say.

A swimmer emerged from the pool and dripped his way into the clubhouse. The sun slid behind a cumulus cloud resembling a camel. Kate shivered and rubbed her arms.

"You're catching a chill," Ingrid said. "Go and shower."

"Will you please excuse me?" Kate asked. She raised her arms and made flappy wings as she walked to the clubhouse.

Ingrid watched her and chuckled. "What a nut."

"Ingrid, did you know Justine was transsexual?"

She opened her eyes wide as if astonished. "How . . . ? Oh yeah, the autopsy. You know, I always think of her as a woman. I mean, she's *been* a woman for—gosh, seven years? Yeah, I knew. I went to school with her—him—in Wilmington. Johnny and I were really good friends. I always knew he wanted to be a girl. It seemed natural to me that he'd make the change, once he could afford it. And he—she—didn't want anyone to know, so I promised not to tell. I told only Kate. Justine trusted me."

"Not even Mike?"

Ingrid flushed pink. "She trusted me, like I said."

I wondered whether she was lying. "Did Kate tell Mike?"

She turned to watch the swimmers. "Kate and Mike don't

talk. He disapproves."

"Disapproves . . . ?"

"Of us. He came to our party, figured out we were gay, snagged Justine, and left. We didn't see him again for a year, until last Friday night."

"So he wasn't close to his sister, yet the two of you were asked to be in the wedding?"

"Oh, that was Justine's idea. She thought the wedding could bring Mike's family back together. If Mike got to know how wonderful I was, he'd support Kate and me as a couple. Stop thinking we were going to fry in hell." She pushed her hair behind her ears, revealing them to be round as an Oreo. Square face, square glasses, squared-off shoulders. Geometrical Ingrid.

"Why would anyone want to harm Justine?"

"I can't imagine." She sounded weary.

Her obtuseness irritated me. "Of course you can. Revenge, fear, jealousy, control, anger, greed. Have I forgotten anything?"

"Accident, self-defense, insanity."

"Any of those apply in this case?"

She folded her arms across her chest. "What's hearsay?"

"Rumor. Or testimony concerning what someone said, not under oath."

"Not the right word then. I don't want to get people into trouble. I could be wrong."

"Enemies, plural?"

"It's just"—Ingrid looked into the sky as if the heavens held an answer—"just the timing of it, like someone wanted to stop the wedding."

"Like Mike? Did he find out about the sex change, get cold feet?"

She shrugged. "Kate and I certainly didn't tell him. Justine didn't either, far as I know."

A gust of wind sent more leaves into the pool. A gray squirrel crept close and chattered at us, whipping its tail from side to side, then crawled into a flower pot and commenced to dig.

"Tricia Scott," I said. "I had a chance to look at her book. She has extreme views."

Ingrid winced. "Go ahead, say it. She's homophobic."

"Is that her true self speaking? Or an attitude she feels she has to adopt?"

"Deep down inside? Her true self. Gays freak her out."

The squirrel had found a pecan in the flowerpot and was nibbling on the shell, rudely spitting bits at us. "How does she act toward you?"

Ingrid shook her head. "She's a Southern lady, and has to be sweet as honey to everyone. But she's also convinced Kate's going to hell, and it's my fault. The most painful part for Kate was that her mother was so excited about Mike's wedding. Tricia adored Justine."

"Quite a contrast then." And ironic, given Justine's gender change.

"We avoid them, and vice-versa." Ingrid stood up, startling the squirrel, who sprinted up a tree and chattered curses. "I have to go. Call if you need anything." She handed me her card. *Ingrid Hoyt, Certified Nurse-Midwife, Master of Science in Nursing, Birthing Center of the Carolinas. A gentle, respectful alternative.*

"Thanks, I will." Birthing center? Where she worked with Justine. Lottie's baby, little Alice in the wheelchair, had been born in a birthing center, not a hospital. There weren't that many of them in the area. Walking to my car, I called Hogan and asked him to find out where four-year-old Alice Ember had been born.

"Just once, give me a challenge," he said.

I stopped by the tennis courts to watch a man lob balls to two young boys. The boys were jumping and shrieking whenever one of them managed to return a ball, having a lot more fun than I was. The man seemed to have inexhaustible patience. Growing up without a father, I was drawn to such scenes. I wasn't aware of any particular sense of loss—that came with thoughts of my mother—but I didn't know how it felt to have a dad. I certainly didn't remember ever experiencing anything like those two kids' excitement.

Anselmo Morales called. A key bit of evidence had just come in from the lab. Justine's fatal dose of strychnine had been in her mug of bitter tea.

"What was the source? Could they tell?" I said.

"The rodenticide you found. It's almost two percent strychnine alkaloid. From the concentration they figure about a half a teaspoon was added, many times the lethal dose. In that concentration, they estimate it was consumed about twenty minutes before she died."

One of the kids managed a pop fly, and over the fence came a yellow ball. I picked it up, pitched it back. Waves all around, big smile from the dad.

"Say, want to watch a movie with me?" I asked.

"Hope it's an action flick."

"Rehearsal dinner, starring Justine Bradley, her friends, and family."

"Sure. Where?"

A mental picture—the two of us curled up on my thrift shop sofa, sharing a bowl of popcorn, laughing at the funny parts, Merle at our feet. I threw away the picture; it was ridiculous. I must be deranged, daddy-shopping for Merle. "I'll bring it to the sheriff's department around eight tonight," I told him.

I dropped my suede jacket off at the cleaner's and headed home. Merle needed exercise and I needed an attitude adjustment. It was a gorgeous afternoon; the temperature was nearly seventy, and breezy gusts sent the orange and red leaves into mini-tornadoes across the community college trail. We'd just finished mile three when my phone chimed. I expected Hogan but it was Wyatt, the innkeeper.

He started out quiet, but strangled, then exploded. "You people have to do something. I told you about the sabotage. Do you know the money I'm losing? This is the final goddamned straw."

I could almost see his purple self-pitying face as he spewed into the phone. "Wait, Wyatt. What happened?"

"Yesterday. We finally get a paying guest. Lady drives up and there's a dead raccoon in the driveway! She freaks and cancels, a four-night booking gone."

"Nothing I can do, Wyatt. Sorry." I'd reached an exercise station so I stopped to stretch my legs and pour some water for Merle.

"Man, this is costing me. I want an investigation! Start with BBAP, those crooks!"

"The what?"

"Bed and Breakfast Association of the Piedmont. An innkeeper cabal. They're trying to drive me into the ground."

Bizarre. I tried to put myself in his place—ragged around the edges, a bit of understandable paranoia—but the best I could come up with was another recommendation to call the sheriff. He mumbled and cursed and finally hung up.

My neighbor Saffron was sitting on her front porch, peekapoo in one hand, wine glass in the other. She waved to me and her dog yapped a few times, sort of a come-play-with-me invitation to Merle. She was cute, if you like the stuffed-toy type. The dog, I mean. Though in the right lighting, Saffron could be cute, too. She was a roundish forty-year-old who alternated between mania (free at last! men! sex! independence!) and depression (life wasn't meant to turn out this way, poverty, wah

wah wah). Right then, a couple of glasses of wine and an hour spent passively listening to Saffron's divorce saga would have suited me to a tee, but later tonight I needed to be alert, to meet Anselmo and watch Kate's video.

After a shower, I lay down and fell asleep. I dreamt about Dana DeGrasso's hot fury and Jax's cold rage. They were caught and cuffed, crammed into a police car, but they escaped and came after me firing guns that spit out yellow tennis balls filled with gopher bait. Justine Bradley floated above us in her wedding dress as Wyatt shook his fist at her. As I dreamed, it all made perfect sense, but as soon as I woke, the logic faded, leaving only surreal images and a feeling of dreamy dread, like something bad was going to happen to me. I didn't enjoy the feeling and hoped it would fade. I wasn't psychic. As far as I knew.

# CHAPTER 11

*Wednesday Evening*

Anselmo's sweater was soft and the same inky green color as his
eyes. He seemed to have nothing on underneath it. He was
growing on me, though I knew very little about him. Maybe
that was why. "Here we go," he said, and pushed Play.

I recognized the inn's dining room, the tapestried walls and
heavy dark furniture. Wyatt and Liesle moved in the background,
serving bowls of soup, placing a basket of bread at each end of
the long table. The sound track was confusing, picking up bits
of a dozen conversations. Kate began to narrate, explaining why
they were there, panning around the table to introduce
everyone. Then the toasts and jokes began, mostly at Mike's
expense, tired old ball-and-chain stories. Scoop Scott, Mike's
stepfather, knew a lot of jokes. "I never knew what happiness
was until I got married . . . and then it was too late!" Ha ha.
Then, "A happy marriage is a matter of give and take; the
husband gives and the wife takes." Ho ho.

Tricia Scott delivered a lecture full of advice for Justine—
attack the issue not the person, keep separate closets (from the
chuckles it seemed Mike was a notorious slob), never go to bed
angry, learn to play golf so you can spend time together. She
threw in a little fifties-appropriate advice—"Make your home
peaceful and comfortable. Greet him with a warm smile and
never complain."

Justine took this well. She laughed and kissed cheeks and

122

poured wine. She had lovely hazel eyes with long lashes, thick dark brown hair she wore tucked behind her ears in a sweep to her shoulders. She wore a cranberry-red dress with a deep V-neck that showed off generous cleavage. I could see why she'd chosen that color for her bridesmaids' dresses—it was perfect for her. Her gestures were graceful, her voice was husky but musical, not a man's voice at all.

"Looks like a girl. Talks and walks like a girl," Anselmo said.

"Is a girl," I said.

Mike sat next to her, his body language expressing familiarity and comfort with Justine as they leaned together to share a joke. He watched her, seeming to admire her lively beauty. Anyone would say they seemed delighted in each other's company.

But not everyone appeared happy.

Kate must have handed the camera to someone else, because she was in the next shot, offering her own toast to Mike and Justine, ending with, "And to the future, when *every* loving couple can legally be permitted the sacrament of marriage."

"Kate," Tricia hissed. "Not now!"

Kate smiled at her mother. "If not now, when?"

"I agree," Scoop said. "Even gays should know the joys of alimony."

Tricia's face was distressed. "Let's not spoil this lovely dinner."

Kate rolled her eyes and brought Ingrid's hand up for a kiss.

"Kate, behave yourself," Scoop said, looking uncomfortable.

"Like you do?"

Mike stood, cleared his throat for emphasis, and raised his glass. "A toast to friends and family. Justine and I are so grateful for your support."

Clink, clink, sip, sip. As he went on with clichés and bromides, the faces around the table relaxed. After the toasts, the camera was passed from hand to hand for unscripted observations. Someone pointed it at Delia and Webster Scott for an interminable amount of time; Delia chattered about a dispute with a credit card company while Webster shone his teeth in a paralyzed grin. I had the feeling he worried what she'd say, and remembered how she'd told me, "I nearly killed her once."

Delia seemed unaware of her husband's discomfort until he patted her hand, then she jerked away from him. "What? What's bothering you now?" she said. "Want me to shut up? Afraid of what I'll say? Well, the truth is going to remain hidden. I like your nephew too much." She blew Mike a kiss.

I stopped the video. "Did you hear that?"

Anselmo looked puzzled. "What was she talking about? The sex change? Did Delia know about it?"

"We'll have to ask her." I pushed Play again.

We saw Webster grin even harder. "Maybe we should let someone else have the floor," he said. Oops.

"Who? You? What are you gonna talk about, golf or girls?" Delia yanked the scarf from her neck and fanned herself vigorously. "Hot flash," she said into the camera. "Power surge. I'm gonna be a tomato for Halloween."

Webster's smile weakened and he waved the camera away, like a celebrity reacting to paparazzi. Shield the little woman, hide her under a basket. But I liked Delia's outspokenness, a refreshing contrast to the too-polite Tricia Scott.

"Here, give me that," Kate said, and the camera jerked around until it was pointed at Gregor McMahon, uptight in his neck brace. "Gregor, you're on," Kate said.

"I propose a toast to the bride and groom," Gregor said. He stood and lifted his glass. "Your meeting was a beginning. Your marriage is progress. Working together will be success." Then he added, "May all your troubles be little ones."

Okay, not very creative, but at least he tried. He took a sip of wine and the camera panned to Justine and Mike.

"Gregor, I'm so grateful you'll be part of our wedding," Mike said.

Justine nodded and added, "This must be sad for you."

Pan back to Gregor, who wore a tense smile, as though he was masking his feelings. "Emma and I had a perfect wedding. In October, like yours."

There was a brief silence, broken by Delia Scott. "Where is she? Did your wife leave you?"

At that point, whoever had been filming decided to cut off Gregor's response to Delia's rude question, and the video next showed Kate raising her glass. "As you know, I am not a traditionalist." She put her arm around Ingrid and kissed her cheek. "But I believe in love, and I believe in going after what you want. Mike adores Justine. I'm proud of my brother for going after her, and for making this commitment. And grateful to Justine for getting us all together." General murmurs of agreement all around, as the camera panned to Mike's parents.

Tricia and Scoop applauded, restored to good humor. "And someday soon, grandbabies!" Tricia said. She leaned around her husband to smile at Justine.

Camera on Mike. He frowned at his mother. "Give us a break," he said in a reasonable tone. "Babies are not on the radar right now."

"Oh, of course not, darling," Tricia said. "We can wait."

Anselmo paused the DVD, freezing Tricia mid-smile. "Tricia is implying that Mike and Justine will have kids?"

"That's what I heard. Seems they don't know about the sex change."

"That's a reasonable assumption. What happened to the guy's wife?"

I told him what little I knew about Emma McMahon, her fatal reaction to an insect sting at a picnic six months ago. He started the video again. The camera lingered on a dinner plate containing the main course, poached salmon and roasted potatoes. There must have been a break in the filming because in the next shot, Wyatt was serving small plates of a layered dessert. "Lottie brought this," he said. Exclamations of gratitude as the camera panned around to Lottie Ember. "It's tiramisu cheesecake in a white cake crust," she said, "topped with a layer of mascarpone, then chocolate whipped cream."

"If I had your job, I'd be big as a truck," Tricia said.

Lottie laughed. "I used to taste everything, but believe it or not, you can get tired of chocolate. On the other hand, my husband . . ." She pointed to Evan's clean plate. He nodded and patted his girth.

I paused the playback. "That's more action than I saw from him this afternoon. He was completely inert. Really depressed."

"Good video," Anselmo said. "Really helps to see her alive."

"Wyatt's been complaining about sabotage, did he tell you?"

"No. He must think you're a better listener."

"He said someone ruined his air conditioner and put a dead raccoon in his driveway."

Anselmo frowned. "Is that relevant to our case?"

"Wyatt says so."

"He also said Justine's death is an attempt to close his inn. We don't believe that, do we?"

I shook my head. "Of course not." I didn't want to seem naïve so I didn't mention my nagging twinge that there might be a connection, though doctoring a cup of tea with rat poison was a quantum leap from fouling up an air conditioner. I decided to keep an open mind. A hole in my head, as it were.

# CHAPTER 12

*Thursday Very Early Morning*

"Donut?" Fredricks pushed the box my way.

"No thanks."

"I grilled vegetables last night. I make this marinade? Think Japan meets Amarillo."

"Cilantro and soy sauce," I said.

"Jalapenos, honey, lime." Fredricks closed his eyes at the memory. "Oh . . . man."

"Sounds good." I thought of my own dinner, cottage cheese and noodle soup. If I were nicer to Fredricks would he bring me leftovers? "I'd love to try it some time," I said.

He didn't get the hint, but instead jotted the marinade recipe down for me. We were waiting in my cubicle to learn the outcome of a predawn raid currently under way on Jax's place, twenty-eight hours after I bought the kilo. I yawned, and sipped the coffee Fredricks had thoughtfully brewed. "When will we hear?" I asked.

Fredricks looked at his watch. "They met up at three-thirty. Say it takes an hour to get to the house and reconnoiter. So it should be about over by now. Let's give them another twenty minutes."

"Sure. Then after that?"

"What do you mean?"

"What's our role?"

"You'll make a positive ID, then we're done, sweetheart. No

role until the trial, if there is one—they'll probably take a deal. What did you think?"

"Then why are we here waiting? I could have come in at noon and identified him."

"Because we're curious. Because we're part of the team. We're supporting the effort."

At that moment I purely detested Fredricks. Sleep was all I could think about but it was going to be a busy day. I leafed through my notebook and underlined things to do next. I had to interview Tricia and Scoop Scott. I was intensely curious to know whether they were aware of Justine's sex change. I wanted to talk to Delia and Webster Scott separately. I looked at my notes—they lived near Wilmington, a three-hour drive. I could go tomorrow.

Fredricks's cell phone chimed and he flipped it open. "Yeah? . . . Oh yeah?" He listened for several minutes. "Okay. Thanks." He snapped it shut and studied me. "Guess what?"

For once he wasn't chewing, so I studied him right back. "What?" I said.

"No Jax, no Dana."

"They were gone?"

"The only person in the house was a housekeeper. She said Jax and Dana left very early yesterday. She thought it was because of a deal the previous night, some girl buying drugs. Jax was beating himself up 'cause he suspected she was a cop but sold it anyway. 'Cute college girls don't buy keys,' he said. 'Someone needs to set her straight.' Those were his exact words, according to the housekeeper, translated into English. She's illegal, by the way, and was turned over to ICE."

"So Jax guessed I was police." What a disaster. Twenty-two thousand dollars to Jax, a thousand to Mo—gone. A night of surveillance, wasted.

"Oh, we'll get them. But watch yourself. It's not unheard of for witnesses to be threatened or worse."

"He doesn't know who I am."

Fredricks pursed his lips. "I'm just saying, be careful, sweetheart."

"Sure, I'll check the closets before I go to sleep." I sounded flip but underneath I felt a buzz of worry begin a slow spin.

"Sleep sounds good. Listen, why don't you go home."

"I will if you will."

Fredricks flicked open his phone and thumbed the buttons as he trudged out of the room. I sank onto the table and closed my eyes to wallow in paranoia. A threat from Jax. If Fern had talked to Jax, had she said anything about me? He might know exactly who I was. Oh, was I tired. And there was no cure except sleep, which wasn't on my schedule.

But it happened anyway. The combo of fatigue and anxiety and an utterly quiet office sent me into la-la land until my phone chimed.

"Hope I didn't wake you," Hogan said.

"Don't worry, I've been up for hours." I yawned and rubbed my eyes.

"You sound like you just woke up. Listen, I'm going to be in a seminar all day so I wanted to get you this information. Got a pencil?"

"Sure."

"Justine Bradley's name change. Get this—she used to be a guy!"

"Yeah, I know. What was her name before?"

"John Nicholas Bradley. She changed it to Justine Nicole Bradley. The state issued her a new birth certificate, with the new name and sex. When did you know?"

"As of the autopsy."

"This is a shocker," Hogan said. "Did Mike know?"

"He says he didn't."

"Well, she sure fooled everyone. Was that why she was killed?"

"I don't know."

"You don't know much, do you."

I sighed. "Why don't you just tell me what you know, Hogan."

"Justine had a life insurance policy, ten thousand dollars. Her brother is the beneficiary."

A brother? Justine's family had been conspicuously absent from the wedding. Hogan gave me the brother's address in Wilmington, and a phone number. "And you asked about Psylex, where Gia Mabe works. They manufacture human proteins from genetically modified plants. No mention of strychnine anywhere in their corporate literature. None of their scientists use it, according to their publications. And it took me seven hours to research that."

Oddly, I didn't feel guilty. "Really helpful, Hogan, I mean it."

"Finally, Alice Ember was born at the Birthing Center of the Carolinas. Where, coincidentally—"

"I know. Where Justine worked. Any connection?"

"Funny you should ask. They wouldn't tell me. But the Embers sued the birthing center three years ago, then settled for an undisclosed amount."

I wasn't surprised to hear that, given the intensity of Lottie's remarks about the "stupid birthing center." And Evan being a lawyer. "Hogan, you're a gem."

"Anything for you, Stella."

Then dump her skinny little ass, I thought. Instead, I said, "Thanks. Enjoy your seminar."

Normally I don't drop in on Fern this early in the morning. Or without calling first. But I had a good reason to catch her off guard. Had she talked to Jax? Drug dealers were insanely suspicious. Did Fern say something that propelled him into hiding? I needed to reinforce my order: *do not mention me to Jax.*

I drove west on Highway 64, against the morning traffic pouring into Raleigh. My favorite part of the drive is the two-mile stretch across Jordan Lake, a reservoir created from the damming of the Haw River for flood control. State land surrounds fourteen thousand acres of sparkling lake and boasts more bald eagles than any other spot in North Carolina. Someday I might have time to get out of my car and enjoy it.

A buttery sun was burning the gray mist from Fern's field and turning the tin roof of the farmhouse into a pearly mirror. I could hear Hillary and Bill requesting attention, or perhaps breakfast, from the donkey pen. I pushed open the front door.

Baking smells came from the kitchen so I headed that way. Fern was measuring coffee; she makes an espresso-strength brew. "What's for breakfast?" I said.

"Darling! A surprise visit!" She gave me a hug, enveloping me in soft pink terry cloth. Her hair was damp and fragrant with lavender, the family scent. "Sit down. I'll cook for you, for a change. I'm making bread."

"I need to stand up or I'll fall asleep. You sit down." I opened the fridge and took out butter, milk and eggs. The eggs reminded me of chickens and Jax. When the teakettle began to whistle, I poured water into a pot for grits, and the rest into the dented metal coffeepot, surely an antique by now.

There was no point in beating around the bush; a direct question would be best. I turned to face Fern. She beamed at me.

"Did you talk to Jax since yesterday?" I said. "Since I warned you about him?"

She sat up straight. "Why?"

Could I tell her? I'd already crossed the line by warning her about him, before the raid on his house. "Did you tell him you couldn't see him again?"

"He called. He asked me to a football game but I said no. I

didn't say never. I'd have to give him a good reason and what could I say?" The kitchen timer dinged. "Take the bread out, would you?"

I took the two aromatic golden loaves from the oven, then poured two mugs of coffee. I added milk to mine until it was a drinkable color. Measured grits into boiling water, and started to scramble the eggs. "Haven't you ever broken it off with someone?"

She tipped her head. "Of course I have. I'll think of something. But honestly, I want a nice chicken house."

I let out a sigh of relief. I was glad she hadn't agreed to a date. There was a good chance she'd never see him again, but nothing was certain. My dilemma was this—how much could I tell her? The more she knew, the more dangerous it was for her. The less she knew, the more dangerous it was for me. I set our plates on the table. "Fern, you can get someone else to build you a chicken house. Harry or Ricky would do it for you." I tilted her chin so she had to meet my eyes. "Jax is very very bad news. And never mention me. It's important. Don't tell him I talked about him, okay?"

She didn't blink. "I get it. I'm not good at subterfuge, though."

"You are excellent at subterfuge. And let me know if you hear from him, okay?"

She nodded. Her mouth was full.

After breakfast I went onto the porch to watch the morning mist over the field. Overhead, a flock of Canada geese honked directions to each other. The highway was a distant hum. I felt safe, as I did nowhere else, yet restless, not wanting to linger, a feeling left over from my teenage years, when anywhere was better than here.

★ ★ ★ ★ ★

It was still too early to start making calls so I drove home. Merle greeted me with ecstatic tail-wags. "Okay," I said, "we'll go for a walk," and he ramped up his dance into a whole-body boogie. If only some of his no-worries attitude would rub off on me.

I drove south on 15-501 to the White Pines Nature Preserve. There were no cars in the parking area, so I let Merle off his leash and he vanished into the underbrush. I could hear him crashing about, and a woodpecker's machine-gun staccato. Between these sounds, the great rustling silence of the forest eased my mind as I ambled along the trail. The deciduous trees sported their fall wardrobes, this season's colors being wine-red and citrus hues that coordinated nicely with the blue-green of the pines and the graceful white trunks of the occasional birch.

The trail was dry but not dusty, and easy walking. Eventually I reached the confluence of the Deep and Rocky Rivers. Merle brought me a stick and I pitched it for him. Beavers had been through the area, leaving a number of chewed-down tree stumps, marked by the ridges of their sharp incisors. Merle existed to hunt and retrieve. Beavers existed to build dams. What did I exist for? To entrap drug dealers, who'd stamp out my life as easily as they'd step on a cockroach? I sat on the banks of the gurgling, murky waters and waited for a perspective that would take me out of my funk.

Driving back north, I started making calls. Delia Scott said she'd be delighted to see me again, and we agreed to meet at noon the next day, at a restaurant in Southport. She said Webster could be available also, later in the afternoon.

Another phone call, to the North Carolina Birthing Center where Ingrid and Justine both worked. I made an appointment with the director, for noon Monday.

I called the number Hogan had given me for Justine's brother and got his voice mail. I left my name and number, telling him I was an SBI agent who had to talk to him about his sister, tomorrow if possible, as I'd be in the Wilmington area.

Tricia Scott's answering machine forced me to listen to a feel-good affirmation. "I am a source of light for others. I am on the perfect path for me right now. I choose aliveness and growth. Please leave a message after the beep." I left my number; perhaps returning calls was on her alive, growing, well-lit path.

My phone chimed and Wyatt said, "Why do I pay taxes?"

"I'm not following."

"No shit, Sherlock. You're missing the point as usual. Last night someone spray-painted 'MURDER! STAY AWAY!' on my sign out by the road. My beautiful sign I paid a thousand bucks for. It's ruined."

"You must have some idea who did it."

"I told you but you don't listen. No one listens." He went on for a while with this annoying pity party. At such times, I think what would Merle do? Merle is my role model for managing blame. Merle doesn't feel guilty unless he's done something wrong. Scolding him results in a long patient look from his golden eyes, a look that says as soon as you shut up, I'm going back to my bunny-in-the-shrubbery dream. No defensiveness, no passing the buck. So when Wyatt finally ended his speech, I promised to look into his claims.

"You think someone is trying to put you out of business. Give me a place to start."

"BBAP. I told you about them. I'm successful. Competition scares those wusses."

I sighed. "I'll look into it, Wyatt."

With Wyatt's harangue echoing in my ears, I gave Hogan a quick call. "Who's the president of the regional bed and breakfast association?"

He click-clicked on his keyboard. "Her name's Camilla Phillips. Pink Magnolia Manor." He reeled off the directions. Camilla's B&B was only two miles from the Rosscairn B&B, on the opposite side of the Haw River. Perhaps Wyatt's claims of a rival's jealousy weren't so far-fetched after all. On an impulse, I turned onto Trestle Road, to pay my respects to the president.

Pink Magnolia Manor was a classic Queen Anne Victorian, with oodles of gingerbread trim, a three-story octagonal turret, and a wraparound porch well-stocked with white rocking chairs. From the front porch, I counted seven colors ranging from white through glossy green to black. It was a house painter's dream, though the peeling condition of the siding, balusters, and windowsills told me no painting had been done recently. A certain bounciness to the porch floor hinted at termites, and a cracked storm window to the right of the front door had been mended with tape. But the hanging pots of ivy and purple pansies and the red front door with its little panes of beveled glass pulled me in with a charming welcome.

Camilla Phillips opened the door. She looked about forty, and size-two slender. She had big blue eyes and the kind of swingy smooth hair I've envied since first grade. She matched her inn, being both pretty and a bit worse for wear, with chipped nail polish and stains on her "Go Heels" tee-shirt. She managed a big grin and effusive greeting. "Come in, come in! Do you have a reservation?"

I had to disappoint her. I flashed my ID. "Can I ask you a few questions?"

She looked discomfited. "What's this about? Is it my son?"

"I have a few questions about your industry. I was referred here by a fellow innkeeper."

"Oh, sure, no problem. Let's sit in the parlor."

She led me into a gracious room with twelve-foot ceilings

and a fireplace surrounded by tiles. Each tile had a different bird painted on it. The furniture was, thankfully, not Victorian and I sank onto a comfortable chenille-covered couch. A layer of dust coating the floor made me feel right at home. From an antique birdcage suspended from the ceiling came the delicate chirping of two tiny birds, caramel-colored with red beaks.

"Say hello to my finches," she said. "I always have some tea this time of day. I'll be right back."

I looked at my watch—eleven-ish. Refreshment would be welcome. In a few minutes, she returned with a red teapot in a quilted cozy and an entire Bundt-type cake drizzled with glaze. She looked at me inquisitively and I nodded.

Melting in my mouth, the cake was moist and tender with hints of cinnamon and chocolate. I had to hold myself back from inhaling it in three quick bites. "What is that flavor?"

"The secret ingredient is blackberry jam," she said. "Now how can I help you? I do have to get back to work in a few minutes."

I told her I was working on the homicide that happened at the Rosscairn B&B. "What can you tell me about Wyatt Craven?"

She looked doubtful. "Is this off the record?"

"I'm not a reporter, and you're not in court. I'm just following up on leads. He's not suspected of anything."

"Well, we've had some complaints. Typically, guests don't complain unless they're treated badly, you know? Stuff happens but you can always make someone happy with a discount or a little gift or a sincere apology. But Wyatt seems to rub people the wrong way. He probably shouldn't be in the business."

A tiny moth floated in my tea so, under the guise of adding sugar, I spooned it out. I took a sip; the tea was delicious and I said so.

"Lady Londonderry. I've heard it was Princess Di's favorite."

"Wyatt's a competitor of yours, right? Do the two of you

refer business to each other?"

She rolled her eyes. "Never."

"Why not?"

"The official reason is our inns are completely different. The Castle's more upscale, with whirlpools and fireplaces. His rates are twice mine."

"Your place is charming." I meant it—compared to the violently plaid décor of a fake castle, Camilla's B&B felt cozy and comfortable, moths, dust bunnies, and all—just like home.

"Thanks. But we attract a different crowd. I get the broke young couples and visiting grannies. He gets the big spenders."

"You said 'official reason.' What's the unofficial reason?"

"When I started my inn five years ago, he paid me a visit. I thought he was being neighborly, and I was friendly. He misinterpreted, asked me on dates. I turned him down. Ever since then he's bad-mouthed my place, warned people away. He's a spiteful bastard."

I studied her. "Bastard" was such an old-fashioned word, like "illegitimate" and "unwed mother" that many people didn't even know its meaning. I'd learned it quite early. I was about six years old when I overheard a playmate's unkind mother whispering "little bastard" to her husband, explaining that my grandmother and I shared the same last name because my mother hadn't been married. It was her whisper, her look, that conveyed the message of shame. So, depending on my mood and how much sleep I'd had, the word sometimes hit a nerve. Soothed by Lady Londonderry and delectable cake, I didn't feel the sting. "So you don't like him."

"Don't like, don't trust, don't send business to, don't want to be in the same room with."

"He's had some problems, claims he's being sabotaged," I said. "Do you know anything about that?"

"Poor baby." She made a mock-sad face. "What kind of problems?"

I thought back to what Wyatt had told me. "Maple syrup in the AC compressor, ammonia in the water softener, and a dead raccoon in the driveway. Most recently, spray-painting his sign." It occurred to me as I spoke, that all these acts were exterior to the house, so anyone could have committed them.

She frowned. "Lord, how awful. He must have lost business."

"Does he have any vindictive enemies?" I added more tea to my cup. It made me feel perky.

"Besides me, you mean?" She laughed. "He's not well-liked, but us innkeepers are a tolerant lot. We don't socialize much—we're too busy—so it's easy to avoid him." She placed her cups and plate on the tray. "You finished?"

I took the hint and stood up. "Thanks for the information. And the cake. Here, I'll help." I picked up the cake plate and followed her into the kitchen. The fridge was covered with family photos and I quickly scanned them. Dogs, babies, kids. And . . . "He looks familiar," I said. I pointed to a snap of a teenage boy wearing a skull-and-crossbones tee-shirt and a sideways ball cap. It was Blue Stone, Wyatt's helper at the Rosscairn B&B.

"My son, Blue," she said. "He's sixteen going on six, or thirty, depending."

I looked at her. Was she clueless or just holding back? She should have told me her son worked for Wyatt. "I've met him," I said. "At the Rosscairn Castle."

"Oh, yeah. He does odd jobs for Wyatt."

"You don't have a problem with him working there? After what you've told me about Wyatt?"

"Not at all. Wyatt pays him on time, treats him okay. I don't think Wyatt knows he's my son. Different last names and all. And it's right across the river—he rides his bike."

"Wouldn't Wyatt know, from Blue's address, that he lives here?"

"Nope. Wyatt never asked, since he pays cash, no taxes. Blue doesn't care. In fact, he'd rather not have deductions."

"Why didn't you mention this earlier?"

"I wasn't hiding it, if that's what you're implying." She aimed her crystal blue eyes at me. "Now, I'm sorry, I have work to do." She led the way to the front door. "Please come back!"

When you're a paying guest, she meant. Surely she didn't want SBI agents hanging out on the pleasant cobwebby porch, watching the hummingbirds, consuming tea and cake, for free.

What had I learned? It was hard to imagine this petite friendly innkeeper dripping maple syrup into Wyatt's compressor. But the mix of competition and obsession sometimes produced unimaginable results—a NASA astronaut stalking her rival, an Olympic skater crippled by a competitor's boyfriend, the screaming weeping fans at the latest Duke-Carolina game. Normal people, overcome by their inner dummy, morph into crazies.

Blue Stone had joined my list of "persons of interest." The list seemed like that game at the State Fair, where moles pop up and down and you get points for each one you can whack with a mallet. On the chance that he was at work, I drove to the Castle B&B, using the back-road directions Camilla had given me. A gravel lane rolled down to an abandoned mill shedding its bricks into the slowly moving water of the Haw River. The lane ended in a crumbling single-lane bridge—built in 1922 according to a sign—that probably didn't get enough traffic to be worth inspecting. No one was coming from the other direction, so I drove onto the bridge and inched across, aware that its splintering wooden guard rails didn't offer much of a barrier.

At the Castle B&B's entrance, Wyatt was scouring the black

graffiti—*Murder—Stay Away*—from his sign. It was an elegant carved-wood sign about three feet in diameter, painted a glossy blue and trimmed in gold leaf. He was working on the first R in "Murder," rubbing gently. I rolled down my window.

"Is it coming off?" I said.

"Kind of. What do you want?"

"Is Blue here?"

He tipped his head toward the castle.

A sense of foreboding passed through me as I clacked the brass door knocker. Murder stay away. No one answered. My apprehension was dispelled by the smell of baking chocolate and butter that led me down the hall to the kitchen area, where I found Liesle mixing up something fattening.

"Oatmeal chocolate-chip cookies," she said. "The first batch is over there—please take one." The mixer began its whirr as she added a cup of chocolate chips to the batter.

I contented myself with a tiny broken bit. Yummy. Then one more. "Where's Blue?" I asked.

"Outside. Sure you won't have another one?"

I declined and pushed my way out the back door. The tents were gone, the tables and chairs put away, leaving only an empty acre of green lawn. Blue was pushing a fertilizer spreader. I waved at him. "Got a minute?"

He shrugged and walked slowly toward me. I motioned that he should remove his headphones and led us to a couple of Adirondack chairs under a tree. He was jumpy, rubbing his legs, rocking back and forth. I perched on the edge of my chair and leaned toward him. "You didn't tell me your mom owned a B&B," I said. "Pink Magnolia Manor, right down the road. And I bet Wyatt doesn't know either."

"No one asked."

"It might be considered a good qualification, that you've got experience in one."

He shrugged and looked off to the side. I peered at his tee-shirt. A skeleton, dripping blood, held a Medusa-head. Do the clothes reveal the man? Was Blue scary like his tee-shirts?

"Your mother doesn't like Wyatt, does she?"

"No, ma'am." He gave me a furtive look.

"Do you know why?"

"No, ma'am." He was looking at the ground now. Anywhere but at me.

"I bet you know who spray-painted the B&B's sign, don't you?"

"No, ma'am."

This repetition was getting old. "How about the damage to the air conditioner? The water softener? The dead raccoon?"

"I don't know."

"Just so it's very, very clear, Blue? Some courts consider vandalism to be a felony. Felonies are serious crimes, people go to jail. State prison."

He stood up. "I have stuff to do. Wyatt doesn't pay me to sit around."

"We're not done. If you aren't responsible, who is? Any ideas? Liesle?"

"Yeah, that's right. She's a hardened criminal, that one."

"Let me see your hands." He held them out. I touched his left palm. "You're left-handed, are you? What's that?" Under the grime, black paint.

"Nothing." He shoved his hands into his pockets.

"Sit down just for a minute, please."

He complied. He was an obedient scared child, and likeable. But that didn't mean he would confess to the vandalism.

"I'm not interested in sending you to jail. I have bigger problems. As long as it stops now. Will it stop?"

"I didn't do nothing."

So he wasn't ready to admit anything. Okay. But maybe he

would stop. I handed him my business card. "I need your help, Blue. Anything you see, think of, hear around this place."

He studied my card. "What's it like, being a cop? Donuts and car chases?" He smiled and the sun glinted off his braces.

"Cookies and cake. Talking to cute guys."

He blushed. "How old do you have to be?"

The question made me pause. Some days I felt older than dirt. Other days, more like a damp chick half out of the egg. He wanted a literal answer though. "It varies by department," I said. "You don't need a college degree but it helps."

"My mom wants me to go to college."

"How are your grades?"

"Okay. Not great."

Recalling the peeling paint and termite-eaten porch at Pink Magnolia Manor, I doubted that Camilla Phillips had a college fund for her son. "I was in the same boat exactly," I said. "Very average grades. No money. But you can do it if you want to."

"When did you decide to be a cop?"

I paused. How much to tell him? My mother disappeared when I was five. Around eight years old, I began having nightmares about being murdered. Fern had tried to help, explaining to me that whoever robbed that Texaco and took my mother was most likely dead, or in prison for similar misdeeds. Not reassured, I had begun clipping newspaper accounts of murders, avidly reading the follow-up stories all the way through arrest and trial. Most people have a box or two of childhood memorabilia. In my closet are cartons marked Unsolved Murders, Murder Arrests, Murder Trials. I would move the envelopes of clippings from one box to another as the police and courts did their work. A helpful librarian obtained reports from the Bureau of Justice Statistics for me. Each year I updated a three-ring binder with homicide and conviction rates, numbers of murders by age, state, and type of weapon.

One persistent statistic consumed me—though homicides have the highest conviction rate of all crimes, over one-third of all murders are never solved. I hated that my mother's death was a cold case. Every day Fern and I lived with the fact that Grace's killer walked free.

"Pretty early on," I told him. "But I almost took a different path. Foolish stuff. Like you're doing." I stood to leave.

He looked up at me. "Thanks."

Good. Message received.


Liesle had already cleaned up after the cookie-making, and the kitchen floor was still damp from a mopping. I heard machine noises at the end of the first-floor hall, coming from the Stirling room. When the din stopped, I knocked on the door.

Liesle opened the door. Her tank top revealed the full rabbit tattoo, slightly dampened with sweat. "Oh, it's you. I thought it would be."

"Why, are you psychic?"

"I am, actually. Stay out there, I'm shampooing the carpet."

I was intrigued. I think psychics are a waste of police resources but this was different. Liesle was here last weekend. What she considered intuition could be subliminal information.

"Psychic in the sense that . . ."

She pulled a hankie out of her pocket and blotted her chest and neck. "Whew, it's hot. Okay, sometimes I know about something before I'm told. Or I feel someone who's died is trying to communicate with me. It's not very developed. It was stronger when I was a kid." She yanked a container of filthy water out of the shampooer. "Mind if I keep going? I'll never finish if I don't."

"Sure, go ahead. Don't suppose you've heard from the dead bride?" I followed her down the hall to a closet with a janitor's sink. She dumped the water, then wheeled the shampooer into

143

the room next door. I helped her move two bedside tables and a chair into the hall.

She pushed her hair behind her ears and studied me. "Something was off about her. You might not understand. With nearly everyone, I sense their unique humanity—it's a mix of fear and love, basically. Even with animals, I can feel what they are about, it's not too different. With her? Something else. She didn't seem real."

This was not helpful. I could hardly take such an insight to Anselmo Morales. "You didn't sense human emotion?"

"To me, she was like this shampooer. Mechanical."

I remembered the video—Justine had seemed quite human. But I wasn't going to argue with Liesle over her own perceptions. "Anything else? When you go into the Falkirk bedroom, do you have any feelings about what happened?"

"Usually, the dead person herself would help me. But her being the way she was, I don't get any messages. It's funny, ever since she died in there, I've sensed peanut butter in Falkirk. It's left over from the death, I think."

"There's peanut butter somewhere in the room?"

"No, no. Of course not. I don't actually smell peanut butter with my nose. I don't go in the room and think someone's been eating PB&J. I think peanut butter. I smell it with my mind. Very strong. You look confused."

She was reading my aura correctly. I couldn't do anything with this. If it were chocolate, I'd think about Lottie and Evan. Booze equaled Mike's step-aunt Delia. Cigars, his stepfather Scoop. But peanut butter? I sighed and let go of this thread.

"Show me where the keys are kept."

She led me into the tiny alcove off the dining room, Wyatt's office. On the back of the door hung a small cabinet. She turned a knob to open it and showed me—for each guest room, a labeled hook; on each hook, sets of keys. One clump of keys was unlabeled. "My keys," she said. "For housekeeping. A key for each bedroom, and the supplies closet."

"And the barn?"

She pointed to a small key on its own hook. BARN was written on the tag. "There's usually two. Blue must have the other one."

"Think carefully about this," I said. "On the weekend of the wedding, do you remember anything unusual about this barn key? Was one missing, or did someone borrow it?"

"Unlikely. I've never known a guest to borrow it. But Wyatt and Blue go in and out of the barn all the time."

"Is it left unlocked?"

"I don't think so. Wyatt's always worried about theft."

I left her to get on with her work. Peanut butter—not a real smell, just a smell in her mind. Lordy.

Wyatt had reached the "s" in "stay away." "Murder" was erased, except for a few stubborn black specks. "If one more thing goes wrong around here, I'm going to torch this place. You didn't hear that, of course."

I recalled my talk with Blue. "It might end now. The sabotage, I mean."

He glared at me with blood-shot eyes. "Gee, golly, that's just super."

Fluffed out with white fur, the cat was enormous, almost as big as a raccoon. It padded slowly across the living room of Mike Olmert's townhouse and sniffed at my shoes. Mike had asked me to stop by. He wanted to show me something possibly useful to the investigation.

"Let me introduce you," Mike said, "to Justine's baby, Brigitte." Brigitte's eyes were pale green and her expression was irritated. I leaned down and rubbed her head and Brigitte emitted a plaintive-sounding "mmrroww." She was toothless except for one pointy canine.

"She's off her feed," Mike said. "I know what you're thinking—with her size that's not necessarily a bad thing."

"What happened to her teeth?"

"It's something genetic—they all fell out. So, this is our house. Justine's and mine. Want to look around?"

I followed him from room to room, to see what I could learn about Justine. She collected elephants—stuffed, clay, glass, metal. Her clothes—deep jewel colors and natural fabrics—filled the closets of two bedrooms. A small deck off the kitchen was crowded with plants in colorful pots. "I didn't want to come back here without her," Mike said. "I didn't think I could face all these reminders. But there was Brigitte to take care of, and these guys." He gestured toward the fish tank built into the wall over a fireplace. Two yellow fish lolled underneath the rocks, their bright color popping them out against the black background of the tank. Each almost six inches long, they seemed large for aquarium fish.

"Canary cichlids," Mike said. "They were Justine's too."

"She had a knack for growing her pets, didn't she."

He chuckled. "They grew for her all right. I guess they're mine now. Sit down, won't you?"

When I sat on the couch, Brigitte climbed into my lap, stretched out like a polar bear, and began to purr. "How are you doing?" I asked.

"Better, thanks." Mike looked calmer than the last time I'd seen him, at the gym, when Anselmo and I had confronted him with questions. As if reading my mind, he apologized for his previous attitude. "I couldn't accept—hell, I couldn't understand—what you were saying, that Justine was transsexual. But the ME—Dr. O'Brien—he convinced me. And I've had a couple of days to think about it."

I nodded encouragingly.

"What she had was like a broken leg. You fix it, you don't limp around in pain and waste your life. She knew who she was."

My opinion of Mike Olmert ratcheted up as he spoke. It was amazing, really, that a man with Tricia for a mother could be so open-minded. I reminded myself—children sometimes turn around and take a very unexpected path. Me, for example. I'm sure Fern never set out to raise a drug agent.

"Yet she didn't tell you," I said.

"She must have had her reasons."

"Did you know her brother?"

He shook his head. "Man, you are queen of the reveal, aren't you? She had a brother?"

"Ten years older, lives in Wilmington."

"No. I didn't know him. You met this brother?"

"Not yet."

"Well, I'd like to meet him sometime."

"I hope to see him tomorrow, and I'll tell him. You had something to show me?"

"Hold on." He went into the kitchen and came back with a plastic bag. "The Castle innkeeper sent me a package of Justine's things. Clothes, makeup. Like I'm supposed to know what to do with them. I'll give everything to charity I guess. Anyway, there was this. It's one of those personalized bracelets, and it's not hers."

The bag contained an Italian charm bracelet, shiny silver modular links on a stretchy band. The bracelet had perhaps eighteen links, and half of them were charms. An apple, inscribed "#1 Teacher." The Miami Dolphins logo. A snake encircling a staff—the caduceus symbol for medical alert. A birthday cake, with a date, April 2. A tiny faded photo of two dark-haired girls and another of a dachshund. No one I'd talked to fit this profile. Ingrid and Kate were approximately the right age, but like Gia Mabe, Mike's stalker, neither was a teacher. I slid the bracelet into my pocket, to be examined later.

"And I want to give you something." Mike handed me a book. "It's Justine's vegan cookbook. She wrote it, and self-published. It's a good book if you're interested in that kind of thing. We got the first shipment just a week ago."

*Enchanted Food* was spiral-bound, with almost two hundred pages. The cover showed a round little phyllo bundle stacked high with green beans, all drizzled with an herby creamy sauce. I leafed through it. Page after page of gorgeous food pictures— stews, cakes, dips. I paused at Tempeh Strudel with Braised Endive, followed by Porcini and Grilled Ramps Napoleon. Four ingredients I'd never tried. The photos were amazing.

I turned it over to see Justine's picture on the back. It wasn't the air-brushed glamour shot I expected. Instead it showed her in the kitchen wielding a chopping knife in one hand and a platter of pita chips and salsa in the other. Her head was tilted and she had a flirty smile, an inviting look. *Come on-a my house, I'm gonna give you tofu cacciatore!*

With a sudden intake of breath, Mike choked back a sob. "This is really hard," he said. "She was so proud of her book."

"Are they her recipes? Her photos?"

"Yes. She made all the food and took the pictures. Everything in the book is Justine's."

"Is it for sale?" I asked. I'm not a cook—Hogan had been the chef in our household. I can make about four things. But perhaps Justine's cookbook would provide a stimulus for me to branch out. I needed a hobby anyway.

"Take it. A gift. In fact, take a carton of them." He opened a closet to reveal stacks of boxes. "I'll put it in your car."

I fished in my purse for some money but he brushed it aside. "Please, give one to everyone who's working on her case. Maybe

she'll be more real and alive to them. Not . . . not . . . you know
. . . just weird."

I tried to thank him but he waved me away. As easily as hoisting a glass of water, he picked up a carton. "Find out who ended her life. Then I'll be thanking you," he said.

I sat in my car and made notes, doodles actually, trying to sort out what I'd learned. A bracelet, a toothless cat, a cookbook, an elephant collection, a secret brother. Irrelevant distractions or vitally important? Mike Olmert, innocent or guilty? I touched the carton of cookbooks, hoping for a flash of intuition, a smidge of Liesle's psychic powers, because deductive reasoning and logic were failing me. Identify Justine Bradley's murderer? I might as well pitch darts at names on a board, trying not to impale an innocent bystander.

# CHAPTER 13

*Thursday Late Afternoon*

Tricia and Scoop Scott lived in Silver Hills, a development with a gate that keeps residents from meeting anyone unlike themselves. The only people who want to come in—the gardeners, maids, nannies, construction workers, vendors—are the ones who have to come in. Innumerable pizza delivery people know the code. Anyone can tear through the gate and snap off the boom arm. Three days to replace it.

I hadn't spoken with Scoop or his wife Tricia since the day of the wedding. They had been out of town, at a conference in Colorado, and had returned this morning. Scoop bowed low and shook my hand. He had a florid complexion and his comb-over made me want to reach for scissors. "Tricia is getting dressed. She'll be right down," Scoop said. His voice was deep, resonant. He held an unlit cigar in his hand.

Verwood and its rural surrounds are home to over forty churches, all Protestant but one, and the first thing a newcomer is asked—what church do you go to? But when you have an Internet church, your congregation is global. Scoop was proud of his pin-studded map of the world, prominently mounted in the hallway of his home. Each pin represented a soul who had joined God's Precious Church via his website, godsprecious .com, for only ten dollars a week, all major credit cards accepted.

He offered to show me the broadcast room, and led me

through their kitchen—the size of a basketball court—through a laundry area, and up carpeted stairs. The spacious room was furnished with a couple dozen folding chairs, a wooden pulpit, and several pieces of old-looking stained glass suspended on the walls like artwork. In the center, a camera on a tripod aimed its eye at the pulpit.

"My sermons are broadcast live on the web. We have music"—he pointed to a CD player—"and Bible readings and guest speakers. You're welcome to join us," he added politely.

"Yoo-hoo," called Tricia from the foot of the stairs. "I'm ready!"

I could see why it took her so long to get dressed. From the artful arrangement of her dyed-dark hair, through perfectly groomed eyebrows, flawless freckled skin, pink linen dress set off by white pearls—every square inch of Tricia breathed maintenance. Her toenails, peeping out of three-inch heels, matched her dress and lipstick. We were quite a contrast—my hair barely tamed into a braid, my all-purpose black pants and leather jacket designed to fade me into the woodwork.

I was trying to ignore my preconceptions about Tricia and Scoop. Yes, Tricia encouraged bosses to foist their religious beliefs onto employees who probably risked losing their jobs if they spoke up. And Scoop's online church accepted donations in exchange for prayers, like Scoop had a direct line to heaven. But it's a free country, there's one born every minute, and it wasn't my job to question Scoop and Tricia's share of the faithfuls' pie.

"When was the last time you saw Justine? Either of you?" I asked.

"Why, Friday night, wasn't it, Scoop? At the dinner?"

"We skipped breakfast," Scoop said. "We're not big breakfast eaters."

"Would you say you knew her well?"

Scoop examined his cigar stub. "As well as one knows any-one."

Tricia looked at him with squinty eyes, like he was a species she wasn't familiar with. "We met her six months ago, in March. We had a party for them, remember, Scoop? For all our friends?"

"Was she well-liked?" I asked.

I could almost see Tricia's hackles rise. "Where are you going with that?" she said sharply. "Justine was lovely. So perfect for Mike. They were in love. We supported them both."

"However lovely and perfect, someone murdered her. Who might have a grudge or want to prevent the marriage?"

Scoop patted his comb-over, crossed his long legs, and looked at Tricia. She studied her fingernails. They exchanged glances. Tricia spoke. "I guess we should mention Gia Mabe. You probably already know about her."

Mike's irrational stalker. "She used to date your son, I heard."

"Mike broke up with her when he met Justine," Tricia said. "I felt so bad for her. We've all been there, haven't we? Heartbroken, abandoned. She didn't take it well."

"I know about her. Anyone else?"

"I can't think of anyone, can you, Scoop?" Tricia said.

Mike had been adamant that he didn't know about Justine's sex change. Had anyone told his parents? Did I want to be the one to tell them? Well, someone had to point out the rhinoceros squatting under the rug. I studied them. Tricia was cucumber-cool, picking imaginary lint from her skirt. Scoop looked a little more nervous, patting down his hair strands.

I took a breath. "I'm sure you know Justine was born male? That she had sex-reassignment surgery?"

Scoop flushed and his hands tightened on the chair arms. He worked the cigar around in his mouth and made a noise, *puh*.

"Bless your heart, I've never heard of such a thing. Come again?" Tricia's smile looked forced and her eyes wandered.

"She wasn't always a woman," I said. "She was born male, named John. She had surgery that changed her into a female."

"I don't believe you," Scoop said. His voice rose, boomed. "That's disgusting. You're disgusting. Mike would never . . ."

Tricia patted his knee. "Scoop, you don't mean that about Agent Lavender. We're just shocked that anyone could say this about our Justine. Such a lovely girl in every respect. Someone has told you a terrible lie."

"She was thoroughly a woman and Mike loved her. I resent your implication," Scoop said. He chomped on the cigar.

I tried again. "She was a definitely a woman. However, it seems to me that it could have been a serious problem for you two, that she was transsexual."

" 'A woman shall not wear anything that pertains to a man, nor shall a man put on a woman's garment; for whoever does these things is an abomination to the LORD your God.' Deuteronomy twenty-two five." Scoop's rich voice thundered. Maybe he was a preacher after all.

"Amen," Tricia said. "An abomination. We just don't believe it. It's unimaginable, right Scoop?" Her face crumpled and she began to cry.

Scoop nodded. His face was purplish. "I'm afraid we'll have to end this visit. You're distressing my wife."

I wanted to crack their two heads together, frustrated by their overwhelming denial, but I couldn't pin them down. Not yet.

I pushed the button that controlled the boom arm protecting Silver Hills. As it swung open and my car rolled onto the highway, I felt a wave of exhaustion so extreme I almost fell into sleep right there. It had been a very long day, starting predawn as I waited with Fredricks for the results of the raid on Jax's house. Breakfast with Fern, a walk in the White Pines Preserve. Tea and cake with Camilla Phillips, and the discovery that Blue

Stone was her son. Blue's denial that he had anything to do with the sabotage at the B&B, yet black paint on his hand revealing his lie. Liesle's claim to psychic abilities, the smell of peanut butter in her mind. A bereaved fiancé, a box of cookbooks. The amazing ability of Tricia and Scoop to deny reality.

I needed a nap. Tonight I had to hit the streets again with Fredricks, and to function at all, I needed to sleep. I planned to go home, walk the dog, then crash for a couple of hours.

Even a simple plan can take a detour. When I pulled into my driveway, I saw the oddest thing. Merle was standing there, tail a-waggin', as happy as ever to see me. Odd—because he'd been inside, doors locked, when I left at four in the morning.

"How'd you get out, buddy?" I leaned down for a slobbery kiss. He didn't tell me but I found out soon enough. My front door was still locked, so I walked around to the back.

The back door was wide open. I hadn't left it open. When I moved in, I had deadbolts installed on both doors. Not an alarm system—Merle is the best possible alarm system, warning me of everything from newspaper delivery to garbage pickup to squirrels on the sidewalk. But I sleep better with deadbolts. And I'd locked both doors before I left. The door was not only open, but busted—someone had shattered the door's glass pane, in order to reach through and turn the latch.

I stepped over the bits of glass into a horrific mess. The kitchen had been trashed. Every dish and glass smashed into smithereens. The refrigerator door hung open, its shelves emptied onto the floor. Milk, beer, and juice puddled around the broken jars of spaghetti sauce, salsa, and pickles. A box of rice, a jar of popcorn, a bag of sugar—all opened and hurled around the room.

It wasn't a typical break-in, some petty crook looking for something to pawn. This was deliberate and nasty. I didn't, couldn't, look at the rest of the house. I took out my cell phone to call 911. When I tried to talk, I had to struggle to get the words out.

I sat down on my front steps, clutching Merle to steady myself while we waited for the police. Merle leaned into me, now and then giving me a reassuring lick. At least he was okay. The damage was just a nuisance, really. But it worried me. Someone had it in for me. This wasn't a burglary. It was retribution.

My neighbor Saffron pulled up in her minivan, with her two girls in the back seat. She parked and walked to her mailbox as the girls ran inside. They were quiet children who never seemed to misbehave. Saffron's troubles were the only ones allowed in her house.

I waved her over. "Were you home today?"

"Yeah, except for taking the kids to school." She leafed through her mail. "Look at these goddam bills. I've got to get a job. Carter is behind on the child support again and we'll get evicted if I don't make some money. You know what really gets me?"

"What?" I didn't care. I wanted the cops to come and be gone, someone to repair the door, and a small army to clean up my kitchen. I longed for clean sheets and a white noise machine playing summer rain.

"Credit card late fees. On top of exorbitant interest. The payment's twenty bucks, and if it's two days late, they charge an extra thirty-nine. Makes me crazy."

"A universal law, Saff. A disincentive."

"Whatever. What are you up to? Keeping the world safe for the rest of us?"

I usually avoided engaging Saffron unless I was ready to surrender an hour. But today I needed someone to talk to. And not about our usual topic, her life. "Someone broke into my house. I'm waiting for the police."

"You're kidding!" She grimaced. "Who would dare?"

"Did you see anyone around my house? Any cars?"

"Around lunchtime there was a white car in your driveway. I didn't think anything about it. I was on the phone with Carter's attorney. I'm trying to get him to pay without going to court. Don't ever get divorced, Stella. The stress will kill you. So, is anything missing?"

"The kitchen's trashed. I didn't go in." I didn't care about any of my stuff, except Fern's paintings, and a desk of my mother's. The rest of it was eclectic junk I'd accumulated since college, nothing of any value, economic or sentimental. "Did you see anyone in the white car?" I asked.

"You know, I didn't look. Normally I'm curious, but I got so caught up in my bill problems."

A Verwood black-and-white pulled into my driveway and two patrolmen stepped out, setting Merle into a frenzy of tail-wagging. I told them what I'd found, and unlocked the front door. The living room wasn't too bad—cushions thrown around, bookcases tipped over. My mother's desk drawers were pulled out and emptied but Fern's paintings had been left alone. The worst of it was a white powder dusting everywhere. One of the cops swiped a finger through it and took a taste. "Flour," he said.

I followed them down the hall. The first bedroom was empty except for a chair and the television, and neither had been touched. The next room, my bedroom, had been tossed—drawers emptied onto the floor, clothes pulled out of the closet.

And the bathroom nearly rivaled my kitchen on the disaster scale. Shampoo and conditioner bottles had been opened and sloshed onto the floor and counter. My junky drawers—full of cotton balls, Band-Aids, sunscreen, makeup—had been upended, some into the toilet. Broken glass, dusted with face powder, littered the floor. White Linen Breeze mixed with Diorissimo assaulted my nose.

While the police dusted for fingerprints, Saffron took me to her house for a glass of red wine. "I told them about the white car," she said. "Honestly, I wish I'd paid more attention. Were you targeted? Because of your work?"

"I don't know," I said. I couldn't think of anyone but Jax and Dana who might have been pushed to such hostility. Had they found out I'd deceived them, had set them up? Could they have harmed Merle, to teach me a lesson? I picked up the glass of wine. It was exactly what I needed. Especially if followed by the rest of the bottle.

Saffron's house was full of color and each room was different. Mustard yellow walls in the kitchen, terra cotta red in the dining room, peacock blue in the living room. White trim and sheer white curtains made a nice contrast with the colors. I told her I liked the effect.

"Paint's cheap," she said. "Anyone can paint. I'll help you if you want."

There was something else different about her house. It was clean, but that wasn't it. The kids' things were out of sight, the furniture wasn't anything special. "You have accessories," I said. A ficus tree in a white urn and a pair of silvery crackled vases. Three Japanese teapots on a wall shelf, a paisley scarf over a tabletop. "I have no accessories. Unless you count broken glass and a coating of flour."

"Aw, Stella. I have two words for you—yard sales. We'll go around together when I find a good one." She patted my hand. I sipped my wine gratefully, then remembered I was supposed to go to work tonight. I called Fredricks and told him what happened. I needed to deal with the break-in. "Any chance I could get a rain check until Sunday? I'm going to Wilmington tomorrow."

"Sure, no problem. Need a hand with anything?" His voice

was gentle and kind, and I almost lost it. My throat felt tight with tears I couldn't allow myself to spill. I thanked him. But I couldn't imagine Fredricks with a broom. I'd have to clean up myself.

The policemen only stayed for a half-hour, long enough to take pictures, make a few notes, and lift a couple of decent fingerprints. I asked them to let me know if they got a match on the prints. I was thinking of Jax and Dana, whose arrest records meant they would be in the FBI fingerprint database.

Saffron insisted on helping me. She parked her girls in front of the TV with a bowl of popcorn and told them she'd be next door. They seemed delighted with this arrangement, and so was I. It would have been hard to face it alone. In the kitchen, hardly anything was salvageable, so we swept the mess into trash bags, wiped the flour off everything, and mopped the floor. I washed the bathroom floor three times to get rid of the oily perfume. My mop smelled really good, for a mop.

My landlord sent a handyman who replaced the broken door pane with unbreakable acrylic. Finally, the house was squared away, all traces of the intrusion stuffed into black plastic garbage bags, the only reminder a hint of Diorissimo. I gave Saffron a hug and made myself a vow to listen to her faithfully at least once a week. Maybe even babysit.

As I put the clothes away in my bedroom, I realized some recent purchases were missing—a black negligee and a pair of too-small jeans, purchased months ago in a brief pitiful attempt to lure Hogan back with my sexy body. Was the intruder really a burglar? A woman? Dana towered over me. She'd never fit into those clothes. Whoever took them—better luck to you, I thought.

# CHAPTER 14

*Friday Morning*

I didn't sleep well. Despite the presence of Merle, Guard Dog Supreme, I was edgy and afraid. I couldn't relax. I could have escaped to Fern's, to curl up in my girlhood maple bed under a chenille bedspread and faded quilt. An appealing thought, regression to a simpler time when my only worry was passing geometry. But I wanted to be tough. I wouldn't be driven out. Instead, I woke up every half hour, breathing spilled perfume and sticky shampoo smells, listening to the wind knocking branches against the roof.

In the morning I took some groceries to Fern. "Here you go," I said, putting away the tomatoes, coffee, cheese, and eggs. "How about pancakes this morning?" I hauled out her old iron skillet, a real workout just lifting it. I found the pancake mix and chopped up an apple to add to it.

"Darling, I finished Tricia's book cover. Tell me what you think." Fern pulled her drawing board onto the table, and removed the sheet of paper protecting the drawing.

Jesus stood in front of a group of men and women, all clad in long robes. He gestured with his arms lifted, palms up, as though delivering a blessing. He was dark-skinned, with short brushy hair, a scraggly beard, a broad forehead and nose, and black eyes. He looked scrawny, sinewy. The style of the painting was more detailed, more meticulous than her usual broad-brush works.

"He looks like Bin Laden without the turban. What's Tricia's opinion?"

"She hasn't seen it yet. I did quite a bit of research, you know. Jesus was Middle Eastern. Jewish, but not like today's Israelis, who are mostly European. He would have looked like an African Arab."

"I hope she likes it, Fern. It's clear you put many hours into it."

Fern studied the painting. "She won't like it at first, but it'll grow on her."

I slipped a stack of pancakes onto each plate and we dug in. I didn't want to tell her about the break-in—it would frighten her—but a warning was in order. "Have you talked to Jax lately?"

"Not since I turned down our date. What's the problem, anyway?"

"I can't tell you." Delicately, I probed. Did she know where he was going to be this weekend? Nope. When was the last time she saw him? Last Sunday, nearly a week ago, when he came with the tape measure. I put my hands on her shoulders. "Don't say I told you to drop him or let him know I'm police. In fact, don't even mention me."

Fern took my hands in hers. "I get it, darling. No need to quiz me like a suspect."

I kissed her soft cheek and left her with the dishes. I had a long drive ahead of me to the Wilmington area.


Delia was already seated when I arrived at the seafood restaurant, a building up on stilts over the Intracoastal Waterway. She'd snared an outdoor umbrella table with a view of pelicans napping on the calm water. A couple of dolphin dorsal fins slid along the glassy surface in no great hurry.

When I apologized for making her wait, she brushed it off. "I was early," she said. "Glad to get out of the house." Blobs of blush stood out like clown makeup on her yellowish, pale face.

The waiter asked if we wanted drinks, and I ordered coffee. Delia hesitated. "Maybe a Diet Coke?"

She told me she and Webster lived nearby. Her voice was shaky, and she cleared her throat repeatedly. "On a golf course. He plays every day. I play a little, otherwise I'd never see him."

We made small talk until the drinks arrived and we ordered our food—shrimp and pasta for me, grilled tilapia for her. The waiter left and I got straight to the point. "When I interviewed you last Saturday, you told me you nearly killed Justine once. Were you joking?"

She grimaced. "I said that? I've got a big mouth, but I don't even remember talking to you. I hit bottom at that wedding, Stella. Webster says I got dressed and sat down with him to wait for the ceremony—but all I remember is popping champagne bottles in the morning. The next thing I recall is being in the hospital. Webster took me there Saturday night."

"The hospital?"

"I was puking blood, Stella. They kept me two days." She didn't say, but I guessed she had cirrhosis of the liver. Cirrhosis causes varicose veins in the esophagus. When the veins burst, the results aren't fun. "I haven't had a drink since. It's very hard, but Webster is supportive. He's dumped out all the booze in the house. And he's paying attention to me. Last night we—" She wriggled in her chair. "You know. First time in months." Her deadpan delivery made me smile even though it was Too Much Information.

Our food arrived and I was ravenous. My shrimp still had their tails on, and I ate one right after another, setting the tails on the edge of the plate like trophies. I tried to slow down. Fern always complained that I ate like the runt from a large litter. "You met Justine previously, then," I said, "before the last weekend."

Delia speared a bit of fish with her fork. "I wouldn't say I met her."

I nodded encouragingly.

"I'll make it short. My husband had an affair with her." She watched me closely, having pulled the pin and tossed this grenade at my image of Justine, the "angel."

I was so astonished I put my fork down. "When? Did Mike know about it?"

"Five years ago, and I don't know."

"What happened?"

"My husband chases women. His brother chases women. Their father chased women. Dad probably still does, in his nursing home, wheeling after any cute lady with her own teeth. It's the Scott nature. They cannot keep it in their pants. I don't mean Web's crude or aggressive. Just that he's always looking. God, I need a drink. What if we get a bottle of wine, split it?"

"Bad idea. So, the Scott nature?"

"Five years ago, Web was the financial officer at a women's hospital in Wilmington. Justine was hired as a nurse-midwife. She was stunning, everyone noticed her. Obviously I don't know the details but what I wormed out of Webster was that he asked her out for a drink and before he knew it they were in bed, in her apartment."

"He told you this?" Now this was a different kind of marriage.

"He had to tell me, because of what happened afterward. It lasted about a month and then she rejected him. Usually he just moves on to someone else but he couldn't let go of her. He got a bit obsessive with phoning, sending flowers, following her around. When she saw him going through her trash, she reported him to the police and they arrested him."

"Was he convicted?"

"No. Charges were dropped. But he lost his job. Well, they

called it early retirement."

"You told me you nearly killed her."

Delia laughed. "I accosted her after he was fired, in the hospital parking lot one night. I nearly hit her—I swung and missed. I was sloshed of course."

"You blamed her."

"I forgot to tell you I'm stupid." She closed her eyes and sipped at her water, her tasteless boring water.

"What did you think, when Web learned his nephew was going to marry her?"

"Excellent question. And what did she think, when she learned Web was Mike's step-uncle? Very awkward. I had to call her. Web couldn't, because of the court order. I made nice. I told her he'd had therapy, I'd had therapy, we'd all had therapy. He was medicated. He was sorry. He didn't want to spoil her day. Maybe we shouldn't come to the wedding."

"But you went. She was okay about it?"

"It was a very uncomfortable conversation for both of us. I asked her if Mike knew she'd slept with Web and she got a little pissy and said of course not. She said we were welcome, she hadn't told Mike about the incident—that's what she called it— and as far as she was concerned, all was forgiven. She wanted the family to be there."

"And Web—was he over her?"

She shrugged. "He still wanted her, like I want a double Rob Roy on the rocks. But he knew better."

"Did he know she was transsexual?"

"What did you say?" She pressed the sweaty water glass against her chest.

"Justine was transsexual, Delia. Did your husband know?"

"You mean she was a man?" She snickered. "Oh my God, Web will die."

"She had the surgery, apparently quite successfully."

"She sure fooled Web. Did Mike know? Who knew?"

"Good question. I'm trying to find out."

The waiter offered dessert. I asked for more coffee. Delia had a twinkle in her eye, probably the first twinkle in a long time. I hated to spoil her mood. "Do you think it's possible your husband killed Justine?"

She thought a while. "No one knows him like I do, and I say—no, it's not possible. He's a gentle man, really. He understands why she called the police. I held a grievance longer than he did."

"Really?"

"What the hell, maybe I killed her! Like I said, that day has vanished from my memory. Can I be guilty, if I don't remember?" She smiled broadly, though her eyes seemed full of fear.

I didn't answer. It was a good question.


It was amusing to watch Webster Scott struggle with his visceral reaction to me. He sat across from me in a coffee shop booth, and I could almost read his mind. On the one hand, I was police investigating a homicide, he'd previously been arrested for stalking the victim, and he'd been in the B&B at the time she was murdered. That made him a potential suspect. Normal reaction—shrivel, retract, hide. On the other hand I was a young woman, and according to Delia that was enough to inflame his libido. He didn't know whether to stare at my chest or clasp his balls.

He tried to cover his dilemma with a shiny smile and small talk. "Your first time in Myrtle?" he asked. "Where you from, anyhow?"

"Mr. Scott—"

"Call me Web, everyone does." He pressed his leg against mine under the table.

I didn't move. "What are you doing?"

His smile dimmed and he pulled away. "Sorry, dear."

"Delia told me about your relationship with Justine Bradley."

Was that a wink? Or a squinty wince? He picked up his decaf latte and took a sip. "It was all a misunderstanding. She and I had a friendship for a while, then she said some ugly and untrue things to me." He went on, about the calls she didn't return and the restraining order that was so offensive—he being a professional man, not a criminal—and the unpleasant incident involving police.

What I heard was a man who wasn't facing reality. Obfuscation and denial were probably second nature to him in any discussion with a woman. No wonder Delia drank. Nonetheless, I tried. "Justine wouldn't have called the police unless she was afraid. Your behavior must have alarmed her."

"I wanted to make things right. She wouldn't listen."

"Were you in touch with her after you were fired?"

"I wasn't fired. I decided to retire, a well-deserved retirement after a long career."

"Just answer the question."

"No, I wasn't in touch with her. We moved to Southport and she moved to Chapel Hill. I was delighted to hear my nephew Mike was going to marry her. Delia talked with Justine and smoothed everything over. Delia's a wonderful woman, just wonderful."

"Were you jealous of Mike? You wanted Justine, didn't you?"

Web shook his head. "Don't be silly. It was over."

His story was essentially consistent with his wife's, not that consistency meant anything. He wasn't helping me solve the murder case. I told him I'd be in touch and left a tip. Delia could break the news about Justine's gender change. Then he'd have another reason to clasp his balls.

Justine's brother and I walked along a row of evergreens in his plant nursery. Underneath a fashionable stubble, Daniel Bradley's face was red, like a perpetual sunburn. He was stocky with firm, not flabby, fat. The only resemblance to Justine I could see was in his eyes—big, long-lashed hazel eyes. One day some scientist will patent the gene for those eyes and make a fortune.

"What can you tell me about my brother's death?" He looked anxious. "I haven't heard anything."

His *brother's* death. He was the first person I'd met who thought of Justine as male. I held out my hand to the feathery leaves of an arborvitae. I couldn't tell him much, because what little we had—the gopher poison in the barn, the list of people with faint motives—needed to stay under wraps until we had sufficient evidence to make an arrest. "Still working on it," I said.

"I didn't know he was going to be married. I wish he'd told me. Er, *she'd* told me. I can never get it right. To me, Johnny was always my little brother."

"Was it hard to adjust to his gender change?"

He frowned. "Hard to adjust? I thought he was incredibly brave. It was a surprise when he told me he was going to take it that far, with the hormones and surgeries."

"And your parents? Were they supportive?"

"Mom died before Johnny had the surgery. Dad still doesn't get it. My parents divorced when Johnny was about twelve, and Dad was pretty hard on him, to toughen him up. Being older, I tried to protect the kid. You know how it goes, just your typical dysfunctional American family." He twisted his mouth into a half-smile. "Johnny had the surgery when he was twenty, after Mom died and left us each some money. He started with breast implants and hormones. Then the sex change. He had some other cosmetic work done. I'm not sure about all of it. I haven't heard from him for several years."

"Was the sex change before nursing school?" I asked. We'd

reached the end of the evergreens, and moved into an herb section. I picked out a rosemary plant for Fern and fondled its sweet piney needles.

"During and after. Dr. Binkley could give you more information." He gave me the phone number of Justine's surgeon.

"One last question." I showed him the charm bracelet. "It was in her room, but it's not hers. Do you recognize these girls?"

He studied the tiny picture intently. "They look familiar but I couldn't tell you who they are. Maybe friends of his? I was so much older that I didn't know his friends very well."

"Why weren't you invited to the wedding, do you think?"

He shrugged. "Your guess is as good as mine."

Justine had been a woman for seven years, yet her brother still referred to her as "him" and "Johnny." My guess—she was terrified at the thought of Daniel meeting her fiancé and his parents, who didn't know she'd started life as a boy, and, it seemed, were unlikely to ever find out. Until she died.

I had one last appointment, in a brick medical building in downtown Wilmington, with a sex-change doctor.

Dr. Frieda Binkley was quite possibly the cutest doctor I'd ever met, a middle-aged version of the child Shirley Temple, with blond curls and creamy fair skin, in a blue dress that matched her eyes. I didn't expect cute. I didn't know what to expect, actually. A female surgeon who specializes in turning men into women? That would make her the ultimate horror-movie character—a castrator. Was she gender-switched herself? I wondered aloud, and asked her why she chose her specialty.

"I was born female," she said. "No gender issues here. I went into general surgery, and for ten years I removed gall bladders and tidied up after gunshot wounds. Then I did a plastic surgery fellowship, and joined a practice with expertise in sex-reassignment surgery. SRS, we call it. Male-to-female, female-to-male. The techniques have been developing and improving for forty years. It's a fascinating field."

I looked around her office for examples, but saw only pictures of kids, horses, and kids on horses. "I don't know anything about it. Would you tell me?"

"It takes a long time, at least two years. The patient starts with hormones to feminize the body. There's a year of psychological counseling and evaluation. Then surgery converts the male to female. Other surgeries such as facial recontouring and breast augmentation are sometimes performed. Electrolysis, to remove facial hair, or back hair if necessary. It's different for everyone."

"It's hard to imagine such an extreme commitment."

"Because you are comfortable in your skin, yes. But about one in five hundred boys is not. A few of them learn enough, and have the resources, to change. In the US today? The estimate is over thirty thousand people have had SRS. Many more attempt to be accepted by society as female, with hormone treatments and cross-dressing. The chances are high you know someone passing as female who was born male."

"Really? It's that common?"

"Gender dysmorphia is roughly as common as cerebral palsy, or blindness, or cleft palate. Those conditions receive insurance coverage, research, and public support. The transsexual? Ignorance. Their lives are lonely. Many teenagers end up on the streets looking for acceptance. There are places in every city where they come out at night."

"As drag queens and prostitutes?"

"A few end up that way. Most lead quiet and desperate lives. They're ministers and pilots and insurance salesmen. They marry and have kids."

I needed only one more answer from Dr. Binkley. "How authentic are the results? Would the woman be able to 'pass,' even in intimate situations?"

She smiled. "Yes, absolutely. There's considerable difference among women, you know, and the average male doesn't know enough to question what's normal. She will look like other women, she will feel and react like other women. Male-to-female is easier in that regard. Going the other way—well, it's not so easy to replicate nature."

She sat back and her smile faded. "It's rewarding work, life-altering. The patients are profoundly grateful. These are people who have known they were the wrong sex since they were aware of gender, around the age of three. Adolescence is particularly difficult, when hormones start to masculinize the body. These women suffered terribly then, as their bodies and faces became more and more male. In fact, these days, many of my patients are teenagers. The reassignment is very successful when the patient is young."

"Like Justine was. Or John."

"Yes. I would call her case a success. She was only twenty. Even before the surgery she was beautiful. Not all of them are beautiful on the outside like she was. Afterward, she was a whole person. I am so sorry to know that she's dead." Dr. Binkley spoke softly as she closed Justine's file.

It was a hundred fifty miles back to Verwood, nearly all of it on I-40, through a sandy flat landscape of scrub brush and loblolly pine, monotonous and trance-inducing, except for the sporadically hesitating engine of my state-owned car. The car would slow and I'd jerk into a small panic because usually there was an eighteen-wheeler on my tail doing eighty and they aren't the most wide-awake drivers.

Two hours of driving would give me plenty of time to think, though my life as a drug agent offered only worries—about Fern, Jax, my own sorry skin. I liked Anselmo. He was married.

His wife was probably a supermodel with wealthy parents, someone trendy and sexually inventive, who wrote brilliant novels or ran her own hedge fund. I'd have to admire him from the sidelines, be content that we could work together. At least I could try to impress him with my investigative talent. Justine's murder was certainly fertile territory for the application of such talent, with plenty of puzzle pieces to push around.

Opportunity? The poison had been in the barn located on the inn property. Blue, Liesle, and Wyatt knew where the keys were and had access to the barn. But just about anyone staying in the inn could have unearthed the key. Or walked in, when the barn was already opened.

The means? The poison had been added to Justine's tea, and she drank it a few minutes before one. You don't make tea and let it sit for an hour; you drink it within minutes. So who had been in her room? Ingrid, of course, helping with her hair. Kate admitted to going in after Ingrid, to get advice about her makeup. Mike said someone knocked at Justine's door just as he was getting off the phone with her. Who was that person? Tricia or Scoop Scott? Tricia had talked about grandchildren on Kate's video of the rehearsal dinner. So it seemed she didn't know about Justine's gender change before the wedding. I could swear, though, what I told them yesterday wasn't a surprise. They were so quick to deny, so annoyed I was bringing it up to them. Stonewalling.

The Embers had sued the birthing center where Alice had been born, and where Justine had worked. Had Justine been involved in the lawsuit, or even in Alice's birth? Had Evan gathered up enough energy to poison Justine as retribution? I'd find out more on Monday, when I talked with the director of the birthing center.

Mike had insisted he didn't know about Justine's gender change. He seemed genuinely sad that Justine was gone, but he, more so than anyone else, had the most at stake in a marriage. And his uncle Webster? Web was fired for stalking Justine and hadn't been able to find another job. Did he harbor an angry resentment?

Going by the "facts," sparse as they were, Webster was perhaps my number-one candidate, just because stalkers don't easily get over their obsessions, and often do murder them. His wife hadn't made it to the breakfast table to police his interactions with Justine. Perhaps they'd had an exchange that sparked his anger. He could have been the visitor to her room after Mike's call. He was, after all, staying in the room next to hers.

Blue was somehow in the mix. Most certainly he'd tried to sabotage Wyatt's B&B. Could the poisoning be part of the sabotage, as Wyatt suggested? An attempt to make the inn guests ill, gone horribly wrong? Blue had been upstairs during breakfast, "fluffing up." I thought about Liesle's psychic sensing of peanut butter. If I learned that Blue'd eaten a peanut butter sandwich that morning, I'd cuff him in an instant.

Too many kinda-sorta motives; not enough evidence. My thoughts drifted to the break-in at my house and my suspicion that it was related to the abortive raid on Jax's house. Perhaps he had recognized me after all. What else could it be?

Just after nine P.M., as I passed the north and south exits for I-95, my car engine began its death throes. It huffed and jerked, smoothed out for a minute, then slowed to thirty miles an hour. Flooring the accelerator didn't help. I moved into the shoulder lane, turned on my hazard lights, and crawled another mile to the next exit, the Johnston County rest area. I rolled to the parking area and stopped, popped open the hood and checked the oil, the hoses, and radiator. They looked fine. I'd have to get a tow truck to take the car to be repaired, then call around to see who could help me get home. I went inside the rest area building to find a phone book.

As I stood by a phone booth, rifling through the automotive listings, I glanced up to see a big woman coming out of the ladies' room. She looked familiar, damned familiar, with that frizzy hair and hollow eyes: Dana DeGrasso, Jax's partner, the woman who'd searched me, taken my gun, wrestled me to the floor. Furthermore, I knew exactly what she was doing here. I-95 runs from Miami to Maine. It's the north-south highway for drug dealers, and its intersection with I-40, three miles away, made this rest stop a convenient location for a drug pickup. No telling how many powder bricks were in her trunk.

I quickly turned my gaze back to the phone book, trying to avoid any worrisome spark of recognition, remembering how she and Jax had scooted after selling to me, the comments of their housekeeper, their suspicion that I was a cop. Dana strode out of the building, and I followed, to get a look at her car and see whether she was alone. I scanned the parking area. I didn't see her anywhere, but the grounds were perfect for hide-and-seek, with floodlights that cast deep shadows among the clumps of shrubbery.

I wanted to arrest her, and needed backup. I called the state police, told the dispatcher who I was and what I wanted to do. The dispatcher said a trooper was patrolling in the area and would be there in a few minutes. I started down the row of cars, checking between them. I held my phone in one hand, while my other hand, inside my jacket pocket, clutched my gun. A nervous reaction to seeing Dana—keep a tight grip on the SIG. I came to the end of the row of cars without seeing her. I went back to the building, edged to the corner, and peered around. No Dana. I decided to let Fredricks know what was going on, and dialed his home number. I was walking to the next corner, starting to fill him in, when I heard a rustling step behind me.

I had half-turned when someone shoved me to the ground and sat on me, sending my phone flying and knocking the air out of my lungs. Gasping to breathe, I recognized Dana's air-freshener smell. I squirmed and tried to flip her off but the woman had the substance of a hippo. She had a very tight grip on one wrist; the other wrist was pinned under me.

"Quit wiggling, you little bitch," she said. "You turned us in, didn't you?"

"What are you talking about?" My mind raced, fueled by fear and acute discomfort. Dana wasn't giving me an inch of wriggle room. Could I talk my way out of this? She pried my right arm out from underneath my body, pulled me to my feet, and wrestled my gun away. The woman must work out—her hands were like vise-grips. I opened my mouth and took a deep breath, planning to let out a helluva scream, when Dana jerked me around and punched me right in the nose. I felt my nose give way, painfully, and my eyes filled with tears. It hurt. A lot.

"Oh, ow," I said. "What do you want?" Maybe logic would help. "You're going to get in trouble for this." My nose was throbbing, it needed ice. "The cops are on the way."

"I'm not worried. You won't be here very long."

I didn't know what she meant but it didn't sound good. "Look, let me go now and you can get away. I don't even have a car."

"Just shut up. You don't get an opinion." She mashed me against the wall of the building, scraping my cheek against the rough brick. "Don't move, just hold still," she said. Any resistance on my part met with increased pressure from her. Then a needle entered my arm, and I felt a bubbly rush. My fear vanished, replaced by euphoria. She could have done absolutely anything to me and I wouldn't have cared. Everything was okay, more than okay, warm and fuzzy, and I floated, carefree, high above all petty worries and fears about a broken nose. My brain soaked up the drug and blazed with joy. My eyelids dropped, my knees buckled, I sank to the ground and vomited all over Dana's sandals.

# CHAPTER 15

*Saturday Very Early Morning*

I was handcuffed and locked up, and I didn't care. Time as measured by clocks no longer mattered. Instead, I started counting the visits from Dana and her needle.

The first time the drug wore off, it was still pitch dark, though I could hear an early bird calling out the approach of dawn. The room's window was locked and covered by a grate, and through it I could see a waning moon and the bright speck of Venus. Thinking I had little to lose, I kneed the doorknob, kicked at the door and called out for help. Dana came in right away with the needle. She wore a red tank top that revealed too much of her big floppy chest, and plaid flannel pajama bottoms. Her hair was wilder and frizzier than ever.

"There's no one to hear you," she said. "Make all the noise you want." She shoved me down on the bed and sat heavily on me. I twisted and earned an elbow in my belly that knocked my wind out long enough for her to inject me with a swift practiced motion. She sat with me for a few minutes as the drug took effect. I asked her about a tattoo on her shoulder, a bulldog wearing a green hat, with "USMC" in black letters underneath, and she talked about being a Marine. I lay there, euphoric and weak, fading in and out of consciousness.

Later I became drowsily aware of my surroundings: a small room without a lamp or overhead light, a stained blue carpet, gray-white walls. The bed was covered by an orange and brown paisley bedspread, unwashed and blotchy with dirt. A dull putty-colored blanket seemed cleaner, so I pulled it open and put it on top of the bedspread. My hands were cuffed so it was impossible to open the window, latched on both sides and blocked by an iron grate screwed tight to the outside wall. Were this a movie, the heroine would produce a little jimmy-thing from her bra and magically pick open the cuffs. She'd raise the window. Then she'd flip the jimmy-thing over and it would be a tiny hacksaw and she'd rip right through that grate, all quietly and in two minutes so she wouldn't be detected, then she'd slither out the window, flip to the ground, immobilize the guards with forceful kicks. Wearing black leather.

But I didn't have a jimmy-thing. And it's much harder to pick handcuffs than you'd think. Actually, it didn't even cross my mind; the handcuffs seemed invincible. I did wonder where I was. Right outside the grated window was a large prickly-looking holly bush, beyond it dirt and a bit of grass, beyond that a chain-link fence and a cinder-block wall painted green, now peeling. Trash littered the area—bottles, fast food containers, bits of paper. I could hear muffled street noises, traffic and sirens and horns, from perhaps a block away.

Fear, the self-preservation variety, scuttled around me like an annoying rat, muffled, dampened and so squashed by the drug that its squeaks barely registered. When the drug wore off, the rat squealed insistent messages about needles, infection, contamination, and survival, stupid. As though Dana could hear the squealing, she would show up soon afterward, needle in hand. The third time Dana came in, she removed the handcuffs to allow me to use the bathroom. Then she recuffed my hands and gave me food—a breakfast burrito, a donut, and some orange juice. I hadn't eaten since the shrimp and pasta with Delia the previous day, so I was hungry and ate everything, even though the burrito was cold and the donut was stale. I asked her what she was going to do with me. "Are you going to kill me?"

"No, I'm not a murderer. Here, this will help." She got out her needle. Fear-rat perched on my shoulder and nipped at my face, until the drug floated me far and away from worries as trivial as death.

Later in the day, she brought me a burger and a strawberry milkshake, delicious and sweet. Once again I asked what was going on, and she apologized for the handcuffs, the locked door—but didn't answer the question. She left and I heard the car start, then silence. She was gone for hours. The drug wore off, and I could hear the rat's hissing begging me to survive. I decided I didn't have much time. She had my SIG. Jax could tell her to take me somewhere remote and shoot me. I knew I had to do something but I was handcuffed and even if I weren't, Dana's size gave her an advantage. The thought of anyone so much as breathing on my throbbing nose brought tears to my eyes. Wussy, yes, but not hopeless—I had brains, feet, my hard head. I lay on the yellowish blanket and created a plan, running through every step, thinking of contingencies.

It was almost dark again when I heard a key in the door and Dana came into the room, dressed up in her clear plastic platform shoes and a swingy wig. I was awake, feeling nauseated and sweaty, not anxious to grapple with her. It would be so easy to go along, nod off. But I'd had enough of Dana's medicine. I wanted my life back. I wanted my life, period.

"Hey," I said, "got a question."

She sat on the bed, her solid haunch forcing me against the wall, and laid a needle on the bedside table. She took a rubber tie out of her jacket pocket. "Sure, make it quick."

"Do you remember when I gave you my umbrella? Showed some kindness? Can you reciprocate, help me out of here?"

"I am helping you. Give me your arm, it's happy time."

She reached for my arm but I pressed my elbows to my sides. "Wait. I've been having cramps all night. I need to go to the bathroom."

"After."

"I'm going to have an accident."

"No, you won't. Be quiet." She leaned into me and I couldn't move. I felt the prick of the needle, and the familiar rush, the nausea, the falling. My muscles loosened, the aching pain in my face vanished, I sank into the security of the drug.

"I'll give you a minute," she said. "Wait until you can walk."

I lay on the bed, my eyes half-closed, waiting for the rush to subside. Trying to remember what I had to do. The rat whined like a mosquito, screeching at me to pay attention, it was now or never. Did I believe the rat? Why not let Dana keep right on visiting me? She's taking good care of you, all's right with the world, said the drug. The whiny rat said, you're an idiot. You're a prisoner injected with opiates against your will. Do something. Now now now now now.

Dana tugged me to my feet and pushed me down the narrow hall to the bathroom. She unlocked one of the cuffs, leaving the other on my wrist. I went into the bathroom, turned on the light, and closed the door. It was your basic filthy bathroom, decorated with scum, grit, mildew and *E. coli*. A look in the mirror showed me a swollen nose, two black eyes, a bruised cheekbone, and a dull tangled mess of hair. I peed quickly then stood and found what I remembered seeing behind the toilet—a plunger. A grotty, black rubber plunger with a beautiful twenty-inch wooden handle. I opened the door a crack and whispered. "I need a tampon. Do you have any?"

"Yeah, sure." She opened a cupboard in the hall, revealing centuries-old cleaning supplies, gummy shampoo bottles, a jumble of raveled towels. And a familiar blue box.

I wasn't feeling much motivation; my brain was in a happy

place and not excited enough to hurt anyone. I needed the opposite of happy thoughts, I needed fear. I thought about Jax. His cruel glass eye, his horrific scar. Would he send a cold-blooded killer to get me, expecting a complacent Stella? I thought about needles, infection, disease, overdose. Fern and how she must be sick with worry. Merle wedged against the front door waiting for me to come home. Was anyone caring for him? Was he hungry? I closed my eyes and waited for my head to stop spinning. I put the base of my left thumb in my mouth and bit down hard, hoping a stab of pain would create adrenaline, enough to do what needed doing.

When Dana handed me the blue box, I lunged, shoving the wooden plunger handle into her heart. Something in her chest gave way, and she fell back with a hoarse cry. I jabbed her in the gut and she doubled over, then I cracked her a few good ones on the head until she fell and stopped thrashing. One of the blows had hit her square in the face, smashing her nose, not quite by accident. She lay quiet, inert, probably concussed but breathing through her mouth. I took a deep breath but didn't slow down because the rat was perched on my shoulder, squealing in my ear, encouraging me to move quickly, so I covered her with the dull blanket and took her keys from the door. I found my gun and my cell on the kitchen counter. Back in control—the feeling was priceless.

I stumbled outside. The early evening was cool and cloudy, damp on my face, silent except for some distant traffic. I debated trying to rouse the neighbors to get help, but the houses were dark, and when one of Dana's keys unlocked the Lexus in the driveway I decided to clear out. I started the car and backed onto the street.

The dashboard clock said 6:30, a time when most people were watching the news, drinking a beer, crawling on the floor with their kids. I wasn't seeing right—no matter how much I blinked, a purplish haze clouded my vision—and my response time felt terribly slow, but I thought I could drive.

I clutched the steering wheel and wondered why I was still alive.

# CHAPTER 16

*Meanwhile, Twenty Hours Earlier*
*Friday Midnight*

Fern counted sheep, visualizing each spindly-legged woolly bundle as it trotted to the fence and jumped over, but she lost interest at number seven. She punched her pillow into shape, untangled her nightgown, then lay still, thinking about her painting class for teenagers. One sweet girl had a brilliant talent, but the other students intimidated her. Grace had been shy like that. Odd how the boys always thought they were better than they actually were, and the girls thought they were worse. She pondered why that was. The boys needed to show confidence and the girls needed to let them? Boys wanted attention, girls wanted friends? Maybe she could talk the girl into entering a contest or two. A few blue ribbons would boost her belief in herself.

It was hopeless. Sleep wasn't going to happen. She got out of bed, made a cup of tea, and settled herself in her glider with a mystery from the library. Soon she was absorbed in the story. One of the characters had stuffed a body under the attic floorboards, and his delusional landlady had just gone up there to look for a 1953 calendar. Would she notice the smell? The floorboard that wasn't put back correctly?

The ringing of her phone frightened her. It's never good news at two in the morning.

"Ms. Lavender? Hank Fredricks." The man's voice was gentle

and somber. "I work with Stella."

Fern managed to ask, "What is it?"

"I have bad news. There's a strong possibility that Stella has been abducted."

She gripped the phone. She must have misheard. "What did you say?"

Fredricks told her the details. Stella had called him about three hours ago, from an I-40 rest stop. She'd recognized a known drug dealer, one with an outstanding warrant, and had asked the highway patrol for help in making an arrest. When the highway patrol arrived, Stella's car was there, but she'd disappeared. Bystanders had seen her being helped, half-carried, by a large woman into a white Lexus.

"What's being done?" Fern could barely get the words out.

"We've issued a missing persons bulletin," he said. "I'm confident they'll find her. I'll call you the instant I know anything. Sorry, I've got to go." He hung up.

"They'll find her"—an echo from twenty-two years ago when Grace disappeared. A broken promise, an outright lie. "They" didn't find her, not for agonizing days, months, then years that Fern barely endured, carrying on only for Stella's sake. Trying to nourish a dwindling hope, trying to blank out the worst, the images and the eternal loss. She couldn't possibly be expected to bear this another time.

Fern threw the phone across the room and wailed with frustration and fear and grief. It was intolerable that she might lose Stella. Fern began a feverish begging to anyone who would listen. Please please please keep her safe . . . What else could she do?

She'd barely heard what Fredricks told her but now she went over it again. Rest area, car trouble. Someone saw a woman help Stella into a white Lexus.

A white Lexus? Jax drove a white Lexus. Stella had told her

to drop him, she knew he was a drug dealer. Not a coincidence. She picked the phone up from the floor.

At six in the morning, Fern heard a knock on her front door. She'd heard about Fredricks from Stella, so she wasn't surprised by his strained shirtfront with its almost-popping buttons. But she hadn't expected a handsome face, in a chubby-Elvis kind of way, or his good manners. They sat in the kitchen at the worn oak table, a potted rosemary plant from Stella's car between them. It was still dark outside, and in the wavy glass pane of the back door Fern saw her reflection, a froth of white hair, a blurry white face. Neither of them had slept all night.

"So you know this character, this Jax," Fredricks said.

She poured boiling water into her coffeepot. While they waited for it to drip through, she picked up Stella's purse, a black leather bag which Fredricks had brought to her. Yellow fingerprint powder had collected in the creases. She pressed the bag to her cheek.

"I met Jax a week ago, at a wedding," she said. "You must know about the case Stella's working on, Justine Bradley's murder? He was utterly charming. He asked me out."

Fredricks startled visibly. "What?"

"Stella knows; she stopped by last Sunday, just as he was leaving. He was here to measure my shed, make a chicken coop out of it." She got out two mugs and poured the coffee. "Milk? Sugar?"

"Just black." He sighed, a big tired exhalation. Fern knew he was exhausted. During the night he'd driven to the SHP District Office in Smithfield, to talk with the troopers and get the things from Stella's car—her phones, her purse, and, curiously, a carton of cookbooks. He'd arranged to have the car towed. He'd spent an hour at the rest stop, watching the evidence team. Then he'd driven to Verwood to meet Fern.

"She told me to drop Jax, that he sold drugs. But nothing specific." To protect me, Fern thought.

"What can you tell me about him?"

Ridiculous responses came to mind. Jax was charming. She'd knitted him a scarf. She should have better instincts after nearly a half-century of dating. A tangle of trivia and guilt. "Not much." She held up the two cell phones he'd put on the table. "What are these?"

"They're Stella's. Both state-issued. One's her undercover phone, the other's for everyday business."

"She has another one too, for personal calls."

Fredricks shook his head. "It wasn't in her car. What's the number? I'll ask the phone company to triangulate it."

Fern gave him Stella's personal phone number. "Don't you need to keep her phones? They might have information—calls or numbers."

"We've already downloaded all the data on those phones. You hold onto them for her."

His implication, that Stella would get her phones back, was such a positive statement that tears came to her eyes. She blinked them back and swallowed. "Where do you think she is? Where are you going to look?"

He pushed his chair back and stood, rubbing his belly like an unhappy Buddha. "We'll find her. I'll keep you informed."

"You'd better. I want to know everything." She handed him a cranberry muffin for the road.

They paused on the porch. The donkeys peered over their fence, watching them expectantly. To the east, a periwinkle sky was dotted with orange clouds, lit up from below by the golden half-sun. It was a gorgeous scene and yesterday Fern would have grabbed her sketchbook. Today, she'd easily forgo the sight of all future sunrises to have Stella's hand in hers. The coffee soured in her throat.

A car crunched its way along her rutted drive. Another early-morning visitor. If it were good news they would call, she thought. She sank into a rocking chair and watched the man get out of the car and slip on his suit jacket.

He had to be Richard, Stella's boss. Stella had described him perfectly—slim, mid-fifties, milky brown skin and close-cut hair. Impeccable in black pinstripe at six A.M. Under normal circumstances, such a sight would catch her breath and activate her flirt gene. Now she felt unexpectedly cold and nauseous; he reminded her of an undertaker. She shivered.

As the man approached them, Fredricks waited with her on the porch. "Sir, have you met Fern Lavender? Stella's grandmother?"

Richard leaned down and took her hand. "How are you doing, Ms. Lavender?" He smelled faintly like a cold sea. His black eyes were intelligent but his concerned expression was profoundly irritating. She wanted action, not sympathy.

"Have you heard anything?" Rude, yes, but she shouldn't have to ask.

He straightened and shook his head. "Not yet. We will." He turned to Fredricks. "We need to talk. I want to hold a press conference."

"No. Abso-fucking-lutely not. Excuse me, ma'am." Fredricks's face flushed purple. Richard turned to Fern. "My apologies. Would you mind . . ."

"Sit down. I'll get you some coffee," Fern said. She went into the house, through the living room and into the kitchen. The window over the sink was open, and she could clearly hear the men on the porch. She took a mug, then leaned over the sink to listen. She could just see their chairs and their heads, close together. Beyond them, the mist was beginning to burn off as the sun warmed the air. This second-worst day of her life was going to be a nice one, God's idea of a thoroughly inappropriate joke.

"Tell me what happened," Richard said. His voice was tense.

"Stella called me around nine-fifteen last night, said she was having car trouble and had stopped at the Johnston County rest area. She said she saw Dana Degrasso," Fredricks said. "Then the phone went dead."

"The woman from the coke buy a few nights ago."

"Right. But she might not know Stella's an SBI agent. Stella's ID was in her car, and it seems Degrasso didn't touch anything in the car—the car was locked, and still had Stella's purse and state-issued phones in it."

Richard shook his head. "The sooner we find Stella the better. And the media can help us."

"Then assume Degrasso doesn't know Stella's a cop. Leave her undercover. A missing person."

"There's no urgency to a missing person. I'm going to report it as an abduction. Give out her name and picture and description. If they know she's police—"

"The word gets out that Stella's a cop and she's dead."

Richard leaned closer to Fredricks. "My friend, here's the hypothetical. If Stella is dead and I haven't roused an goddam army to find her, I will rightfully be crucified."

"Her death would *look* bad?" Fredricks spit it out.

Richard studied him. "You misunderstand."

"I heard what you said."

"Where is she? You have ideas?"

Fredricks stood and rolled his shoulders. "I will find her."

"I'll give you twelve hours. Then I load the big guns."

"I'm glad I don't have your job."

Richard snorted. "You're not alone in that sentiment, my friend."

At that, Fern decided she had to rejoin the conversation. She poured coffee into the mug, put it on a tray with a small pitcher of milk and the sugar bowl, and went outside. "I know you both have work to do, so take the coffee with you," Fern said. She wanted them to leave. Standing around on her porch wasn't finding Stella.

They gulped down the coffee and thanked her. She watched them get into their cars, then walked over to the donkey pen. Bill and Hillary nuzzled her with their white mouths as she leaned into the fence, crumpled by exhaustion and fear. She closed her eyes and concentrated on Stella. "You're fine, you're fine, you're fine," she whispered. Her prayer. She would will Stella home safe.

Fern dreamed she was at the controls of an airplane, a huge passenger jet flying a few feet above a forest of trees, seconds from crashing. She didn't know what to do, she couldn't fly a plane, she was paralyzed. The plane lurched as it brushed the trees, plunging toward the ground and she couldn't even scream. "Ahhh," she tried to say. Nothing came out. A dog barked. And barked. And barked.

She woke up disoriented and still afraid, slumped in the chair by her fireplace. The barking continued, a tinny metallic recording coming from the kitchen. She stood up slowly, then realized what she was hearing—Merle, Stella's dog, a ring tone. One of Stella's phones. She scrambled into the kitchen and grabbed it. "Hello?"

"Stacy? Is that you? Who is this?" It was a woman's voice, rushed and panicky.

"There's no Stacy here," Fern said. "You must have the wrong number. What number were you calling?"

The woman gave a number, triggering a memory—Stacy was Stella's cover name! This was one of Stella's drug contacts, maybe a link to Stella in some way. She had to hold onto her.

"Okay, just checking. We never know who's calling or what they want," Fern said. "I'll take a message. What's your name?"

"Tell her Bebe called. She met me with Mo. And he's disappeared!" The woman nearly shrieked this last in anguish. "I wanted to warn Stacy. I think Jax has killed him."

"Who is Mo?" Fern mashed the phone into her ear. At the mention of Jax, she wanted to reach into the phone line and pull this woman through by the hair.

"He's my husband. I been sleeping in the car. I got nowhere to stay, no money, and a baby coming any minute. I thought maybe Stacy could help me."

"She's not here." Fern's emotions were mixed. Did she care about Bebe's plight? She couldn't spare the pity right now. But anyone who could put Jax and Stella/Stacy in the same sentence needed to be clutched, tightly. Yes. She wanted to be Bebe's new best friend. "Did you tell the police your husband was missing?"

Bebe let out a barking laugh. "I don't talk to cops. They ain't my friends. What do they care about a tweaker!"

"A tweaker?"

"Mo does meth. A tweaker. He went off to meet Jax two nights ago." Bebe coughed, a smoker's terrible hack. "Thing is, we got nothing. I'm scared to go back to our apartment."

" 'We'?"

"I got a little boy, Oliver."

"Don't you have any family?"

There was a silence on the other end.

"You still there?" Fern asked.

"Yeah, sure. Just thinking about my asshole father. Sorry, that's what he is. No, I don't have family. What's your name, anyway?"

"Fern Lavender." Fern's thoughts flew. Did she want to help Bebe? Bebe might know something. She thinks Stacy's a drug user like her husband. Fern took a deep breath. "I'll give you a place to stay for a couple of nights, until you get settled." As she uttered these words she felt a tinge of fear to be stepping into Stella's undercover world. At the same time her spirits lightened; it felt good to take action, not just sit by the phone waiting for a call that might never come.

Bebe hesitated. "Where do you live? And who with?"

Fern reassured her as best she could. "Out in the country, by myself. You'll be safe." She gave Bebe directions, and hung up. She clasped her hands to her chest, feeling her heart pound. Stella would have my head, she thought, my addled head.

Thirty minutes later, as Fern was changing the donkeys' hay, a blue station wagon, its paint faded and grimy, crept down her gravel driveway and stopped. The driver's door opened and a woman pulled herself out. She wore a rumpled sweat shirt and jeans, and looked as exhausted as Fern felt. She was thin except for her enormous belly. A small bony boy emerged from the car and took his mother's hand, staring at Fern with black eyes in dark-hollowed sockets. The pair of them could have been right out of a Depression-era Okie dustbowl.

"I'm Bebe and this is Oliver," the woman said, looking wary. "Stacy lives here? With you?"

"I'm Fern. Stacy's not here right now." Fern tossed one last forkful of hay and set the pitchfork in a corner of the shed. She shut the gate and latched it. "Do you need a hand with anything?"

Bebe's face relaxed a fraction. "You're a good person to help us out." She tugged open the car's rear door and retrieved two stuffed grocery bags. "These are our clothes. We got nothing else, not even a blanket. We slept on the seats. Though I wouldn't call it sleeping."

"Come inside," Fern said. "Are you hungry? Want something

to eat?" She addressed the child.

He nodded but didn't speak.

"He's not much of a talker," Bebe said. "You're hungry, aren't you, Ollie?"

"Come in. I'll fix some eggs."

They followed Fern inside. "This is a nice house," Bebe said. "Reminds me of my grandpa's old place in Rocky Mount. Quiet. You're not scared staying here by yourself? I'd be scared. Not as scared as last night. Try sleeping in your car 'cause you can't go home." She barked a laugh as she took out a cigarette.

"You'll have to smoke outside. Better still, quit. Can't be doing that baby any good," Fern said.

"Yeah, sure." Bebe put the cigarette back into the pack and dropped it in her purse. "Listen, thanks a bunch. I swear I haven't closed my eyes since Mo went off."

"Want to wash up?" Fern pointed down the hall and hoped the answer was yes—the little fellow was grimy. Bebe led him by the hand to the bathroom. Well, at least Bebe and Oliver were taking her mind off Stella, and after they ate, she'd see what Bebe knew about Jax.

The child ate his eggs quickly, followed by two slices of toast and strawberry jam. He'd saved the bacon for last but it didn't survive long either. He held out his plate. "More, please," he said, the first words Fern'd heard from him.

"Drink your milk first," Bebe told him. She'd cleaned her plate, too. She sagged against her hand, her elbow on the table. Fern stirred the second batch of eggs. The bread slices popped up in the toaster, and she sliced them in half and buttered them. Oliver watched her spoon jam onto his toast—"Enough?" and he nodded and began to eat again.

"Stacy live here?" Bebe asked.

Fern shook her head, no. She wanted to talk about Stella but couldn't figure out how to phrase things. She rinsed the frying pan and set it in the dish drainer. She took the milk to the table and poured Oliver another cupful. He was slowing down, she noticed. His eyes glazed over, unfocused as he sipped the milk. "How about a rest now?" Fern said. "Come with me." She led them up the stairs to Stella's old bedroom. Dusty, but it didn't matter. At least the double bed was made up, covered with a soft chenille bedspread.

"This is nice." Bebe removed Oliver's shoes and pants and he slipped under the covers. Thirty seconds later his eyes closed. "I'll get a smoke, then lie down with him for a while."

Fern followed her outside to the back porch. "You've got your troubles, Bebe."

"I'm scared. I can't go back to the apartment." Bebe lit a cigarette and inhaled deeply.

"When's the baby due?"

"Three weeks."

Fern could think of nothing to say. She couldn't bring herself to utter greeting-card sentiments about bundles of joy. A new baby seemed like the last thing Bebe needed.

Bebe looked away and blew a cloud of smoke. "I'm missing Mo right now." She put her hand over her eyes and her face crumpled.

"What happened to him?"

"He went to meet Jax at a burger joint two days ago. I haven't seen him since. That bastard Jax, his ass is mine. I've got a gun in the car. I'll kill him."

Guns, drugs, murder. Just like that, Fern had entered a new universe, Bebe's world. It was time to fess up about Stella's disappearance. Bebe might be able to help. Fern thought how she might phrase things without revealing Stella's job. "Stacy's gone missing. Last night."

Bebe attempted a deep breath that turned into a cough.

"That's terrible. Just last night? Maybe she's partying somewhere."

"No, the police think Jax maybe had something to do with it because Stacy saw his friend Dana at an I-40 rest stop just before she disappeared. The police found her car but no sign of her." Sharing this sort-of truth with Bebe made Fern feel perversely hopeful.

"That motherfucker!" Bebe let out a stream of curses for a good minute as she extracted another cigarette and lit it, puffing out a goddam this and cocksucker that. At least the little boy was out of earshot. Fern remembered Grace's "goddammits," used appropriately as a tower of blocks fell. The three-year-old had picked it up, of course, from listening to Fern's muttered swearing when she ran out of cadmium red at a crucial moment. When was that, forty years ago? Before Fern learned how hard life could be.

Bebe calmed down and put her hands on Fern's shoulders. "Here I am taking all your time and you worrying about Stacy."

"Do you know how to find Jax?" Fern asked.

"I know where he hangs."

Fern felt a jolt of excitement. "Have you told the police?"

"I don't talk to police. And promise me you won't either, or I'm outta here." She dropped her cigarette and stepped on it, then leaned over awkwardly to pick up the butt and put it in her pocket. "Let's say I take the rest I badly need, then I'll drive you around, okay? If you buy the gas." Her breath smelled like rotten fish, and Fern tried not to cringe.

"Sounds better than doing nothing. Go lie down." Fern would have preferred to hit the road that instant but Bebe looked like she was running on fumes.

While Bebe and Oliver slept, Fern turned on the television. She flicked through the channels, looking for news. Even channel 14, the all-news-all-day station, didn't mention her missing granddaughter. Fredricks had said that law enforcement had been alerted. She'd forgotten to ask exactly what that meant, whether they were actively searching or just adding Stella's name and picture to a long list.

She had to move so she wouldn't think. Thinking led straight to what-ifs—what if Stella had been hurt and what if she was frightened and what if she never came home again? No thinking, just move and concentrate on the job. She put hot water and a splash of oil soap in a bucket and went upstairs to wash the hall floor that years ago she'd painted red, the red now worn away in places showing green paint underneath. She backed down the stairs, washing each step clean enough to eat from. She drank a cup of coffee standing up, looking out the window at the donkeys and Bebe's car. It was filthy. Fern grabbed plastic bags and went outside.

Paper bags from fast food restaurants were jammed under the seat. Dozens of wrappers spoke to a candy bar addiction. She wasn't surprised to see roaches scuttling away as she gingerly eased a rifle onto the ground, then pulled out the cups, burger wrappers, peanut shells, empty cigarette packs. She took Ollie's few toys inside and dunked them in a bleach solution. She vacuumed the floor mats and seats, until she started to feel faint and realized she hadn't eaten in hours. She went inside, boiled, peeled, and ate two eggs without tasting them, then went back to work, soaping and hosing off Bebe's car, washing the windows in and out, spraying bug killer under the seats.

But it wasn't working; she felt panic in her gut, rising into her chest. She went into her painting room and rummaged in the closet until she found a blank canvas. A dark blue background, a face outlined in black. A child in a yellow dress, holding a doll. Broad strokes suggested the cloth, the feet, the hair. Highlights of white, shadows of dark umber. She always spent the most time on the eyes. These eyes were sea-green and sunken, the skin red with greenish undertone. This child was Stella, this child was Grace. She painted until she felt wobbly. Her eyes were dry as corks. She picked up Stella's purse and took it to her bedroom. Clutching it to her chest, she lay down. Stella be well, Fern said to herself, over and over. Her heart beat, too fast, and the terror of what-ifs lurked at the edges of her consciousness. She stared at the ceiling.

Fern dreamt she lost a baby, a miniature one no bigger than a fingernail. She'd put it down somewhere, couldn't remember exactly. Someone might've stepped on it or vacuumed it up. Or dropped it into the sink, or swept it under the rug. She couldn't see someone so small because everything was fuzzy and she couldn't find her glasses. She heard it crying, that hiccupping cry of the newborn. People walked around her house ignoring the crying. She tried to tell them to get out but she couldn't make a sound.

She awoke awash in sadness, sweating, the room over-warm from the late afternoon sun. Stella's purse had fallen to the floor, spilling its contents—the familiar red wallet, a notebook, lip balm, pens. A charm bracelet in a plastic bag. She couldn't bear to think about Stella and what she might be enduring.

She looked at the clock—it was almost five in the afternoon. From the living room just outside her door she heard Bebe speak to Oliver in a low voice. It was a comfort to have someone else in the house, some company to give her something to do. Perhaps Oliver would like a donkey ride. Bebe could drive her to Stella's house to get Merle. Do something to make time pass, to help her endure the wait.

She found Oliver kneeling at the coffee table, drawing with her colored pencils on the back of an envelope. "I'm coloring," he said. "I'm being quiet."

"You're being wonderful. Where's Mommy?"

He pointed to the front door with a green pencil, without taking his eyes from his picture.

Outside, Bebe tipped a cigarette at her car and gave Fern a gap-toothed smile. "Some good fairy's been working. Looks better than new. I thank you. Sorry I'm broke, but I used to do hair. You need a trim? In return?" Bebe said this nonchalantly, blowing a stream of smoke into the air.

Oliver came onto the porch and held up his drawing for Fern. It showed three people figures with lumpen arms and legs. One was clearly Bebe, with a big belly. One was small—Oliver. And one had a magnificent crown of fluffy hair—yes, she needed a trim.

"These?" Fern asked, touching the four-legged animals.

Oliver pointed to Bill and Hillary. "Them."

"You have quite a talent," Fern said. "I teach drawing, so I know. Bebe, I'd love a haircut."

"Bring me scissors, a mirror, and a towel?"

Fern didn't expect much and didn't care. Whatever happened, her hair would grow again. She sat down on a chair on the porch and Bebe draped the towel around her neck. Fern was pleasantly surprised to find that Bebe did a fine job, sectioning carefully, taking off about an inch everywhere, scissoring into the ends for a softer line. Fern admired herself in a handheld mirror. "Very nice."

"Ah, well. Your hair is fantastic to work with. So thick and wavy. Stacy got her hair from you."

The reminder of Stella renewed Fern's sense of urgency. No news was good news, right? Stella was alive somewhere. "You said we could go look for her? I'll get us a quick bite to eat first. Ollie can bring the pencils."

"Let me fix some supper," Bebe offered. "I'll go see what you've got. You sit out here and relax." She stubbed out the cigarette on a tree trunk and went inside.

Ollie looked a bit pinker now that he'd had a meal and a nap. He was still scrawny but the circles under his eyes had faded. He peered through the porch balusters like they were jail bars, taking in the tree stand along the edges of the field, the donkey pen, the shed.

"Want to go for a walk?" Fern asked, holding out her hand to him.

They walked along a path worn by deer and the occasional fox. They saw two rabbits and a cardinal. They looked down into a groundhog hole, up at a wren's nest. Oliver didn't let go of her hand until they spotted a damp patch infested with rolly pollies. He squatted to study the bugs, then picked one up. When it curled into a ball, he popped it into his mouth and swallowed it.

"Oliver! We don't eat bugs!"

He stuck out his bottom lip, jumped up and ran ahead of her, down the grassy path winding through the field, back toward the farmhouse. He stopped at the donkey pen and stared through the fence. Fern opened the pen's gate, fit a bridle on Bill, and hoisted Oliver onto the donkey's back. As she led the donkey slowly around the pen, Oliver gripped the donkey's short mane, grinning with gleeful terror.

The presence of the child helped to soften the hard truths of the day, and after they finished eating the spaghetti Bebe had made, she offered to drive Fern around. "I promised to show you some places Jax might be. Come on, let's just take a ride, long as I don't have to go in."

Bebe steered the station wagon down the driveway, through the jungle of towering pines. It was Sunday evening; Stella had been abducted fewer than twenty-four hours ago. It seemed like a lifetime. They stopped in Verwood at Stella's house. Fern left Bebe and Oliver waiting in the car while she went to the back door and looked inside. There was Merle in the kitchen, tail wagging. Merle's first priority was outdoors. Poor doggy, he'd had an accident in the hallway. Understandable—she didn't know the last time Stella had been home to feed or walk him. Fern cleaned up the mess, found the dog food and filled his bowl. Merle devoured the chow in a noisy gobble, and Fern gave him a bit extra. He sucked it up, slurped some water and looked at her expectantly. "Come on," she said. "You can stay with me." She took his leash from the hook by the back door. Stella's dog wasn't the same as Stella, but Fern felt she was doing something, at least.

Oliver's expression was a mix of pleasure and alarm as Merle bounded into the back seat and gave him a big lick. Fern ordered him to lie down, Merle settled on the seat and Oliver patted his head tentatively. Bebe backed out of the driveway and headed down the highway, west.

"There's three places I know where Jax hangs," Bebe said. "He's got a house in the woods. That's where he sells out of, 'cause he can see folks coming. I don't much want to go there, 'cause they can see us coming!" Bebe barked a ha-ha. "There's his ex-wife's house up eighty-seven. She watches her grandkids and I can't see adding a kidnapped woman to that pack." Again the harsh ha-ha. Bebe rarely smiled or laughed, but somehow Fern trusted her the more for it. "So that leaves this house on Waters Street. Let's swing by, take a look. You can pretend you want to buy blow."

Fern laughed. This time Bebe cracked a real smile, showing her horrid teeth. They sped along the highway, heading into a pink-streaked crimson sunset. Bebe soon turned onto East Waters. "There's the place," she said, slowing to a crawl, pointing to a cinder-block house. It sat back on the lot, elevated from the street. It had been painted yellow once, but time had weathered away much of the paint and summer's humidity had mildewed the trim. A vacant lot on one side, a chain-link fence and overgrown shrubbery on the other. Curtains hung limply in the windows, and there were no signs of life.

Bebe stopped the car a hundred yards further down the street. She rolled down the window and lit a cigarette. "Wanna go see who's there, if they know anything?"

Fern would do anything for Stella at this point. "Sure. What should I say?"

"Here's the deal." Bebe blew a perfect smoke ring out the window. "Go to the door and check things out. If no one answers, you go around and look in the windows, see what you can see."

"What if someone notices me?"

"Tell 'em you're from the city. Water department. Social worker. Make something up. Believe me, the people in this house won't care as long as you act the part."

Fern knew her white hair, red sweater and blue jeans didn't add up to the look of a city worker. "What about I say my dog's missing?"

"Whatever. The story they would most believe is you want to buy product."

Fern cleared her throat nervously, wondering what the hell she was doing. It was one thing to sit on her back porch and talk about looking for Stella; it was another thing to creep around a run-down crack house in the dark.

"We'll stay in the car with the dog. I gotta tell you though, if I see Jax, I'm hitting the gas pedal. Now go on. Take this so you can see." Bebe handed Fern a lighter.

In the few minutes since they'd parked, night had fallen, leaving the street in darkness. Fern saw very few lights; most of the houses seemed to be abandoned. The darkness offered protection as she walked down the sidewalk to the cinder-block house. Bottles, cans, and paper littered the yard. A flat of withered marigolds lay by the steps. Someone bought those, Fern thought; someone once wanted something pretty and living here.

She knocked on the door but no one responded and she heard no signs of life. She carefully tried the doorknob—the door was unlocked. Dare she? She dared. She opened the door, flicked on the lighter, and saw a small living room, furnished with a sagging couch, a table, a television. The place stunk of mice and mildew and spoiled food.

No lights—no sounds—the house was empty. Disappointed, she decided to take a quick look around, then get out quickly before someone noticed the light flickering through the rooms and called the police. Holding the lighter above her head, Fern walked down the hall, freezing when she heard the distinctly human moan of a person in pain. A current of sudden fear washed through her. She couldn't tell where the noise came from. She stood very still and listened, feeling a drop of sweat trickle down her back, her breath coming too fast, the blood throbbing in her head.

"Unh, unh." A groan, more drawn-out this time. It came from further along the hall. Something on the floor—a pile of clothing? She stared so hard in the guttering light that her eyes hurt. She saw a shoe, a foot. Dear God, it was a body, covered by a blanket. Could it be Stella? Fern switched on an overhead light and pulled the blanket aside.

Not Stella, but a large woman with a bloody nose, frizzy hair puffing out of a wig, smelling like a Christmas tree. She moaned and whimpered something Fern couldn't understand.

Fern crouched down, her hand over her mouth, wondering what to do. The woman was too big, too inert to move. A doctor was needed. She would get Bebe to call an ambulance. "I'll be right back," Fern said. She dashed into the living room but as she reached for the doorknob, a violent pounding on the other side of the door began. She froze against the wall as the pounding continued, insistent and demanding.

# CHAPTER 17

*Saturday Evening*

I hung onto the steering wheel and tried to drive. East Waters Street was empty but it took me a while to make the left turn onto Raleigh Street, looking both ways and then doing it again. My reaction time was way off. I drove very slowly, blinking constantly to keep my eyes focused. I was desperate to put some distance between me and the cinder-block house. I wanted to get back to Verwood. I wanted to hug Merle. I wanted to take a shower. I could smell myself, odors of sweat, fatigue, and dirt, but more than stink needed to be scrubbed away.

One mile later I came to my senses, pulled into a grocery store parking lot and unclenched the steering wheel. Who should I call first? I tried Fern but she didn't answer. I left a message. Next, I called Richard. He picked up right away. As soon as he heard my voice he interrupted me. "Stella, thank God. Are you okay?"

Was I okay? I decided not to be too literal. "A couple of scratches. I'm okay."

A moment of silence. "And since last night? Explain."

'Splain. I 'splained about Dana, the drugs, our tussle, my imprisonment. "I stole her car, actually."

"Hold on. I'm going to make another call."

I leaned back in the seat and closed my eyes, then felt a overwhelming thirst. I got out of the car, clutching the phone to my ear, and went into the grocery store. I was doing fine until vertigo zapped me and I staggered into a shelf of cat food and knocked a bunch of cans onto the floor. People stared at me with looks of pity and a woman asked if I was okay, did I need help? I thanked her and waved her away, then sat on the floor for a few minutes until the dizziness subsided. I made my way to a self-serve coffee counter, found a paper cup and a water fountain, and filled the cup. I drank and drank, all the while pressing my phone to my ear.

Richard came back on the line.

"Do you need a doctor?" he asked.

"I don't think so. But I shouldn't be driving. Perhaps I should just wait here."

"You're not far from Fredricks. He'll pick you up." He paused for a beat. "I'm glad you're safe." Richard rarely reveals the existence of a caring heart under his Italian silk tie. It made me smile, for the first time in twenty-four hours.

Within minutes, two cars pulled into the parking lot. I recognized Mo's beat-up blue station wagon but was surprised to see Fern and Merle hopping out of it, accompanied by Bebe and a scrawny little boy. Fern threw her arms around me and I hugged her right back, inhaling her lavender scent, burying my face in her soft white hair. She's my only living relative, after all.

From the other car, a police cruiser, emerged Fredricks and a uniformed cop. They all started talking at once, except the child, who looked at me solemnly, studying the needle marks on my arms until I felt oddly ashamed and asked to borrow Fredricks's jacket. Though chilly and shaky, I finally felt safe, with Merle pressed against me on one side and Fern's soft body on the other.

"This is Oliver," Fern said as soon as she stopped crying. "He's Bebe's little boy."

I didn't know where to start. "What are you doing here?"

"I broke into a house that Bebe knew about, and found this

woman who was hurt, then the police came busting in and called an ambulance for the woman, then someone called them and said you were here. So we followed them."

Bebe nodded agreeably, warily eying the cop through the smoke of her cigarette. "Glad you're okay," she said. Oliver clung to her leg.

"Uh-oh," I said, suddenly feeling dizzy. The ground tipped up and I staggered.

Fredricks caught me. "We're going to the hospital." He steered me into the back of the patrol car and the cop punched on his siren and swung out of the parking lot, accelerating with an abrupt motion that didn't help my equilibrium. I braced myself against the front seat and closed my eyes.

"I don't need a doctor," I said. "I'm fine."

"Frankly, you look like crap. You have two black eyes, did you know that? And your nose is . . . well, not as cute as it used to be."

"Dana slammed me at the rest stop." I gave him the story. There wasn't much to tell, really, and I didn't want to dwell on being a captive, a victim.

"She injected you? My God, Stella. What with?"

"Haven't a clue. A painkiller. Happy stuff."

"Why? I mean, was she trying to get you addicted?"

"She didn't say." We'd reached the hospital, and Fredricks warned the cop driving the cruiser that this might take a while, but the cop said he'd hang around. Inside the emergency room, Fredricks worked some official magic and a nurse ushered us into an examining room. She offered us water and said she'd do what she could to get a doctor in, but Saturday nights were busy and she couldn't promise much. I slid onto the table and lay back, curling onto my side.

In the harsh fluorescent light Fredricks's skin was gray, and black encircled his eyes. He slumped onto a chair.

"I don't mind waiting here by myself," I said. "You go home."

"Don't be ridiculous. I'm going nowhere."

"When did you find out I was gone?"

"How about I tell the complete story. Since it looks like we have plenty of time."

"I'll try to stay awake."

"My wine group came for dinner," he began.

"Right, it was the night of your special dinner." Normally I wouldn't be able to endure such a recital but I was feeling quite grateful to Fredricks at the moment.

"We had drinks in the living room."

"The boys?" I knew Fredricks had his kids most weekends. He'd told me that a year ago his wife had left him for a stockbroker, a tennis-player with six-pack abs, a nine-to-five job, and most of his hair—attributes Fredricks lacked and his wife apparently required.

"Very hyper from all the people. But I settled them down. Then I plated the food. Roasted squash puree topped with goat cheese and caramelized onion. Cornish game hens, with a glaze made from Riesling, currant jelly, sage, and thyme. It was beautiful."

"Sounds good." Even the game hens. I was hungry.

"I added a mound of wild rice." Fredricks stared dreamily into the distance, remembering. "Did I tell you I painted my dining room red? Sort of a tomato soup color. Black linen place-mats, black plates, black candles. Everyone oohs and ahhs, and I pour the first wine, a Viognier. The dinner is off to a brilliant start. Then my phone rings."

"It's me."

"You never call me at home. So I took it."

"I'm at the rest stop and just saw Dana."

"Right. Then the call drops. I called back but your voice mail picks up. So I have to think about my priorities. Were you in trouble? What could I do from Durham?"

"What did you do?" Lying down, my eyes kept sagging shut, so I sat up and took a long swig of water. I wanted to hear Fredricks's story.

"I called the Troop C District Six office of the Highway Patrol. They said you'd already asked for backup and a trooper was on his way to the rest stop. I went back into the dining room and ate my dinner. Then I served the apple galette, with shaved candied ginger and some homemade ice cream. I poured a Riesling. I told them about a tasting challenge I'd won.

"But all the while I worried about you. As soon as I could decently leave the table, I called SHP again and was patched through to the trooper who answered your call. He'd found your car, locked, but you were nowhere in sight. He asked around and someone had noticed Dana helping you into another car. You looked drunk."

"She jumped me and injected me. I don't remember anything after that." Except urping on her feet.

"I notified Richard, pointed my guests at the coffee, and went to work."

"Was it on the news?"

"Good question. Richard and I had a disagreement about that. It went on the news as an abduction."

"With my name?"

"Name and picture. But no mention that you were an agent."

If Jax had seen the story, if he had talked with Dana, he now knew the real name of the woman she'd grabbed. Not Stacy, but Stella Lavender. I closed my eyes and pretended to be Jax. *Dana, my dear, look at the news. Her name is Stella Lavender. Could she be related to Fern Lavender? I dimly recall . . . doesn't Fern have a granddaughter? I didn't really notice . . . what was her name . . . Stella? Yes! Very interesting, this development. Dana, you stupid bitch, what have you done?* Yes, it might have gone like that.

Or another way I wasn't ready to consider quite yet.

"How did you find out where I was?"

"I realized your personal cell phone wasn't in your purse, and you might have it with you. So I asked the cell phone company to triangulate it. It took them hours but as soon as they said 'East Waters Street' I knew. It was quite a surprise to find your grandmother and Bebe Bernigan there before us."

"Ah, Fern and Bebe. Quite the odd couple. Does Bebe know I'm police?"

"I didn't tell her."

I hoped Fern hadn't either. A problem for another day. We waited for a long time. I dozed, then woke. He slept too, his head resting on his folded arms at the foot of the examining table. Finally, an Indian doctor pulled the curtain aside and asked me what was wrong.

I felt like an idiot telling him my nose hurt.

"What happened?" he asked. His touch was so gentle I barely winced.

"I ran into a door."

He looked at Fredricks, then back at me. "I'd like to talk with her alone, sir."

"Hey, relax," I said. "We're both police. I got into a scuffle with someone."

He looked down at the fresh track marks on my arms. "Oh please. Do I need to call security?"

"Hold on," Fredricks said, pulling out his ID. "Surely you heard on the news—the woman missing from a rest stop? It's her. She was held and drugged."

"I don't have time to read the papers," he said. "I'm on call one night out of four. When I go home, I sleep. But you know what? You are such a mismatched pair you have to be telling the truth."

Once we got all that out of the way, the doctor was very nice.

"Ice won't help at this point," he said. "I don't see any bleeding and I don't think anything is broken. Wait about three more days until the swelling diminishes, then see your regular doctor if you're worried. Can I get you a painkiller?"

"Not necessary. I'm trying to quit," I said.

Finally, just before midnight, my chariot reached my doorstep. All was back to normal, except that raging paranoia seized me as I opened the door. Fredricks had pointed out the obvious. Dana knew she'd grabbed the girl who'd bought a kilo from Jax. Fredricks had managed to keep my identity as an SBI agent out of the news, but Jax could know my unusual name, could connect it with Fern's, and remember meeting me. Though I wasn't in the phone book, it wouldn't be difficult to find out where I lived.

Fredricks checked the doors and windows; all was secure. Still, I thought about asking him to sleep on the couch. I decided I'd keep my weapon close by for the rest of my life and woe be unto anyone who broached my personal space. Exception—Merle, my darling dog, who whimpered happily as I leaned down for a slobbery kiss.

I brought the SIG into the bathroom. I didn't like what I saw in the mirror. My face was a blue-red-purple mess, my arms were dotted with injection sites, my ribs and back were bruised from the various falls, thumps, and squeezes Dana had administered. But these battle scars would fade. It felt so good to know I'd busted her in the face and she was going to prison.

I filled the tub and added lavender bubble bath—it's supposed to be warming and calming. I sank into the water and allowed the bubbles to do their trick.

# CHAPTER 18

*Sunday Morning*

The lavender worked wonders. In the morning I woke up feeling almost normal, willing to tackle my life again. Life intruded quickly when I listened to my phone messages. While I was on my little vay-cay with Dana, everyone else was busy creating havoc.

Ingrid wanted to know if I could recommend a private investigator. She didn't say why.

Tricia Scott needed to talk. It was important.

A county sergeant was going to interview Dana when she got out of the hospital, to see what she could tell them about Jax; did I want to watch?

Hogan had some information regarding real estate that I'd be interested in.

The facts of my twenty-four-hour abduction and rescue were beginning to filter out, thanks to the Internet, and a reporter wanted an interview. At least a dozen callers asked if I was all right.

Lieutenant Anselmo Morales wanted a face-to-face.

Monica Reardon, director of the North Carolina Birthing Center, reminded me of my appointment at noon tomorrow. Whoever put me on her schedule apparently forgot to note I was with the SBI, because she seemed to be under the impression that I was pregnant—she asked me to bring my insurance card.

Everywhere I looked, someone wanted a piece of me, and my calm unraveled in a hundred directions. So, after a cup of coffee, I took Merle out for a run. Both of us needed the exercise and the endorphins. Others were using the exercise trail—moms pushing jog strollers, seniors walking briskly, and one fellow, a real athlete, lapping everyone else. The sun was charging up the planet, and the northern hemisphere had entered the autumnal phase of its solar circuit. Nearly all the trees were leafless. My alert level had dropped from red (paranoid) to orange (cautious), so I didn't check the strollers to make sure they contained babies, or look for gun bulges in the seniors' jackets, though I made sure no one was following me by running clockwise, opposite the flow.

What were my priorities? Hogan could be handled with a phone call. No interview with a reporter, ever. That left Anselmo at the top of the to-do list. Then Tricia. The sergeant, yes. Finally, I'd call Ingrid.

The sight of me startled Anselmo. "Wow. You look like you were in a car wreck." He motioned toward a chair. We were in his office in the Essex County Law Enforcement Center, an impersonal and bureaucratic room that could have been a generic office except for a poster-size photograph of a pretty blue sailboat on a sparkling sea. It was tilted and moving fast into a cotton candy sunset.

"I look worse than I feel."

"Your grandmother caught DeGrasso, I heard."

"Essentially, yes." I shook my head, still amazed by that.

"And how are you?"

"Nothing's broken. I feel good, actually. Unless I smile."

"I'll try not to make you smile, Stella." He made a serious face and I tried not to smile. I was starting to feel comfortable around him, mostly for all the things he wasn't. He wasn't insecure. He would never make a remark about my (lack of) height. He wouldn't push my buttons like Hogan, or condescend like Richard, or ply me with food like Fredricks. Probably he didn't know me well enough, and for now, I was happy to keep it that way. Distance equaled respect.

"I'm thinking about taking up martial arts," I said. "What do you recommend?" I was fit enough—I could outrun most criminals—but, as Fredricks had suggested, I needed some good judo moves so the next time a Dana type mashed me into a wall I could flip her to the ground and plant my foot on her ginormous backside.

"I've seen one Steven Seagal movie. Lots of air chops and kicking. I prefer this." He patted his gun holster. "What did you learn in Wilmington?"

"Friday seems like a month away. Let's see." I consulted my notes. "Delia Scott told me that her husband and Justine had an affair five years ago when they both worked at the same hospital. Then he was fired for stalking Justine. He hasn't had a job since then. Quite a surprise to everyone when Justine turned out to be his step-nephew's fiancée."

"And they came to the wedding?"

"I wondered about that. But Delia didn't seem to blame Justine for anything. She was quite realistic about her husband's problem and its consequences. I talked with Webster. He's harder to read. Delia told me he was chronically unfaithful. He swore that Justine had forgiven him and he no longer had feelings for her. He was happy that she was getting married and wanted him to attend the wedding."

"Keep him on the list."

"Exactly." I told him about my visit to Mike's townhouse. "Our victim wrote a cookbook. A vegan cookbook." I rifled through my bag and pulled out *Enchanted Food*. "Here, Mike wanted me to give these out. You can keep it."

He studied Justine's picture on the back cover. "She was a writer? A chef?"

"And a photographer. Look at the pictures."

He tuned the pages. "I never heard of these ingredients. Kudzu? I thought that was a weed."

"My grandmother makes jelly with the flowers. Mike also gave me this." I handed him the plastic bag containing the Italian charm bracelet. "The B&B owner mailed it to him, along with the rest of Justine's belongings. But Mike said it wasn't hers. See? Wrong birthday. Justine didn't own a dog, she wasn't a teacher."

"Whose is it?"

"And how did it come to be in her room at the B&B? I'm going to put a researcher to work on it, see if he can come up with some candidates." Whenever I mentioned Hogan, I tended to blush but perhaps pink cheeks weren't so obvious under purple eyes. "I also talked to Justine's doctor, the one who performed her sex reassignment surgery. She was adamant that Justine would have been completely believable as a woman."

"That supports Mike Olmert's contention that he didn't know she was transsexual."

"And one more thing. Justine had a brother. I talked with him while I was in Wilmington. He didn't know about the wedding, in fact he said he lost track of his sister a few years ago. Actually still he refers to her as his brother."

Anselmo raised his eyebrows. "Confusing."

"He still calls her 'John' and thinks of her as male."

"No wonder he wasn't invited to the wedding." He stood and stretched. "Want some coffee?"

More caffeine would starve off my incipient headache. "Sure."

He poured me a cup. "Poisoning cases take a long time," he said. "Ann Miller Koontz was finally sentenced five years after she poisoned her husband." He referred to a recent Durham murder case.

"There was no evidence. Just her lover's confession to his lawyer before he committed suicide."

He took a milk carton out of a little fridge and handed it to me. "No evidence in this one either. Neither forensic nor circumstantial. A confession would be helpful."

"Maybe someone will feel guilty."

"It happens," he said. "We need a lucky break."

"Pretty boat," I said, pointing to the picture. "You sail?"

"Yes—her name's *Blueblood*. Like that spot right there." He reached out and touched my bruised cheek. "I'll take you out on her sometime."

I felt a bit faint. Must have been low blood sugar.

The boom arm swung up to let me drive into Silver Hills, past the starter castles and mini-Greek temples with four-car garages and drought-parched lawns. Tricia Scott opened her door. She wore a pastel floral shirt and pink pants, shoes, and headband. An Easter egg vision, except for her spray-hardened hair.

"Oh! I've been praying for you," Tricia said. "Thank God you're all right. Except . . ." she pointed delicately to my face. "Are you okay?"

"Thanks, yes, it will fade. You wanted to talk to me."

She invited me into the kitchen and offered me coffee. I glanced at her desk and there was Fern's preliminary sketch of the painting that Tricia had commissioned for her book. Curious, I took a closer look. Fern had toned it down somewhat— Jesus' hair was less scruffy. His eyes had a manic glint and he looked furious. He looked like General Patton with a beard.

Tricia looked over my shoulder. "I love it. It perfectly captures his leadership qualities. I'm going to have her add some women soldiers in the background. With weapons."

"Weapons?"

"Spears, swords, that kind of stuff. I've decided to emphasize female empowerment in my book."

"A cause I can support." I took a grateful sip of the coffee. "Where's Scoop?"

"He's upstairs, getting ready for his weekly broadcast. Come and see. Online congregation, hymns from a CD, some sermon he prints off the web. It's an utter perversion." She jumped up and left the room.

"Oh, I don't know . . ." I said, but Tricia was halfway up the stairs to the big room over their garage, and her last comment made me curious.

Scoop celebrated our entry into the room by throwing a hymnal against the wall. "Oops, sorry," he said. "I didn't hear you coming. The fucking microphone is broken. Call Mike and get him over here to fix it pronto."

"No problem." Tricia left the room to place the call.

I wasn't taken to church as a child—Fern summarily rejected all organized religion as patriarchal and oppressive to women— but I did know that preachers weren't supposed to throw hymnals and swear like Tony Soprano. Scoop had pasted pictures to the wall—Jesus with the fishermen, holding a child who looked frightened, counseling a blank-looking Martha. Not particularly inspirational, and I have to say, not a very realistic portrayal if Fern's research had been accurate.

I wanted to ask Scoop why Jax was at his stepson Mike's wedding, but didn't want to connect myself to Jax. I tried an oblique approach. "My grandmother Fern met a fascinating man at the wedding. He's going to help her build a chicken coop. Jack something?"

He took the cigar out of his mouth and studied it. "Jax Covas."

"Ah, that's it. An interesting man. A church member?"

"Uh, yes." He turned his back to me and looked out the

window, then picked up a notebook and leafed through it, looking anywhere except at me. I was about to push him a bit further when Tricia returned.

"Mike's on the way," she said to Scoop, then took my arm and led me to a chair in the last row, away from the pulpit and her husband. "I have to tell you something. Here, sit by me." Her eyes were wide and excited. She whispered low, for my ears only. "I had a revelation this morning, Stella. I know what you're thinking—that only Mormon elders have revelations, but middle-aged evangelical women can summon them up too, especially when they are questioning the fundamentals."

At that moment Scoop let out a string of curses like a twelve-year-old trying out new swears. "I have to be online in ten minutes! They want to see me screw this up!" He punched the heavy wooden pulpit. "Ow, goddammit!"

"Darling, please. We have company here," Tricia called to him.

"If I lose members, I'll lose money, I have mortgages to pay. I'll go bankrupt. Where the hell is Mike?"

"He'll be here in two minutes. He said he could fix it." Tricia barely blinked at his rant. "Anyhow, Stella, starting with first principles, marriages everywhere are full of pain. Do you agree?"

I nodded. The whack job behind the pulpit provided excellent proof. She leaned toward me confidentially. "My first husband left me for the church secretary's tits, a fact as clear as glass to anyone who cared to look. It was humiliating. At least Scoop is discreet, bless his treacherous little heart. And I apologize, he's under stress right now." She paused, glancing at her husband. His comb-over had loosened and long greasy strands dangled off the side of his head as he fussed with his equipment and muttered imprecations. She pursed her lips and turned back to me. "Really early this morning, maybe four o'clock, the cat woke me up. She was hopping around on the bed, tossing a poor dead shrew here and there. I pitched it into the trash then went back to bed and began to pray. What can I do, what can I offer to the world, that would make a difference?"

"I don't know." I was bemused by the change in her expression. Her eyes were alight, and the constant tension had left her face.

"It's a rhetorical question, honey. I prayed until the sun came up, and then it came to me in a revelation. A new business. I will lead Christian tours to beautiful places. Fly away from this cold loveless house to warm beaches like Cancun and Maui and San Juan. Bible readings, meditation, couples counseling. Think of the website—mai tais, toes in the sand, courteous Christian natives. An attractive couple exchanging loving glances."

The front door opened. "We're up here," Scoop called down. "Hurry, I've only got a few minutes." His aggravated voice disturbed Tricia's reverie and she frowned.

Mike lumbered up the stairs and into the room. His face was pale, his beard stubbly, and he looked exhausted. He glanced at me. "Wow, what happened to you?"

"Accident," I said. "Looks worse than it is."

"Gia's following me. She's really lost it. I don't know what she'll do."

"Is she out there now?" Tricia asked. We went to the window but the afternoon street was quiet, only a couple of children riding bikes.

"Are you going to fix this thing or not?" Scoop held up the microphone.

"What's wrong with it?" Mike asked.

"It doesn't fucking work, Einstein."

"Don't talk like that in front of my mother." Mike examined the various electronic components of Scoop's makeshift broadcasting system. "Look. You have to plug in the transmitter." He held up the cord. "See? Plug? Goes in outlet." He demonstrated.

Scoop grabbed the microphone and attached it to his collar. "Testing, dear Jesus, thank God it works."

"Maybe you should thank me too," said Mike. "I was sound asleep when you called. And you woke up Gia. She spent the night on my couch."

Gia was his house guest? I felt lost, adrift in a sea of neurotic behavior.

"Let's get out of here," Tricia whispered to me. "Let's go plan my first tour. Cancun sounds good, doesn't it?" She pulled me out of the room, ignoring Scoop's "where the hell are you going?" I followed her downstairs into her office. I was getting impatient, and ready to leave as soon as Tricia told me what was so important.

"You called me," I said. "Something significant, was it?"

By this time she was online and perusing flights. "Look, four hundred ten dollars, only one change in Miami." She was entering a credit card number when I noticed motion outside, through the window facing the street. It was Gia, walking toward the front door, walking fast, as if on a mission. Her eyes glistened with mania in a waxy-white face. My heart lurched when I recognized what Gia cradled in her arms.

A shotgun.

At that instant I had my own revelation—there was about to be a massacre. Time slowed to a crawl, the way it does when things get exciting. Gia opened the front door. As she came into the hallway, I shoved Tricia to the floor behind her desk. I knelt down beside her and unholstered my SIG. I could see Gia's feet; she paused at the office door, then moved away. As I heard her climb up the stairs to the broadcast room, I picked up Tricia's desk phone and dialed 911, requesting help pronto. Anticipating the boom of a shotgun at any moment, I started up the stairs to try to save Mike's life.

I flattened myself against the stairway wall and leaned cautiously around the doorway. Gia stood six feet away, her back to me, still cradling the shotgun like a baby. She had walked into Scoop's live broadcast over the Internet. From the CD player came a pure soprano voice singing about lambs and blood. The camera, aimed at the front of the room, captured the empty floodlit pulpit and behind it, Scoop, crouching down low, his hands shielding his bald head. He began to inch and worm along the floor toward the stairs like a Marine under fire. Mike had flattened himself against the back wall, and was slowly sliding toward the floor.

But Gia didn't threaten them. She walked to the camera and turned it around so it faced the back of the room. She sat down in front of the camera, set the butt of the gun on the floor and her chin on the muzzle end of it, like she was going to blow her head off. She pushed her hair behind her ears and stared into the lens. "I'm going to end my pain right now," she said. "You'll be sorry, Mike Olmert!"

"Move now, move fast," I hissed to Mike. He dashed past me, down the stairs, and Scoop scrambled to his feet and followed. I stood in the doorway, unsure, wishing I'd brought my Taser. I didn't want to injure her.

As they fled, Gia's eyes fastened on me. She pointed to me. "You! You can't have him!"

I kept my gun out but didn't threaten her. Death-by-cop might be one of her current goals and I had no interest in helping her achieve it. Getting closer might increase her paranoia and push her to act.

"I can help you," I said, "if you put the gun down."

For an answer, she twisted her head back, resettled her chin firmly on the muzzle, and reached down toward the trigger. Her arms were too short. She glared at me as if it was my fault. As she focused on me without blinking, I considered the distance between us and how quickly she could upend that gun and pull the trigger in her hyperalert state. A shotgun blast at ten feet would turn me into hamburger. I remained still, holding the SIG in both hands in front of me, watching her eyes and her hands and her feet. It was a stand-off, and until her attention wavered or she threatened my life, I could only wait. A siren wailed faintly in the distance. Then another, a duet. I felt a trickle of sweat between my shoulder blades. A muscle at the corner of my left eye began to twitch. Gia and I watched each other like mongoose and cobra. The sirens grew louder as the seconds passed, then abruptly cut off as the police cars pulled into the driveway and I braced myself for the hostage protocol, the tear gas, the swarming SWAT team.

From behind me came the sound of footsteps on the stairs. I turned; it was Tricia. "Stay back," I whispered, moving to block her entry into the room, but it was a wide doorway, and I had to keep my eye on Gia, so Tricia easily stepped past me, sat down beside Gia, and put her arm around her. "You're hurting," she said, "let's talk to God," and she began a murmurous prayer asking for help, for strength, for grace. I was astonished at her fearlessness. And Gia didn't turn the gun on Tricia. She eased her chin off the barrel and closed her eyes and listened, visibly trembling. Their image streamed live onto the Internet, the camera capturing the bowed heads, the words of entreaty, Gia's ragged breathing, the shotgun pointing at the ceiling. It was a powerful scene that I hated to break up but Tricia had distracted Gia enough so I could make a move. It took less than a few seconds—seconds that seemed like an eternity—to slip into the row of chairs behind them and creep as silently as possible, while shielding my face from the camera. I grabbed the shotgun just as the police burst into the house.

★  ★  ★  ★  ★

Gia was taken away in handcuffs. The manic glare in her eyes had faded to a depressed resignation. While waiting to be interviewed by the police, I slumped in a chair and listened to Tricia and Scoop digest the experience.

"Someone was recording the broadcast and the whole thing went online," Scoop said, fiddling with his comb-over, pressing the long side-pieces into place.

Doesn't look good, Scoop, I thought, that you crawled out of the room and let your wife deal with the shotgun-totin' psycho. "No such thing as bad publicity, I've heard," I said.

"Certainly not for my darling," Scoop muttered.

Trish smiled so wide I could see where her caps ended. "Already I'm getting calls. I'm going on TV tonight with a couple other women who've repelled home invasions."

"That's what I'm talking about," I said. "Your tours are going to book up fast."

Scoop looked from me to Tricia and popped the cigar out of his mouth. "What tours?" he asked.

The interview room was an uninspired space, with scuffed dull beige walls, no pictures or windows, no reading material. Anyone in that room would be forced to face her own thoughts. Through the one-way glass I watched my nemesis, Dana De-Grasso. Clutching her waist, she rocked in her chair and picked at her nails, flicking fragments of nail polish into the air. Dark purple bruises embellished her face and her frizzy hair was clumped and greasy-looking.

The interrogating sergeant was a burly man in need of a shave, with a stale smell like he'd been working for eighteen hours. "I'm going to propose that she give up Jax Covas's whereabouts in exchange for cigarettes and this." He held up a box of fries, a burger, and a milkshake.

"That's what she gave me to eat, so she must think it's food," I said. "Don't let her know I'm police, please."

Dana had been kept in the hospital overnight, then brought to the county jail. For the past hour, she'd been sitting in the interview room, waiting to be questioned once I arrived. The sergeant opened the door and went in. I watched on a small TV screen at his desk.

Dana's dead eyes flickered at the sight of the box of food, and she sat up a little straighter.

"Hi, you doing okay?" the sergeant asked.

Dana said, "Yeah, I guess. What's this about?"

He looked incredulous. "Huh? You don't know?"

She shrugged. "I kinda know." She eyed the food. "I'm hungry. Is that for me?"

"You're in deep, lady. Kidnapping is a federal crime. I'm talking life sentence, madam. I'm not gonna ask you why you snatched that poor young woman and beat her up and injected her with your shit. Why doesn't matter to me. We know you did it. Nothing good is ever gonna happen to you again."

Belligerent, bullying—the sergeant was breaking every rule in the interviewing canon. Fortunately he wasn't going after a confession. Dana's expression was defensive and sullen.

"She's okay, isn't she? I didn't hurt her," she said.

"She's not okay. You're going to prison, honey. You'll be old and gray when you get out if you're unfortunate enough to live that long. Unless you cooperate. I've got some leeway on the charges. First degree, second degree, unlawful imprisonment. Big difference in sentencing. You understand?" He took out a pack of cigarettes and matches, placed them on the table, but didn't offer her one. Dana seemed to withdraw into herself, marshal her resources. She didn't look as if she found any.

"What do you want from me?" she asked.

"What were you thinking? What was the plan? The point of

this crime?"

Dana didn't answer.

"Were you going to kill her?"

"No, absolutely not. I'm not a murderer."

"Were you going to turn her over to your boyfriend?"

"I don't know who you mean."

The sergeant made a show of leafing through his yellow legal pad. "Juan Xerxes Covas."

"You mean Jax?" She hunched her shoulders and rocked in her seat. "The hell with him."

"Where is he?" The sergeant plopped the pad onto the table, poised his pen to write, and looked at her expectantly.

"I kept trying to call him, to ask what I should do. You know. Let him know I had her. But his service was dead, I couldn't even leave a message. He must have killed his phone."

"He lives with you, right? Where would he go? He have family?"

"He has an ex-wife around here somewhere. He's got family back in Guatemala."

"An ex-wife here somewhere? You mean in the States?" The sergeant unfolded the bag and took out some fries. He opened a packet of ketchup and squeezed it into the fries. He ate a couple without looking at her, then licked his fingers.

"I mean here in North Carolina. He visits her now and then for stuff with their grandkids. But he never told me nothing about her." Dana gazed miserably at the wall. "I'd give him up in a minute, believe me. He knows I've been arrested and he doesn't even get in touch? Or send his lawyer to bail me out? 'Got your back,' he used to tell me. I thought I was doing him a favor when I picked her up. That's treachery, man."

"He *is* a double-crossing SOB. Tell me where he is and I'll take care of him for you." He unwrapped the burger and inserted a straw into the milkshake.

Dana was silent for a minute. "There's a place he hangs."

The sergeant pushed the burger, shake, and fries across the table.

"Ten-fifteen East Waters," she said. She stuffed a handful of fries into her mouth.

She'd given the address of the cinder-block house where she'd stashed me. A stupid lie. But it was too late to renegotiate; she was well into the burger. The sergeant knew it too. He picked up the matches and left the room, closing the door behind him. "Let her rub her knees together if she wants a light," he said to me. "You hear all that?"

"I did. The ex-wife. We'll get back to you with her ID." Hogan could find her, I was sure.

He handed me his card and pulled on a sports coat. "I'm available if you learn anything but right now I'm out of here. It's my daughter's eighth birthday and there's a cake that looks like Hannah Montana's guitar in my car."

On the TV screen, Dana was chawing down the burger. She picked up the milkshake and sucked on the straw. I remembered when she brought me one, held it to my mouth so I could drink it, delicious, cold and sweet, how grateful I'd felt for that small pleasure. She'd locked me up for twenty hours. For that, she was facing twenty years in a different kind of lockup.

I didn't feel the least bit sorry for her.

# CHAPTER 19

*Sunday Evening*

"Intriguing perfume," the waitress said. "What is it?" She was a chunky woman with a baby-smooth face and long red hair swept behind her ears, wearing a tuxedo. The other waitress was in a floral miniskirt, lace tights, and painfully high heels that made her long legs look even longer. The bartender had on pearls and a black strapless dress displaying her thoroughly tattooed arms. It was lesbian night at Why Not, a gay club in downtown Durham, and apparently the staff had been instructed to dress up.

Since I wasn't wearing any perfume, I didn't reply to the waitress's question.

"Touch of Pink," Ingrid said with a beguiling smile. She had asked me to meet her in the bar to discuss her search for a private investigator. In an adjacent room, swaying, twirling women danced to an all-girl band playing covers.

"Very nice, dearie." She turned to me. "And what happened to you?"

"It's a long story."

She frowned at this non-answer, as though my rainbow-hued face was possibly my own fault. Ingrid ordered white wine and I warily asked for ginger ale. With alcohol in my bloodstream, who knew what I'd do in this friendly bouncing place—relax, have a grand time like everyone else, dance with some cute girl . . . ? So I thought it best not to drink.

Ingrid sat across from me in a booth. Compared to the waitresses, she was dressed conventionally in jeans and a white ruffled blouse over a tee-shirt that sported some letters. "What's on your tee-shirt?" I asked. She pulled her blouse open and showed me—2QT2BSTR8.

"Clever." My clothes were even more conventional but I fit right in, as half the women in Why Not were wearing black leather.

"Usually me and Kate come here together for date night," Ingrid said. She looked longingly at the women, mostly in couples, sharing the rooms' tables. "But I think she's found someone else."

They call it heartache for a good reason, and mine wrenched with sympathy as her words carried me into familiar emotional terrain. I could identify with every pang, every teardrop, every spasm of loss. "How do you know?"

"She's been so distant. This morning she literally pushed me away. I love her more than anything, Stella. I want to know what's going on. Her sun is in Aries, you know."

"Oh?" I was with her, up until the sun-in-Aries part.

She took a big swallow of her wine. "Kate's impulsive, acts without thinking. I did her natal chart, and at the moment of her birth, Cancer was ascendant. That's why she has a hard shell and a mean pinching claw. But she's soft and loving on the inside. Except the past few days when she didn't even kiss me good-bye."

"Have you tried talking to her?"

"She says nothing's wrong."

And I'd heard that one too. The cowards won't confess. "This is recent?"

"Ever since last weekend, which by the way was the worst weekend of my life. Even before the murder. I loved Justine but it was too much, listening to Kate's parents fawn over her.

They've always been horrible to me and Kate." Her square face was flushed, her eyes puffy with tears behind the dark-rimmed glasses.

"So she says nothing's wrong. Has she acted like this before?" I was beginning to feel like a marriage counselor, the last thing in the world I'm qualified as.

"Stella, I have a confession. Promise you won't kill me." Ingrid took my hand and squeezed it.

"Of course I won't kill you."

"I lied. When I said I never told anyone about Justine's sex change? Here, I'll show you." Ingrid pulled a video camera out of her purse and turned it on. She pressed a few buttons and handed it to me. "Watch this. I taped it that Friday night, after the rehearsal dinner. Mike had left, Justine had gone to bed."

On the tiny screen I saw a pan through the parlor, past stuffed Scotties staring fixedly at each other, focusing on a clutter of wine glasses reflecting flickering candlelight. The camera pulled back to show Kate, Tricia, and Scoop sitting together on a sofa.

"This is my last night in a family of four," Tricia said. "Tomorrow we'll be five."

Ingrid, from behind the camera, said "What about me?"

"You count, Ingrid," Kate said, looking at the camera. "Five in our family now, six tomorrow."

Tricia looked dismayed. "Don't spoil this moment, please."

"It's a good time for a prayer," Scoop said, folding his hands and bowing his head. "Dear heavenly Father," he began.

From behind the camera, Ingrid said, "Ask for tolerance," and Tricia winced.

"Forgive us our weaknesses. Give us strength to fight depravity, to bow to thy will, to cast out the demons that possess us." His resonant voice was self-assured.

The camera wavered and I could hear Ingrid whimper. Scoop stopped praying and frowned at the camera.

Ingrid blurted "I hate you! I hate you! You are so . . . so . . . wrong about everything. Ignorant!" She continued filming, as though to record her anger. "You think she's so perfect but she's not. I'm sick of being treated like a leper. I went to school with her and Justine used to be a *boy*. There, now pray for *her*." Ingrid's voice was shrill, breaking with tears.

Scoop stared at the camera. His brow was furrowed and his mouth was open, giving him a stupid and uncomprehending expression.

"That's the most absurd thing I've ever heard," Tricia said. She pursed her lips and shook her head. Kate stood and reached out to the camera, the world tilted, and the screen went black.

I handed the camera back to Ingrid. "Wow. What a scene to capture on tape. Their expressions were priceless."

"Tricia asked what I meant and I told her. That Justine was just hormones and a few knife-flicks away from being John, the boy who used to try on my makeup. Kate had to explain the surgery. It was pretty funny." She grinned a rare, lovely smile.

"Did they tell Mike?"

"They didn't believe us. Or didn't want to believe us. They were horrified."

"But now Kate's angry with you."

"She thinks Justine was murdered because I told. But I'm glad I did, because secrets are sick."

I sipped my ginger ale as I processed what Ingrid had revealed. Both Scoop and Tricia would have been repelled by Justine's sex change. They could have bowed out of the wedding, or called a halt to it, but they'd shown up in ministerial robes and a big brown hat and smiles. From what I'd seen of Scoop, he was one of life's rougher players, a bit of a grifter with a temper. I imagined him sweeping into Justine's room and delicately sprinkling a speck of strychnine into her tea. It didn't seem his style. In her book, Tricia was full of harsh intolerant rhetoric, though in person she seemed kind of sweet, ignoring her husband's bad humor, planning her cruises to sunny climes. She didn't seem as controlling as she'd have to be to murder someone. "Does Kate think one of her parents poisoned Justine?" I asked.

"No, she says they refused to believe me. But she thinks someone tried to stop Mike from marrying Justine, because I blabbed. Not necessarily her parents. Someone else was listening, someone outside in the hallway at the time, I heard the floorboards creak. I don't know who."

"Mike?"

"Oh no. Mike had gone home."

I thought about who else was in the Castle B&B that night. Lottie and Evan Ember, with their little girl Alice. Webster and Delia Scott. Gregor McMahon. Wyatt. Had one of them overhead Ingrid blurting out the news about Justine? None seemed to have the kind of vested interest in Justine's surprising history that Mike would have, or Tricia and Scoop. I sighed. This was good information, another piece of the puzzle, but I couldn't see where it fit.

"How well do you know Gregor McMahon?" I asked.

"I knew his wife Emma very well. I introduced them, in fact, a couple of years ago. But he was one of Mike's friends, and they . . ." She shook her head and sighed.

"They what?"

"When Kate and I became a couple, some people sort of dropped us."

The waitress brought Ingrid a refill. "From Melanie at the bar, with the ponytail," she said. Ingrid looked over and waved half-heartedly.

"How does Melanie know you and I aren't together?" I asked.

"She's an old friend. She knows you're not my type." She sipped from her glass. "Anyway, I checked my horoscope today.

Mars is retrograde."

I raised my eyebrows.

"Confused emotions and relationship conflicts. But screw that. I'm a Libra and I need balance. Something's going on with Kate and I want to know what."

I beckoned the tuxedoed waitress over and ordered my own glass of wine. This was turning out to be a more complicated conversation than I'd anticipated. "What about following her one evening, like tonight?"

"Jump out of the bushes, yell 'gotcha'?" She shuddered. "Libras hate confrontation. But if I had facts and proof, I could walk away with some self-esteem. Despite a broken heart."

I didn't agree with her. Facts and proof of Hogan's infidelity had rinsed away any doubt, but all the self-esteem in the world wouldn't have softened the desolation I felt. "It could be something else, Ingrid." I wanted it to be anything else, some common cause of a downtick in a relationship.

"Like what?"

"Problems with her work. Distractions. Something she can't talk about yet."

In the next room, the band took a break and a karaoke competition started up, featuring a half-dozen unique renditions of "I Will Survive." Women began to drift into the bar to escape, and I watched them, half-curious. They looked like anyone anywhere. Short-tall, fat-thin, young-old, diverse in looks, skin color, clothing, and hair. The feminine rainbow. Then I caught sight of a familiar face.

"You might be able to save some money on a PI," I said. "There's Kate right now."

"Where?" Ingrid rose half out of her seat.

"Stand up and you can see her." Kate had slid into a booth across the room, in the corner. Because of the angle and the distance, I couldn't see who was with her. The miniskirted waitress set two draft beers on her table.

"Oh God, oh God." Ingrid covered her face with her hands. "I knew it."

"Hey, chill. It could be something completely innocent." But I knew how she felt, that drained sinking suspicion that you're being cheated on and you're about to find out who with.

"You look," Ingrid said. "Just go over and say hello. Please?"

So I did. I picked up my glass of wine and wound my way around tables until I reached Kate's booth. Fearing the worst, I expected to see some sweet young thing. Well, he was neither. Mike, Kate's brother, sat across from her in the booth, his heavy forearms like bowling pins resting on the tabletop. They were so intent on their conversation they didn't notice me. A silly grin took over my face as I realized that Kate wasn't unfaithful. I felt like cheering. Instead, I said hello.

"Hey, Stella," said Mike. "I was just telling Kate what happened this morning. Some excitement, no? You saved my life."

I objected. "Your mother was the brave one."

"Mom's the real deal, all right. Getting her fifteen minutes of fame."

"Ingrid sent me over."

Kate flung her arms up in the air as if she'd made a touchdown. "Ingrid's here? Where?"

I pointed to our booth where Ingrid was peeping around the corner. When she noticed Kate looking at her, she ducked back.

"What's the matter with her?" Kate asked.

"She thinks you're cheating on her," I said. It's always best to get these things out in the open.

"Hardly," Mike said. He stood and hollered across the room. "Ingrid, get your skinny butt over here!" Heads turned at the sound of a man's voice, and Mike laughed. "It's pretty obvious I'm not a gay woman, right? I'm here to learn. Kate tells me Justine liked this place."

"She could relax," Kate said. "No one would judge her." She looked at Mike, seeming to mean that comment for him.

Ingrid threaded her way across the room. She looked from Mike to Kate. "You're meeting with your brother?"

"Yeah, we had something important to talk about. Sit beside me, sweetie." Kate moved over to make room. Mike made space for me beside him. The waitress brought a big platter of nachos and I dove right in. I was still feeling hungry after my stay with Dana; she hadn't fed me very well. The salsa-avocado dip was to die for and I ate a third of it immediately.

Ingrid leaned into Kate's face. "What's going on? You've been making me crazy!"

"I know and I'm sorry. Forgive me?"

Ingrid shrugged. "Um, maybe. I was scared." She looked like she might cry.

"Hey." Kate put her arm around Ingrid's shoulders. "I had something to work out."

"Why couldn't you talk to me about it?"

"I didn't want to get your hopes up. See, I changed my mind. About us having a baby."

"Really? Really?" Ingrid's face lit up like a neon star and she wrapped her arms around Kate. "And that was why you were so pissy all week?"

"Oh honey, I'm sorry. I wanted to make sure I could find a donor. It was complicated because of—you know—the week-end."

"And did you find a donor?"

Kate looked from Ingrid to Mike.

"She did, and it will be an honor," Mike said with a big smile. Ingrid burst into tears and Mike looked at Kate anxiously.

"Don't worry," Kate said. "She's very happy."

"That's so—so nice," Ingrid sobbed. She half-stood and leaned over the table to kiss Mike's cheek. "I can't—I can't—"

He sat stolidly. "What, I have to buy you dinner first?"

We all laughed. The miniskirted waitress brought their food, a burger and fries for Mike and a chef's salad for Kate. Ingrid ordered a veggie burger but I declined. This little family grouping didn't need me hanging around asking awkward questions. But while I had them all in one place and in a good mood, I had one last question for Mike and Kate. "Justine's gender change would have mattered to your parents. A lot. What would they have done to stop the wedding?"

Mike smacked the table with a fist as meaty as a coconut. "You think they killed Justine? They didn't want her in the family so they killed her?"

"Don't be ridiculous!" Kate waved her hands back and forth like a metronome. "Mother was in the guest parlor with me until an usher took her outside and seated her. And Scoop was outside with the guests. There was no opportunity."

"I'm sorry." Mike rubbed his eyes and face. "This business has me spinning. Of course my mother couldn't have done it. But who would want to?"

"What about Gia Mabe?" Kate asked.

"Yeah," said Mike, "she's got my vote."

"Starting around twelve-thirty, she was taking pictures," I said. "I've seen them—they're time-stamped. By the way, Mike, the pictures give you an alibi too. You're in every one." I thought back to Gia's office, her camera, her metallic breath as she leaned close to me and whispered his name. "Scoop is in most of them as well."

I tried to visualize the half-hour before Ingrid heard Justine's cries. Who knocked on her door? What was the conversation before the one-half-teaspoon of powder was sprinkled into her tea? Did the killer watch her drink, wait for the first agonizing convulsion? Then leave the room, join the wedding guests and wait for the inevitable? No one emerged from the murky fog of my imagination. Anyone with a shadow of a motive had an alibi; none of the others had motives.

I felt like a fourth wheel sitting with this little family unit, so I ate one last chip and slid out of the booth. Two mommies and one daddy, three more parents than I had. Lucky baby.

"Thanks, Stella," Ingrid said. "If I can do anything for you . . ."

"Don't forget to invite me to the shower," I said.

I pulled into my driveway. It was nearly midnight. On the front porch, sprawled on my rickety wicker lounge, Hogan slept, an irritating yet pleasing sight. Irritating, because he would probably disturb my fragile emotional equilibrium. Pleasing, because I could get him to do a security check before I sent him home.

"Let me guess," I said. "You stopped by to say good-night to Merle."

He opened his eyes and sat up. "I was worried about you. And I have something to tell you."

"Did what's-her-name find a new mate online?"

"Funny. Can I have five minutes and a drink of water?" He stood and stretched, and his tee-shirt rose to show off a couple inches of his trim middle, the middle that was no longer mine to wrap around.

"Sure. Come along while I walk the dog."

Merle writhed with pleasure to see us both come through the door. Hogan flicked the hall light on, then flinched when he saw my face. He gently tipped my chin up to examine Dana's handiwork. "What the hell? It's worse than I thought."

I gave him a glass of water. "I'll be okay. External injury, heals quickly, should be all better in a week." I attached Merle's leash and grabbed a plastic bag. "Come on."

Overhead, heavy clouds had gathered, covering up the milky moon. The air was wet and chilly and soon it would rain hard.

Hogan started out at his usual fast walking pace but I'd had my run for the day. I asked him to slow down so I could keep up. "What's the big news that couldn't wait until the morning?" I asked.

"I found out why Jax Covas was invited to Mike and Justine's wedding."

Immediately I forgot my fatigue, my pains, my aching heart. "Why?"

"He's using God's Precious Church to launder money."

"What?" Scoop and his "church" had been so clearly pretentious, but more along the lines of a low-budget scam.

We stopped to let Merle investigate a message left on a mailbox. "The church is a front," Hogan said. "Jax pays rent to the church, ten-twenty times the going rate. Then the church pays him to develop some property for a building—a two-acre lot down near Bonlee. I checked it out—the lot's a skinny strip and surely isn't being developed. Still scrub pine."

"How did you ever find this out?"

"Oh, I have my sources. Friends in good places." Though it was dark, I knew Hogan was smirking with pleasure at his cleverness. "In the middle there's a real estate management company called Carefree. Here are the five addresses owned by the church, according to the Registry of Deeds, all managed by Carefree." He pulled a list out of his pocket and when we reached a street light I scanned it, recognizing only 1015 East Waters, where Dana had taken me. "I had help from the Financial Crimes Division. They were impressed by Scoop's creative accounting. They're going to prepare a case against him, if the IRS doesn't get to him first." Hogan pointed to an address at the bottom of the list. "Where you bought the kilo, Stella."

I imagined Scoop Scott in an orange jumpsuit, behind bars. Would Tricia visit him faithfully, endure a pat-down of her knit pantsuit? Or would she have another revelation, dump Scoop, and relabel her cruises for a different kind of afterlife? Born Again—Getaways for the Newly Divorced. "Did you learn anything about Jax?" I asked.

"Aside from his arrest and jail record? The guy doesn't exist. No credit cards, no phone records, nothing."

"He might have been out of the country."

"I checked with ICE too. They didn't have anyone by that name."

I felt a wet drop on my head, and another, and pulled my jacket over my head as the skies opened with a soaking downpour. We jogged back to my house and left our shoes on the porch. I filled the teakettle and put it on the stove. "I have something to show you, too." I handed him the Italian charm bracelet. "It was among Justine's things in her room at the Castle B&B. The innkeeper mailed it to Mike Olmert a few days ago. But he said it wasn't hers."

Hogan studied the charms one by one. "A woman, a teacher, a Dolphins fan with a dachshund. Born April 2."

"Can you trace it?"

"I'll try. I bet there were a couple hundred baby girls born that day who grew up to be teachers. But a Dolphins' fan? That will narrow it down."

"Very funny." The kettle began its insistent whistle and I filled each mug with hot chocolate mix and a marshmallow. "Impossible request, I know. Except for a genius."

Hogan smiled, running his hands through his hair. He knew I wasn't exaggerating. He blew on his cocoa to cool it.

"Oh, Mike Olmert wanted me to give you this." I handed him a copy of *Enchanted Food*.

He leafed through it. "Thanks. Gorgeous pictures. I love food porn."

Wow, what an opening. I was sorely tempted but I'd been

practicing maturity so I let it go. "Hey, is Justine's chili recipe in there? Lottie Ember said it was the best she'd ever tasted."

He checked the index, then found the page. "Here is it. Look at these ingredients—bourbon and cashew butter and chocolate!"

"What's cashew butter?"

"It's like peanut butter. For thickening."

Like the peanut butter Liesle had "sensed" in the room where Justine died.

Then I laughed at myself, at my desperate grasping at any straw, even one suggested by an amateur psychic. The chili recipe looked easy. I could make some for my neighbor Saffron, to repay her kindness in helping me clean up my house after the break-in.

"How's the investigation going?" Hogan asked.

"The more I learn the less I know." I added some milk to my mug and took a sip.

"Sounds like a Zen bumper sticker."

"This link between Scoop and Jax is intriguing but I can't see how it relates to Justine's murder."

"Maybe she balked at the last minute, decided she didn't want to marry into a criminal family."

"So someone killed her?" I asked. "I can't see it. She probably could've cared less where Scoop's money came from. I know I wouldn't. There's more important things in a marriage than your stepfather-in-law's business." I looked at him with my most innocent expression. "How is Candy, anyway?"

He looked embarrassed and annoyed simultaneously. It was kind of cute. "Fine," he said. "She's fine."

I could have asked more questions. *Then why are you here at midnight? Is she as slutty as she looks? Do you two still email each other your deepest dirty desires?* But I reined in my impulses and said nothing. It felt grown-up to keep my mouth shut except for, "More cocoa before you go?"

He took the hint and left. I performed my own perimeter check, slid the deadbolts home, and stored the SIG under my pillow. Whispering sweet nothings into the ears of my canine alarm system, I invited him onto the bed. Tuning out the frightened squeaks about Jax and Dana and Mo, I fell into a deep sleep.

# CHAPTER 20

*Monday Morning*

I was looking forward to spending some time with Fern. I'd barely given her a hug Saturday night before Fredricks rushed me off to the hospital, and I needed to reassure her I was okay, find out why Bebe was with her, make sure she hadn't heard from Jax, cook something. Richard had given me medical leave for another day, so I didn't have to think about buying dope until tomorrow night. I'd bring Merle so he could run in Fern's fields and chase critters. I'd plant myself in a rocker on her porch and watch the dog cavort.

Hogan called when I was halfway to Fern's. "I must admit failure," he said. "I couldn't find a record of Jax Covas's divorce."

"Darn," I said. "I did so want to impress that sergeant."

"But he married a woman named Lynda Christina Pons in 1972, in Amarillo, Texas."

"Brilliant! Now tell me her North Carolina address."

"Alas. Couldn't find her. Two failures in one day."

"A record for you, isn't it?"

"It's a personal worst. But I got hits on the bracelet."

I felt a jolt of excitement at this bit of news. At the same time I noticed a herd of brown cows, my marker on Highway 64 for a cell phone dead zone. "Hold on, I've got to pull over before I lose you." On one side of the highway, a forest of scrubby trees sported autumnal gold and scarlet, and on the other, fat hay rolls dotted the fields. No cell phone towers in sight. I got out of the car and walked back a hundred feet. One curious cow took a few steps in my direction to get a closer look. "Okay, shoot," I said.

"Remember the charms? I started with two bona fide facts. The mystery woman's a teacher, born on April 2. So I contacted the Educational Testing Service, since all teachers have to take one of their exams, the PRAXIS. I asked them to tell me the names of anyone who took the PRAXIS who had that birthday. They wouldn't tell me without a subpoena."

"You knew that would happen."

"Not always, you'd be surprised. So I put my mom on the case. She called a friend of hers who works in the Department of Public Instruction, and told her she'd found this teacher's bracelet with a birth date. Her friend came back with six names, and one of them you'll recognize."

"Your mom rocks. What's the name?" I inspected a grassy spot for cow patties and sat down.

"What *was* the name. She's dead. Emma Grantham McMahon."

Gregor McMahon's wife, who died at the picnic six months ago. I thought back to my interview with Gregor. He'd said he'd first met Justine at the picnic, on the day Emma died. I had assumed that's when Emma first met her, too. How did her bracelet end up in Justine's B&B room, six months later? This could be nothing. It could be everything.

"Can you dig a little more? Look for a connection between Justine and Emma. Something has to make sense."

"Even geniuses have limits, Stella."

"Aw, come on. You owe me. For all those years I washed your socks."

He laughed. "And I cooked your dinner. Okay, I'll work on it and get back to you." He hung up.

From a twiggy shrub nearby came a performance equal to any symphony as a mockingbird trilled brilliantly through his repertoire. Soothed by a warm breeze, I lay back in the grass and closed my eyes to listen. An approaching car slowed, then pulled over and stopped just past me. A woman leaned out the door. "Need a hand?" she called.

I waved her off. I guess I did look needy, lying back behind my car in the grass. I shut my eyes and waited for my intuition to work, but nothing emerged from my subconscious about Gregor McMahon, the furry corporate economist, part-time professor, best man at Mike's wedding. Yet I thought I should look at Gia Mabe's camera one more time.

I stood and brushed myself off. The curious cow stared at me. "How now?" I asked. "How now?" Her jaws rolled as she chewed thoughtfully on her cud.

A sharp wind whipped my hair into a froth as I trotted along a woodsy path in the Eno River State Park, trying to keep up with the director of the North Carolina Birthing Center. She'd suggested the walk for a bit of midday exercise. Monica Reardon was an aged flower-child, with wispy, flowing gray hair, a long denim skirt, crinkled blouse, and clogs. From a piece of string around her neck hung an amulet, a cobalt blue glass bead with a white and yellow eye like an egg. "We give one of these to each new baby," she said. "It's an evil eye bead, to protect against evil spirits. Looks like you could use one right now. How do you feel?"

I gave her my now-standard response—looks worse than it feels, only hurts when I smile. The bead seemed the perfect size to choke an infant. Guess that was why the birthing center carried liability insurance, which was on my mind when I scheduled this interview.

"You know I'm investigating the poisoning murder of Justine

Bradley. I need to know whether there was any relationship between Justine and Lottie Ember, one of your patients. Alice Ember was born here, and her parents sued." I didn't ask whether they'd given Alice her very own bead.

She grimaced and shook her head. "Justine had just started working here when the Embers came in to have their baby. But she wasn't the midwife, I was."

"So Justine wasn't involved in the lawsuit," I said. Monica set a brisk pace, her arms pumping and a long heel-to-toe stride, longer than mine, so every now and then I had to insert a little jog to stay abreast.

"Well, Justine was named in the lawsuit, because she had made notes during some of Lottie's labor."

Lottie had certainly not mentioned that when I first interviewed her. Well, I hadn't asked her directly, had I? I assumed she'd first met Justine at the picnic like the rest of Mike's friends. Lesson to self—never assume. "Did the Embers win their case?" I asked.

"Partly. It went on over two years, what with discovery and depositions and counterclaims." She clutched her hair. "Turned me completely gray. It was awful."

We reached the Eno River, low and slow because of the drought, and paused at a wooden viewing platform. A red-tailed hawk flew overhead, following the river. At its "scree, scree," I looked up. An eagle had entered its territory. Though the eagle was much larger, the hawk dived at it repeatedly until the eagle soared away. A reminder that you don't have to be the biggest to win, just the one with the most to lose.

"So they received a settlement?" I asked.

"A million dollars."

Not much, given the severity of Alice's disability. I asked how the amount was arrived at.

"I know what you're getting at. These cases sometimes settle for five, ten million or more. But my insurance company took a hard line after Justine was deposed, because she backed me up completely."

"What was the basis for the lawsuit?"

"The Embers claimed I ignored warning signs during Lottie's labor."

"Such as?"

"Fetal heart rate changes."

"Did you monitor the baby's heart rate?"

"Of course, but we don't use electronic fetal monitoring. It's not in the protocol for a normal low-risk childbirth. Instead, we intermittently auscultate."

"Auscultate?"

"We have a handheld ultrasound device that amplifies the sound of the fetal heart. During the second stage of labor, I made a note in the record every five minutes. The baby's heartbeat was well within normal limits, with no unusual accelerations or decelerations. The Ember's attorney subpoenaed the records, and tried to make a case that they'd been altered, because the handwriting was different for some of the entries. But Justine backed me up. She had made some of the entries, I had made some. We showed the attorney other records where the same practice was obvious. They had to let it go; the fetal heart rate showed no distress."

"So, due to Justine's testimony, the Embers had to settle for considerably less," I said. A motive for murder? After all, the Embers came to Mike and Justine's wedding. So they didn't seem to be holding a grudge. Unless they planned all along to attend and exact some retribution during the wedding weekend? That seemed improbable. But everything about this case seemed improbable, starting with the murder of a bride.

We started back toward the park entrance. The rude wind was now at our backs so it was a bit easier to keep up with

Monica's long stride. "I don't think they should've gotten a dime," she said. "I did nothing wrong, it was a perfectly normal birth. These things happen, and it's normal to want to blame someone, but a million dollars? Our insurance costs are second only to our payroll."

She stopped and took a deep breath, standing straight with her hand on her back. "Women have managed to give birth for a hundred thousand years without Pitocin and fetal monitors. I wanted to give them a technology-free option. But it's been a constant struggle with the medical profession, the state, the insurance agencies and lawyers. No one wants us here except the mothers." We reached a small park, a nook with a fountain, and we sat down on a bench. "Justine's going to be hard to replace."

"Because everyone liked her?" I asked.

"Hmmm. She wasn't warm and huggy. But she was very good. She took the time to explain things clearly. Women, even the first-time moms, knew exactly what was going on. Knowledge goes a long way to reduce fear. She could talk them through it."

"Did they know she was transsexual?"

Monica whipped her head around and her face looked a lot less friendly. "What? Are you kidding? She was a man?"

"She was born male. She transitioned to female about seven years ago."

She fondled her evil eye as she pondered the implications of this news. "Honestly, it's impossible to believe. She was so feminine. I never would have guessed. Why was she murdered?"

I shrugged. "We don't have a viable suspect. So the answer is, I don't know."

Monica Reardon was polite enough, and forthcoming, but she didn't offer me an evil eye bead. And I could have used it.

★ ★ ★ ★ ★

I called the sheriff's department and inquired about Gia Mabe. The duty officer told me she'd been taken to the hospital in Chapel Hill and admitted to a psychiatric unit. So I spent an hour obtaining a warrant to search her home for the camera, then drove to her address, an old brick school renovated into condos. The street had begun a slow evolution into gentrification. A Realtor, an artsy-crafts store, and a bistro with a chalkboard menu on the sidewalk were neighbors to a dusty-windowed appliance stockroom and two dead storefronts. I showed the warrant to the building supervisor and he unlocked the door to Gia's apartment.

I halted at the threshold to drink in the gorgeousness of the place. Apparently a biotech salary could buy some fine details—re-pointed brick walls, granite countertops, and recycled antique pine floors. The generous open space was furnished with a long low couch covered in thick dove-gray plush, a twiggy rocker, and glass coffee table, all grouped in front of a ceiling-high stone fireplace. A farmhouse dining table nestled amid a jungle of leafy green plants well-nourished by the sunlight pouring through a solarium wall. It was restful, pleasant, nice. Unlike Gia. In the midst of the plants I noticed a little movement, then sharp white teeth in a pink mouth as a black kitten yawned. It stood, arched its back in a stretch, then walked over to me to investigate. I touched its bony little head and it began a mad purring.

Gia's camera sat handily on the kitchen counter. I turned it on and searched her photographs. A week-ago Saturday, wedding day. Mike, Mike, Mike, starting at twelve-twenty. Twenty minutes later, Mike was on the phone, making his call to Justine. Then Mike was standing in front of the guests with his stepfather Scoop in his ministerial robe and the sullen Evan Ember. Just the three of them. Gregor McMahon and his cervical collar didn't show up in any of the pictures until exactly one o'clock. The moment of the scheduled start of the wedding. Wherever he was until then, it wasn't where Gia wanted to aim her lens.

Once I found the camera, my legal right to search ended. However, I didn't think a quick look through Gia's effects was out of order. I didn't plan to uncover any evidence against her, just snoop a bit and see where it might lead. The hallway was a gallery of framed photographs, all seemingly from the pre-breakup period, evidence of Gia and Mike together in happier times. One photo had been enlarged to sixteen by twenty and placed in the center of the rest. It showed a group of people sitting around a bonfire, toasting marshmallows on sticks. Firelight illuminated their faces. I noticed Gia and Mike sitting close together, smiling at each other. Kate and Ingrid were in the picture too, Kate's arms mid-fling as Ingrid sipped a beer. And was that Gregor McMahon? *Sans* cervical collar, wearing tee-shirt and baggy shorts, he looked relaxed and happy. Even Lottie and Evan were there—Lottie in maternity clothes, Evan many pounds thinner. They leaned into each other, posing for the camera, each holding a marshmallow on a stick to the other's mouth. Lottie's pregnancy made it easy to date this photo-graph—when I met Alice in Lottie's chocolate shop, Lottie told me she had just turned four. There were three other women in the picture but I didn't recognize them. Gia had lost more than a lover when Mike and she parted; she had lost a family of friends.

The kitten followed me into Gia's impressive walk-in closet, bigger than my bedroom, where I found more evidence of Mike-fixation—boxes of memorabilia, including random pieces of his clothes and junk mail. Gia had a nice wardrobe, I observed idly, neat and well organized, though very corporate, not really my style of clothing. Then I noticed a pair of jeans still sporting price and size tags. Really nice jeans, medium wash with a distinctive turquoise thread. Hmmm. I checked out the pockets—rounded, with a circular appliqué and stitching like rays from the center. I recognized these jeans. I liked those jeans, just as much now as when I had bought them. They were *my* jeans, stolen from my house in the break-in.

I sat down on the floor of the closet to reorder my thinking. Gia had broken into my house and trashed it. Not Jax. A heaviness left me, a burden I didn't even realize I'd carried. I wasn't afraid of Gia, despite her love-crazed shotgun-totin' ways. She was scary like a tarantula—to be avoided, certainly, but not that interested in my demise. Jax, on the other hand, was a different species, a predator species.

In a dresser drawer I found my nightgown. Black lace with spaghetti straps and a scalloped hem, still wearing store tags. Mine. Gia, you are where you belong, on a locked ward. "Woohee," I whispered, picking up the kitten and pressing my cheek into its fur. "Your mommy's also a burglar." It stretched out a paw and touched my nose.

I would let the Verwood police know they could close the case of the break-in to my house. Gia's troubles with the law were only beginning and she'd probably lose her job if convicted. She'd have to sell this pretty apartment. Would kitty need a home? Kitty's black fur had a reflected luster like velvet. Velvet, that would be a good name for a black kitten. I found a stash of cat food and opened a can of salmon dinner. Velvet lit into it with a growl. I refilled a water bowl beside the fridge, added another for good measure, and on my way out I found the super and asked him to feed the kitten until Gia returned.

I picked up a bagel and a coffee at the bistro next to the condo building, and took them back to my car. I was pleased to have the jeans and nightgown back, and pleased that the mystery of who trashed my house was solved, but the jeans were too small, and there was no point in putting on a spaghetti-strap black lace negligee just to sleep with Merle. He preferred flannel.

At the red mailbox I slowed to turn into Fern's lane, but braked when I saw a car coming toward me, a super-sized black SUV scraping its way through the scrubby brush. I reversed and backed out onto the highway shoulder to let the mammoth vehicle pass. Its dark-tinted windows reflected the light, and I couldn't see inside. One of Fern's admirers, no doubt.

I pulled up to the farmhouse and opened the car door to let Merle out. He bounded toward the donkey pen, stopping every few feet to sniff and explore. Fern came out onto the porch. I noticed right away that something was wrong. Her blue eyes were too big, her expression too strained, and when I hugged her, her body was trembling.

"What's wrong?"

"You just missed Jax," she said.

"That was Jax in the Navigator?" I tried to control my re-action but Jax's appearance at my grandmother's was no friendly little visit.

"He dropped off some roof tiles and screening. Said he'd be back later. Asked where you were." She took my hand and squeezed it tightly. "Bebe's hiding somewhere. I can't find her or Ollie."

Certainly she's hiding. We should all be hiding. I took a deep breath. "Fern."

"I know," she said. "I pretended everything was all right. So did he."

It was one thing to wrestle with Dana as she injected me with opiates. One thing to lock eyes with the demented Gia, wait for her to drop her guard and her gun. It was something else entirely to know that Jax had my grandmother in his sights.

"We're getting out of here now," I said. "Pack something quick. I'll find Bebe."

She nodded and went into the house. I followed and started up the stairs, calling out, "Bebe! Where are you?"

In the bedroom where they'd been sleeping, the bed was neatly made, with my old teddy bear and a couple of Barbie dolls that had been in the attic resting on the pillows. I stood still and listened but heard only a tick, tick, tick as a honey bee knocked against the window, trying to get out. My heart pounded a similar rhythm. "Bebe! We're leaving!"

At the end of the hall, behind a narrow door, was the attic, an unfinished space under the eaves. I opened the door and peered in. The space was hot, dusty, and cluttered with over a century of boxes, trunks, dressers, coat racks, mirrors. "Bebe," I said, "Jax is gone and I'm going to take you somewhere else for a while. Somewhere safe."

I heard a rustle from behind a chifferobe, and the little boy crawled out. He met my gaze with a solemn expression. "We're playing hide-and-seek," he said. "Mommy said to be very quiet."

"Where is she?" I asked.

He shrugged.

"Well, come on. We have to find her." I poked around, looking inside, behind, and underneath, but Bebe wasn't in the room. We went out into the hall, and I decided to check the bathroom.

Behind the shower curtain, Bebe sat in the bathtub, knees and arms folded around her big belly. "It's goddam uncomfortable in here," she said. "This tub is cast iron. Help me out." I held out my hand and she tugged herself up and stepped awkwardly out of the tub.

"Mommy, you were supposed to find me," Oliver said. "You didn't tell me you were going to take a bath."

"Sorry, sweetie." She leaned to kiss his cheek, then turned to me. "Did I hear you say we were leaving? Ollie and I are one hundred percent in favor of that plan. When I saw Jax out the window I thought my short miserable life was about to end." She was bone-pale, her eyes shadowy. She took Oliver's hand and started down the stairs as I placed a quick call to the Chatham sergeant to let him know about the SUV.

We left Bebe's station wagon parked in the driveway. Fern had hastily shoveled an extra two days' worth of hay into the donkey pen, and Merle had reluctantly climbed back into my car. Bebe installed Ollie on his booster seat, and the four of us plus dog set out. I checked the highway for black SUVs, as the last thing I needed at the moment was a car chase. But the road was clear, so I pulled out, and headed east.

Fern took a deep breath and let it out. "It was one of those 'I know he knows I know' moments but neither of us could let on. He comes tootling up the driveway, backs up to the shed, and starts unloading materials. I go out to see who it is and I can't believe it. Like nothing happened. Tell me what's going on, Stella."

"Are you a CI?" Bebe asked.

"What's a CI?" Fern asked.

"Informant. A snitch. No, I'm not. I can't talk about it any more." The complexity of the situation was giving me a headache. Did Jax know that Dana had kidnapped me? Why hadn't he killed me? Had he killed Mo, as Bebe suspected? Perhaps someone else had killed Mo? Maybe Jax knew I was police and left me alive since killing a drug agent would be a far worse crime than selling, and he wasn't stupid. But I was certain of one thing—he knew Stella Lavender was Fern Lavender's granddaughter, and he'd dropped by Fern's to send that message.

"Where are we going?" Fern asked.

"You'll love it." I didn't want to stash Fern, Bebe, and Oliver in a crummy motel room with nothing to eat but delivery pizza, and nothing to do but watch TV and peep fearfully through the polyester drapes every time a car pulled up. They needed a safe haven, where no one would think to look. I knew the perfect place.

# CHAPTER 21

*Monday Mid-Afternoon*

We tromped up the steps of Pink Magnolia Manor. "This is nice," Bebe said, looking around at the big porch with its wicker furniture, ferns, and ceiling fans. Oliver clung to her, his eyes huge. I rang the doorbell.

After a few minutes, Camilla's face appeared in the door's glass window and she opened the door, rubbing her wet hair with a towel. She smiled but it seemed forced; this was the second time I'd showed up without calling first. "Oh my, what happened to you?" she asked.

I was getting tired of the question. "An accident. Looks worse than it is." I introduced Fern, Bebe, and Oliver. "They need two rooms for a few nights." Surely Jax would be found by then, limiting the damage to my credit card.

She ushered us inside. A cinnamon-yeast aroma pervaded the house. "Smells good," Oliver said. He smiled shyly, and twisted himself behind Bebe's skirt.

"I'm making sticky buns." Camilla turned to Fern. "We've met before. Have you stayed here?"

"I have." Fern chewed her lip as she searched her memory. "With Harry Edwards. Would have been six years ago." She winked at me. "Two nights, for my birthday."

Bebe sank onto the chenille-covered couch. "Ooof. Ollie, look at the pretty birds."

He put his nose to the cage as the finches chirped and

preened. "Theys looking in the mirror," Ollie said. "They see themselfs." He giggled and the birds fluttered.

"Easy, Ollie, don't touch the cage. Say, what kind of place is this? It's much nicer than any shelter I've ever seen," said Bebe.

"A bed-and-breakfast," Fern said. "Like a little hotel. Non-smoking."

Camilla studied her reservation book. "I have a couple of rooms upstairs that share a bath if that's all right. For as long as you want them. Breakfast at eight." She dug in her pocket. "Here's a key to the front door."

I led my troop up the stairs. On the landing, a stained-glass window sprinkled rose, blue, and amber lights onto the worn brown carpet. "Fairy lights," Bebe told Ollie. Her room had two twin beds with white quilted coverlets. She kicked her shoes off and sank onto one of the beds. "Lord have mercy," she said, "I am not moving for the next three hours. Ollie, lie down over there. We're taking a nap."

His eyes were big as he took in the room, the flowered wallpaper, the hobnail lamp. I helped him remove his shoes, and pulled the coverlet back. Clutching the teddy bear, he climbed up and lay down on his side to face his mother. Despite Bebe's bad habits, she'd raised an obedient child.

Fern's room had plum-colored walls, a double bed, and walnut dresser. Dotted Swiss curtains filtered the sunlight, and the bed covering, a paisley quilt, looked new. "Very nice," she said. "But I hope we don't have to stay here too long." She looked at me searchingly, distress etched on her face.

"Me too. I have a feeling Jax will be found soon." My feeling was more like hope than assurance. There was an outstanding warrant for his arrest, but aside from alerting the county sheriff, there was little else I could do. Fredricks had told me that he wasn't known to the drug task force, that their informants had never mentioned him. My purchase of coke from Jax revealed

him as a new player. Now that he'd been spooked and disappeared, they didn't have the information to find him.

Fern and I went outside to a brick patio warmed by the
afternoon sun. Merle napped by my feet as we lounged on
cushioned iron chairs. Camilla brought us a tray with chicken
salad sandwiches, brownies, and a pot of Lady Londonderry
tea, my new favorite. The chicken salad had grapes and walnuts
in it, and the brownies were frosted in chocolate with white
marshmallow swirls.

"Lovely," Fern said. "Sit down with us."

Camilla pulled a chair over and poured herself a cup of tea. I
held out the plate of brownies but she declined. "I don't eat my
own baking," she said. "When I first opened my B&B, I went to
an innkeeper conference. Everyone I met there was huge from
eating their own cooking."

"I've always wanted to open a bed and breakfast," Fern
mused.

"Quite a common fantasy. I hear it all the time. But just have
a morning like mine, you'd run fast in the other direction."

"Bad morning, was it?" Fern said.

"This couple brings their two-year-old, a real rug rat. His
mom says to fix him eggs and hash browns, but he throws them
on the floor." Camilla illustrated with a broad swoop of her
arm. "Hollers 'pancakes!' Mom says 'no pancakes' and he
screams so loud I'm surprised there's still glass in my windows.
She gives in and I make pancakes. Kid pours his own maple
syrup, a half-cup at least—real maple syrup—eats two bites and
screams 'down down down.' Mom puts him down and Mr.
Sticky-hands heads right for my music box collection. I jump
ahead and grab the music boxes, more screaming from kid and
a dirty look from Mom. I wanted to swat the kid so bad, right
on his little behind . . ." Camilla shook her head. "When people

ask if I take children, I always say 'if they're well-behaved.' I'm going to change it to 'if the parents are well-behaved.' "

"So the fantasy isn't real," Fern said.

"The reality is that running a B&B is a twenty-four-seven job for very little profit. I mean, we have enough, Blue and me. But insurance, utilities, everything is high. I was glad when Blue got a job."

"Across the river, at the Castle B&B," I told Fern.

"He can ride his bike over there, and it pays for his braces, his skateboard, his clothes." She opened a slim booklet. "Time for research. I have vegans coming for a week. That's seven breakfasts without eggs, cheese, or meat."

"Oatmeal and soymilk," Fern said.

"Good, thanks. Our B&B association put this out a couple of years ago." She held it up, a pamphlet entitled "Special Diets for the B&B." She leafed through it. "Here we go, vegan breakfast items. Couscous with fruit and nuts. Tofu scramble. Okay, with the oatmeal that covers three mornings. Four to go."

"I have something for you," I said. "Be right back." I went out to my car and opened the carton containing Justine's vegan cookbook, *Enchanted Food.* Surely there were breakfast menu items in here. I glanced at the table of contents. Appetizers, Soups, Entrees, Vegetables. Special Meals—Children, Picnics, Breakfast, Party. The "Breakfast" section had twelve pages of recipes. I handed the book to Camilla. "Keep it," I said.

She thanked me and leafed through the recipes, then studied Justine's picture on the back cover. "The girl who died at the Castle B&B, right? Kind of ironic that she was so particular about what she ate. The rest of us eat whatever and live for years, she eats healthy and . . ." She stood. "I've got to get back to work. Find me if you want another pot of tea."

I thought about Camilla's words. It *was* ironic, that Justine's death was the result of drinking her cleansing tea. Despite being so careful about her food, she'd ingested a substance that killed her within minutes. Was the irony deliberate, an intentional aspect of a calculated act of murder?

"I know you can't tell me everything," Fern said. A breeze whipped her hair around her face. She fished in her pocket for an elastic and fastened her hair up. "But I feel so ignorant. What has Jax done?"

I studied her for a moment. Blessed with wide cheekbones, a piquant smile, and big blue eyes, Fern had always been the pretty one in the house, the cheerful flirt, the free-spirited sprite. But the past few days had taken their toll and it showed in her tired eyes. She looked frail, and for the first time I noticed a delicate spider's web of wrinkles on her face. She must have been devastated by my abduction, then terribly frightened to see Jax step out of the SUV onto her driveway, asking for my whereabouts. I wanted to put my arms around her and assure her all would be well for the rest of her life. But I couldn't, not yet.

Slowly I told her the story, how Mo had led me to Jax and I'd bought a kilo of cocaine from Jax and Dana. "When Dana saw me at the rest stop, she grabbed me, because she and Jax were convinced I'd given them to the police. I was the only witness who could testify about the drug buy."

"What were they going to do to you?" Fern picked up the teapot to pour another cup.

"Who knows? Jax never showed up, it was just Dana."

"Are the police looking for Jax?"

"Yes, but he's gone into hiding. The only thing Dana told us was that he sometimes visited an ex-wife around here."

Fern set the teapot down and looked at me with an excited gleam in her eye. "He mentioned her to me! Hmmm . . . what did he tell me. She takes care of their granddaughters. He showed me a picture. Just as cute as could be, identical twins, with red hair and freckles and missing front teeth. Like a Norman Rockwell painting."

"Identical? How old?"

"Around six."

I popped the rest of the brownie into my mouth and pondered Fern's words. There couldn't be many red-haired twin girls in the area. I could start with pediatricians. Or the schools. Red-haired. Girls. Sifting through the detritus that fills up my memory, I came up with an image—a double-door stainless steel refrigerator covered with pictures of red-haired girls, a matching set grinning gap-toothed into the camera. A camera held by their grandpa? Could there be two such sets of twins? What was her name . . . Lynn, she'd told me. The oxy lady. Was she christened Lynda Christina Pons?

I couldn't help myself. "Hoo-wee!" I jumped up and spun in a little victory dance. Merle woke up and woofed. "Fern, you are awesome. I think I know who the ex-wife is. She'll give up his whereabouts, and he'll go to jail."

She studied my face. "Are you sure?"

"Wow, what a lucky break." I felt a shimmer of optimism. "I'm going out for a while. You and Bebe stay put, okay? I'll leave Merle with you."

For an answer, Fern crossed her eyes at me, picked up her teacup, and drank. I could almost feel her gaze on my back as I walked to my car. If I were a mind-reader, I'd swear she didn't want me to leave.

In a simpler universe, the cops would bust oxy lady Lynn's butt and wring her until she gave up Jax.

This universe? Not simple.

Fredricks's cubicle in the SBI building was decorated with photos of his boys. He was a proud dad. His computer screen, however, rotated through a show of wine-themed slides, one after another: bottle labels, dewy grapes, misty vineyards, and glasses of wine. I was admiring an artistic arrangement of purple-stained corks, listening to his end of a phone conversation, when I heard the wrong answer. Lynn's name had been flagged in our database as the subject of an ongoing investigation into prescription drug sales, evidence courtesy of yours truly. When Fredricks made a courtesy call to the leader of the team to inform him of our plan to arrest her, I could hear the sputtering and cussing from across the room.

"I guess that means no," Fredricks said, holding the phone away from his ear.

More buzzing sputter.

"Thanks. We'll hold off." He hung up and shook his head. "He says no go. They're building a case against pharmacies, as well as a dozen dealers. The FBI and DEA are involved. If Lynn Pons is arrested now, the case will implode. We don't go anywhere near her."

My mood plummeted into a moshpit of anxious frustration. "Did I tell you Jax showed up at my grandmother's house? I had to move her and Bebe and Oliver into a B&B."

Fredricks nodded. He tipped his chair onto its back legs, creaking ominously under the strain, and stared at the ceiling. He appeared to be thinking about Jax's whereabouts but I wasn't sure. Perhaps he was thinking about pâté, or truffles. "The sheriff's patrols will find him," he said.

"I've bought from his ex-wife three times. She knows me, we chat a little, mostly about her nice jewelry. I'm thinking I might be able to get Jax's contact info from her. Not in a pushy way. Just in conversation."

He let his chair down with a thump. "Absolutely not."

"Why not?"

"If you alert her, the massive wrath of the enforcement arm of the federal government will descend upon me." He pointed to the phone.

"I won't alert her."

"The answer is no."

"When are we going out again?"

He looked at his calendar. "Tomorrow night, if you feel up to it."

"Let's make a buy at Lynn's."

"No."

Reluctantly, I nodded, hating the answer. My fault, for asking the question.

I wandered toward my own cubicle, to kill a few minutes until my appointment with Richard. I loathed my cubicle. Every time I sat down to read memos and write reports, I turned into Eeyore, toiling in gray pessimism. On my cork board were some snaps of Fern and Merle, and a few pictures from a trip to Jamaica with three friends after graduation—posing with Noel Coward's statue at his home, Firefly, perched over a balmy blue bay, climbing Dunn's River Falls, having our hair braided on the beach. Who was that dark-haired girl, the one on the left in the red bathing suit? She looked happy. She wasn't worried about drug sellers or murderers or her reputation in the SBI. She was having fun on her vacation. I had to give up hopes of another vacation when Hogan and I split. We'd been saving for a trip to Ireland, but after our breakup, we divided the money. My half went to pay for roof repairs at Fern's farmhouse.

I knocked on Richard's office door but he couldn't hear me over the screech of his grinder so I let myself in. Richard frowned as he measured the freshly ground coffee into a French press. I paused to admire him, a vision in a subtly checked tan linen suit and tassel loafers. A puff of brown silk swelled out of his breast pocket. His shirt was pale green with tonal stripes, and more stripes—tan and blue and green—lay diagonally across his tie. Checked suit, striped shirt, striped tie—you have to know what you're doing to make that work. He reminded me of a peacock, fine to look at and admire until you were warned away by a shrill scream—the equivalent in Richard's case being his dour expression and stinky cigar.

He carefully poured boiling water into the press, then stirred the slurry with a chopstick. He placed the filter assembly on top and set a timer. Finally, he turned to me. "Stella. You look terrible."

"I know. Getting better though."

"I want to hear about the homicide investigation."

I knew he didn't want to be bored with the details. "I've talked to a lot of people and learned more about the victim, but we have no reason to charge anyone. No witnesses, no evidence. No one's even pointing fingers at a suspect."

"I heard the victim was transsexual. Has to be a factor, no?"

"The guy she was going to marry says he didn't know. And I think he's credible."

"Morales is okay with progress on the case?" He picked an invisible piece of lint off his French cuff and smoothed down his tie.

"Neither of us is," I said. I was getting an uneasy feeling. I never liked talking with Richard in the best of circumstances—he rarely had good news for me—and he hadn't assigned me to support Anselmo Morales because he felt charitable. He thought I'd be able to get results. I wondered if Anselmo had complained about the progress but thought it better not to plant that thought in Richard's mind by asking the question.

The timer dinged and Richard pressed down on the handle, pushing the filter through the coffee carefully and evenly. He poured himself a cup, added about three drops of cream, and sipped. "Aahhh." He put the cup down. "So, bad weekend for you." He paused but I didn't respond. "I'm considering moving you out of the drug business."

Four years with Richard had taught me that his ideas didn't always fit well with my plans. The idea of leaving my job as an undercover drug agent was appealing only if I moved to something I preferred, like homicide. "Why?"

For an answer, he pointed to his finely shaped nose, then to my banged-up one. "We have an opening in arson. How'd you like a trip to Connecticut to train with an arson dog?"

Crunch through cinders while Queenie sniffed for accelerants? I gave a little chuckle so he'd think I thought he was joking. "No thanks."

"Arson is a good career move."

Oh really? Queenie would get all the credit. I failed to see how that could be good for my career. "I really like working on homicide investigations," I said. As I spoke I felt a qualm of doubt—was I any good at it? Surely by now I had interviewed Justine's murderer and just as surely that person was still walking free.

"Think about it. I have a few days to fill the opening. Let me know by Friday." He picked up his cup and swiveled in his chair to admire his view of the employee parking lot. My signal to leave.

I went back to my cubicle and sank into a chair. Richard's suggestion had drained my energy. I closed my eyes and rubbed my forehead. *Come on, Stella, focus.* I pulled out my notebook and flipped through its pages, scanning my notes on a dozen or more interviews. I underlined the dangling threads, circled the thoughts to pursue, and made question marks on facts that needed checking. At six P.M. my stomach was growling, so I picked up my notebook and left the building. Merle needed to be walked. I needed to be anywhere else.

★　★　★　★　★

Since 1895 when its first brick building was erected on a hilltop in the middle of a cluster of dogwood, oak, and tulip trees, the Gardner University campus had grown to more than 90 buildings on 320 acres. Clutching a campus map in one hand and steering with the other, I trolled nearly every one of those acres in search of a legal parking space, until I finally gave up and swung into a half-empty Employees Only lot. Since it was after eight P.M., I hoped the campus police wouldn't care too much about my lack of a parking sticker.

A brisk breeze had cleared away the haze and overhead the heavens were full of stars, a sliver of moon, and the twinkle of airplanes floating to and from Raleigh–Durham airport. I strode along the walkways to Edmonds Hall, an imposing building of pink brick with cream trim, and caught Gregor McMahon on his way out, locking his door.

"You're late." He looked at his watch. "I don't have much time." I was struck, as before, by how stiff and formal he was, an impression not helped by his cervical collar. And how furry, utterly covered with a pelt of black hair.

"I won't be long," I said. A woman poked her head out of the office next to his and looked at me with curiosity. I didn't look like a student. I looked darned cute in a jacket dress, dark blue with short sleeves, and blue and white spectators. I had even made an effort with my hair and tamed most of it into a twist. Gregor nodded at her but didn't introduce us. He unlocked his office, shooed me in, and shut the door. He sat down behind the desk, and I took the only other chair. His desk was clear except for a phone and a pile of manila folders. Behind him, a small table held a laptop and a framed photograph of Gregor and a young woman, both in hiking attire, crouching on a rocky plateau with a vista of sky and clouds behind them. The woman's face was shadowed by her hat brim but I could see a friendly open grin.

"Is that a picture of Emma?" I asked.

His face softened. "We went hiking almost every weekend."

"I have a question about her. How well did she know Justine Bradley?"

He shook his head. "I don't understand."

"Emma's bracelet was found in Justine's room on the day she was murdered. I'm wondering how it got there."

He looked at me with dead eyes and an expression of distrust. "You found Emma's bracelet? The charm bracelet? Where is it?"

"In an evidence envelope at the sheriff's department."

"I want it. She wore it all the time."

"When did you last see it?"

He grimaced. "The day Emma died. I assumed someone in the hospital took it. It was in Justine's room at the B&B?"

"Did they know each other?"

"No. I don't think—no. I mean, I saw them talking at the picnic but Emma was friendly with everyone. When can I have the bracelet?"

"When we find out who murdered Justine." I kept my voice even.

He closed his eyes. "My neck is killing me tonight. Anything else?" He did look miserable, his skin greasy and pale under dark stubble.

"I'm sorry. Just, can you think about this for a minute? Who else can I ask?"

Silence as he appeared to be thinking. Finally he opened his eyes. "Ingrid Hoyt."

"Because . . ."

"She was a friend of Emma's. In fact, she introduced us."

"When and where?" Just another tangle in this mess of knots.

"Four years ago, in July. Some friends from State had rented a big beach house on Oak Island for July Fourth week. Kate and Ingrid were there too, and one night Ingrid called some of her Wilmington friends to join us for a beach bonfire. Emma came and we met and started talking and . . ." He pulled a handkerchief from his pants pocket and blew his nose hard. "She was really special. I'm sorry."

"That's okay. I understand." I remembered the picture in Gia's apartment, the happy group around the bonfire toasting marshmallows, drinking beer.

"It sounds really corny but she was my sunlight. When she died, my world died. I would like to have the bracelet." He folded his arms across his chest and winced.

I wondered what Emma had seen when she met him. I saw a fur-covered pain-wracked man with an unpleasant manner. Perhaps he was just unpleasant to me. Perhaps the pain was recent. "I'll see that you get it," I said.

# Chapter 22

*Tuesday Mid-Morning*

Bebe had offered to fix breakfast and Camilla had been easily convinced to let her.

"Country style," Bebe said. She held an unlit cigarette in one hand and a brown crayon in the other. As Ollie leaned over her arm, she carefully colored a horse. She had a nice technique, outlining first then filling in. "Cheese grits, ham, fried apples, eggs, biscuits."

"We all loved it," said Fern. "Then banana pudding."

"Oh dear. Dessert too?"

"It's a B&B. Breakfast needs to be special," Bebe said. Ollie handed her a red crayon and she started on the horse's mane and tail.

"It was good," Ollie said, watching every expert stroke of Bebe's crayon. "I like this place."

"Where is Camilla?" I asked.

"Shopping and visiting her father in Salisbury," Fern said. "She said there weren't any check-ins so she'd be gone until this evening. We have this lovely home all to ourselves. She left me a project." She pointed to a box emitting a flowery fragrance. "Packages of bath grains. She bundles them together and sells them."

Since I was just hanging out, waiting for a call from Justine's brother, I offered to help. The bath grains were in small envelopes illustrated with a line drawing of a magnolia. Fern had found some watercolors and was painting the envelopes, giving each flower a wash of pink. She handed me a piece of pink sheer ribbon. "Tie this around five packets, then stick on a price label."

"I can handle that." The ribbon's silver edges were wired so that it held a nice bow and I could scrunch the ends. "How's this?" I held up my first effort.

Oliver looked up from the coloring book. "Pretty."

"You have to go, Ollie?" Bebe asked. He was clutching himself. He nodded. "Come on, then." She heaved herself to her feet and he followed her down the hall.

"He's a nice little boy," I said.

"He is," Fern agreed. "You know, something is bothering me, Stella."

"What?" I looked at her. She was her usual blooming self this morning, her skin fresh, her eyes clear. Yesterday's worries had been dispelled with a good night's sleep and a country breakfast. Whatever was bothering her, it had to be minor.

"I'll tell you now, while Bebe's out of the room. When Camilla started me on this project, she told me to get the scissors out of her son's dresser. After she left, I went up to his room. Do you know what I found?"

"Dirty socks?"

"Go up to the third floor and look in his dresser. Top drawer."

"I can't do that."

"Go on. Then come back and tell me what you think."

"What is it? Dirty pictures? Pot?"

"You won't believe me if I tell you. See for yourself."

I shrugged. "Okay." I climbed the two flights of stairs, up to Camilla and Blue's rooms at the top of the house. The wide hall landing was their living area, furnished with a comfortable sofa, desk, and TV cabinet. An open door led into a bedroom where a flowered nightgown had been flung onto a chair and a clutch of makeup littered a cherry wood dresser. A second door was closed, and I opened it tentatively, feeling squeamish at invading Blue's private space, but at the same time curious to know what was bothering Fern.

The room was furnished in golden oak with a dark blue area rug and bedspread, and very neat. Drawings had been thumbtacked everywhere, pictures of futuristic cars and spaceships, robots and aliens, meticulously detailed and wonderfully colored. I knew Fern would instantly recognize his talent, but that wasn't what she'd found in his dresser.

I caught a glimpse of myself in the mirror—my face was a mess of greenish-yellow bruises. Ugh. I pulled open the top drawer to expose a couple of *Playboy* magazines. Certainly those had not bothered Fern. But when I lifted the magazines I saw what she meant—five thick wads of cash, fastened with rubber bands. I flipped through each, seeing twenties and fifties, about five thousand dollars. A shocking amount of money that I was certain Blue didn't earn working for Wyatt at the Rosscairn Castle B&B. There could be no *good* reason for it, only really bad ones like theft, drugs, blackmail.

Murder?

I returned the cash and magazines to the drawer, left the room, closed his door, and leaned against it to ponder my next step. This situation would make a good law-school exam question. Camilla hadn't invited me to rifle through her son's belongings. The money wasn't in plain sight. I didn't have a warrant. Ergo, my knowledge of the money wasn't something I could use legally.

But I could take a much harder approach with Blue. I'd suspected he was implicated in the vandalism at the Castle B&B. Now it seemed he was a greedy fool, deep into serious crime. Blue's involvement in a felony would ruin his life and crush his mother's spirit. I wanted to rattle his bones until he gave it up—where did this money come from?

Downstairs, Bebe and Ollie had returned from the bathroom and were once more absorbed in their coloring. Fern caught my eye and I shook my head. We weren't going to talk about the money right now. I was feeling agitated and restless, in no mood to hang around and tie pretty bows until Blue came home from school in five hours. The three of them didn't need me; they were occupied and safe.

"Call me if you need anything," I told them, and picked up my car keys.

My car was a ten-year-old Civic. Whenever I thought about trading it in on a newer car, I'd envision my bank balance, depleted by regular debits for purchases of dog food and Fern's home repairs, and be happy I didn't have a car payment. A state salary only went so far. The Civic got great mileage, so I didn't feel guilty about driving around aimlessly, talking to myself, mulling different theories out loud.

*Ingrid finds dying Justine. Kate next-to-last to see her; someone came in later. Poison came from barn. Blue took poison? Handed poison to killer?* I turned onto 15-501 heading south. *Tricia and Scoop have reason to stop wedding; however, both have alibis during time window. Would Lottie Ember leave Alice alone, trot upstairs and poison bride? To what end? Lottie doesn't seem crazy.* Turned west onto Highway 64. *Gia, however, is crazy. But she's taking pictures. She doesn't take her eyes or camera lens off Mike for an entire hour.* Took the next exit, turned right. *Ingrid friend of Emma McMahon. Ingrid friend of Justine Bradley. Emma, dead. Justine, dead.*

*Ingrid.* The needle pointed to Ingrid.

My wanderings turned out not to be so random after all. Impelled by frustration and a strong desire to put Jax behind bars, I turned into the stone-walled entrance to Victory Ridge. Fredricks had not forbidden me to drive by Lynn's house, park a few houses away, and get out of my car. At that point I stopped thinking about what Fredricks had forbidden. Since I'd bought oxycodone from Lynn a few times, she might trust me. What if I just asked her for the name of a cocaine dealer? She might give me Jax's phone number. Or I could tell Lynn that I knew him, but his phone number wasn't working. Just bring his name up idly, as I admired the pictures of her grandkids and stocked up on painkillers.

A red minivan was parked in the driveway but no one answered the clack of the brass door knocker. I heard muffled voices from behind the house, then the unmistakable sprong sprong of a diving board. I went around to the side, encountering an eight-foot privacy fence and a man clipping shrubbery. We exchanged "holas" then continued with our tasks—his, attacking an overgrown half-dead butterfly bush, and mine, peering through a chink in the fence.

The pain pill business must be lucrative. I saw a twenty-five-foot pool surrounded by a flagstone patio. Teak benches and planters under a vine-covered pergola. At the pool's shallow end sat Lynn, wearing a black bathing suit and a floppy white hat and dangling her feet in the water. At the deep end, swimming laps—Jax Covas.

He touched the concrete, flipped, and started back. He swam like a machine, not particularly fast but strong and steadily. When he reached the opposite end he rolled again, and on this lap he faced me as he turned his face out of the water for air. Was it my imagination or did his one good eye seem to drill through the chink in the fence, espy me spying on him?

My heart began pounding like an unbalanced washing machine on spin cycle. I took a quick step back from the fence and sped back to my car to call the Essex County sergeant.

"I've located Jax Covas. But there's a problem. We can't arrest him where he is." I told the sergeant about Lynn and the complications of the investigation into the prescription drug sales. He asked me to wait, he'd have a unit in an unmarked vehicle there within ten minutes to follow Jax and arrest him.

I scrunched down in my seat to wait. The air was waterlogged, the sky dark, and thunder growled in the distance. Jax would get out of the pool when the rain began. My phone rang—it was Justine's brother returning my call. He was the only person I knew, besides Ingrid, who might know something about Justine's relationships prior to her engagement to Mike. He was at his nursery, he told me, sorting bulbs for a sale on the weekend.

"Remember the charm bracelet I showed you?" I asked. "Turns it out belonged to a woman named Emma McMahon. Do you know her?"

"I don't recognize that name."

"Emma was a friend of Ingrid Hoyt's. From Wilmington."

"If Johnny knew her in Wilmington . . . it would have been during high school or earlier."

*Duh. High school.* "Before she married, Emma's last name was Grantham. Emma Grantham."

Daniel paused. "Oh, sure. Johnny had a friend named Emmy Grantham. They went to junior prom together. I remember her. Bubbly, funny."

"They dated?"

"Well, Johnny didn't really date girls. But he tried to fit in. Emmy was a friend."

"What about the picture—could one of the two girls have been Emma?"

He paused. "Emmy had long dark hair like the girl in the picture. It was a long time ago, you know, and I didn't know her well. I'd hate to send you down the wrong path."

"Did they remain friends? I'm trying to figure out why Justine had that bracelet."

"I don't know, sorry."

Emmy Grantham, Emma Grantham McMahon. Had to be the same. I'd thought Emma and Justine first met at the fateful picnic when Emma died. But they'd known each other well, when Justine was John. They'd been friends. So surely, when they met at the picnic, Justine recognized Emma. Did Emma recognize the new John, the feminized version with long hair, breasts, a new nose and chin, and a brand-new rock on her third finger, left hand? Did she react, or look twice, or ask a leading question?

Justine had to be consumed by fear that Emma could ruin it all for her. Then how convenient for her that Emma had a fatal reaction to an allergen. How convenient for her that Gregor couldn't find his car keys to get the epi-pen out of his car. How convenient for Justine that Emma perished that day.

I was so focused on sorting these bits and pieces into a theory that I almost didn't notice Jax come out of Lynn's house. He got into the red minivan, backed out of the driveway, and headed toward me. He was using his phone, and probably not paying attention to the cars on the street, but I turned away as he passed, just in case. I started my car and eased onto the street. As soon as he was around the corner I made a quick U-turn and began to follow, staying well back. I punched the number of the Essex County sergeant into my cell, to give him the bad news that we were on the move. "Stay on the line. I'll get dispatch and find out what happened," he growled.

It had begun to rain, fat drops that smacked my windshield hard. Jax swung onto Highway 87 and headed south. I kept a considerable distance between us, as traffic was light and the red minivan was easy to follow. After five minutes he made a right onto Gum Springs Road. A minute later I made the same turn and realized two things simultaneously—the red minivan was nowhere in sight, and my connection with the sergeant had broken. Dead zone. Ahead lay miles of road through fields and farms, dotted with the occasional business—a carpet store, a massage school, a nursing home. I slowed, scanning the landscape for the red minivan. I tried to get my phone to work but "searching, searching" scrolled across the screen. Yeah, everyone's searching.

Searching paid off as a flash of red down a little-used lane caught my eye. I backed up and turned into the lane, no more than a couple of ruts in the underbrush. I could see the parked minivan about twenty-five yards ahead, next to a sagging weathered barn, in a cleared area. Brambles scratched the side of my car as I inched my way slowly and uneasily. I knew he had been alone in the van, but he could be meeting others and I had no desire to confront Jax and his minions by myself. Backup—where were they? My useless phone was still searching. I stopped the car and rolled my window down. It was utterly quiet—no voices, no rustle of leaves, no birds—but the harsh stink of burning gasoline filled the air. Perhaps the fumes had driven away the birds. When a cloud of black smoke began to billow up from behind the barn I decided to act. I backed up my car almost to the road, where it couldn't been seen from the cleared area, yet still blocked the lane. I opened my trunk and slipped into a Kevlar vest. I took out my duty belt and stripped the first aid kit, knives, and baton from it, leaving the Taser and cuffs. I unholstered my SIG and edged my way along the lane, pressing into the undergrowth to minimize my profile. When I reached the edge of the clearing, the air was slowly being poisoned with acrid smoke that burned my eyes, grabbed my lungs in spasm, and nauseated me with its metallic almost sweet smell. I wondered what he could be burning in this sputtering rain.

The barn was fifty feet away, the minivan parked beside it. Jax was somewhere on the other side. Eenie-meenie-miney-moe. I went to the right, flattening myself against the side of the barn. Now I could hear the fire crackle. My eyes watered and my lungs burned as the smoke enveloped me, pulled up into the atmosphere by the low barometric pressure of the coming storm. I swallowed to hold back my queasiness, and very cautiously looked around the corner of the barn. An element of surprise was inevitable but I also wanted it to be all on his side.

Jax stood in the drizzle with his back to me, a gas can beside his feet, and no obvious weapon—his hands were empty. He watched a flaming pyre, the burning of a partly blackened, recognizably human body, its legs and arms outflung and rigid as if in shock, its torso aflame, resting on a pile of boughs of pine and cedar, bits of two-by-fours.

I stepped into the open, holding my SIG out straight with both hands. "Hands in the air! Now!"

He turned to face me and I saw recognition flash across his face. He smiled. "Stacy, what a surprise. Or are you Stella today?" His voice was smoothing and so smarmy I felt like popping him right there.

"Who's that?" I motioned to the burning body. "And get your hands up."

He looked back at the fire, ignoring my command. "That is not your business, Stella. Now, it is perfect that you are here. I need to talk with you. Come, let's sit. Put your weapon away." He motioned to his minivan, and began to walk quickly toward it.

Talk about arrogance! How did he know I wouldn't shoot him in the back? I swapped the SIG for the Taser and gave him one last chance to pay attention to me. "Don't touch the car."

He reached out to the car door handle so I squeezed the trigger like I meant it, overrode the five-second cycle twice, and the silvery threads fluttered as wattage pulsed through his body over a hundred times, giving him the mother of all full-body charley horses. He toppled and writhed, shrieking reflexively until I stopped, and before the effects could wear off, I pulled him to his feet, not easy as he was essentially quaking dead weight, and relieved him of a loaded Rohrbaugh R9, then cuffed his arms to the car door handle. He collapsed onto the wet ground and glared at me with his one good eye. I imagined he was angrier at the loss of control than the neuromuscular pain caused by the Taser.

I ran back to the fire. Despite the splashings of gasoline, the flames had died down to a mere smolder. It's difficult to burn a body, especially a near-emaciated one with as little fat for fuel as this one appeared to have. I found a thick dead branch and pushed the body off the embers onto the ground. The truly awful stench made me gag. I can't adequately describe what it smelled like—perhaps something like pork marinated in chemical waste.

The body's extremities—its arms from the elbows down, and its lower legs—were not burned. The forearms were heavily and colorfully tattooed. The tattoos, red and black abstract designs of spikes and swirls, looked familiar. I covered my mouth and nose with my hands and leaned in more closely to study them. I'd seen those designs before, draped across the front seat of a dented station wagon, when Bebe drove Fredricks and me to buy the kilo, just before Mo tied a blindfold across my eyes. Those red and black tattoos had decorated Mo's forearms.

This was Mo's body that Jax had been trying to burn.

The smells and the smoke and adrenaline suddenly overwhelmed me, and I felt dizzy. I staggered away from the fire, around the barn to escape the noxious fumes, stopping only to vomit up a sour liquid, choking and gagging again and again as my body tried to expel the poison of this place.

Cuffed to his minivan, Jax was going nowhere, but I needed backup to bring him in. My cell phone was still searching so I ran back to my car to drive out of the dead zone. Once I reached Highway 64 and passed the herd of brown cows, I parked and called the Essex County sergeant, giving him directions to Jax and Mo's burning body. I told him I'd meet him there. It was raining harder now, and wind gusts rocked the car.

I wasn't in any particular hurry to get back to Jax. Let him ponder the burning body, contemplate his future in the courts, and drown in the drenching rain. I had an important call to make—someone had to break the news about Mo to Bebe. Perhaps Fern would do it more gently than I could. I dialed the number of the Pink Magnolia Bed and Breakfast. It rang a dozen times until the answering machine picked up. I hung up and redialed twice. Surely Fern and Bebe were there—they didn't have a car and they were essentially hiding out.

When she finally answered the phone, Fern was out of breath. "Stella! You'll never guess what—Bebe's water broke! Ricky's going to be here in about a half hour to take us to the hospital. Can you meet us?"

"Uh, don't know." I changed my mind on the spot—it was a terrible time to tell Fern and Bebe about Mo. It could wait a few hours. Let Bebe have her baby first.

"As soon as he gets back, Blue's going to watch Oliver. Everything's under control, don't worry."

"Where did Blue go?"

"He's gone to return the money."

"He took the money with him?"

"Well, sure. How else would he return it?"

"Where did he go?" I tried to sound calm.

"He arranged a meeting at the Rosscairn Castle B&B. Stella, he's so sweet. I told him I'd found the money and asked him did he earn it. He just blushed. He knew it was wrong. I asked him did his mother know about it? He said no, please don't tell her. And then he made a call, put the money into a backpack,

273

and hopped onto his bike."

Blue. Rides. His. Bike. While carrying thousands of dollars, a payment connected with Justine's murder, I was certain—the deed itself, or assistance in committing it, or silence. Had Blue committed murder for hire? Or, had he seen something he wasn't supposed to? I didn't know which alternative was the most alarming. I had a very bad feeling about Blue and the person he was biking to meet at the Rosscairn Castle B&B.

"When exactly did he leave?"

"Oh Stella, you sound mad. Don't be mad. He's doing the right thing."

I gritted my teeth. "Fern, he's in danger. When did he leave?"

"About two minutes ago."

I snapped my phone shut. From the Pink Magnolia to Rosscairn Castle would take less than fifteen minutes by bike. I was five miles from the Pink Magnolia. Blue had probably taken the Trestle Road shortcut over the single-lane bridge. I thought I could catch him before he got to the Castle. Let the county cops take care of Jax. He was not my priority.

I floored the accelerator and flew just fast enough to avoid hydroplaning in the water sheeting the pavement. US 64 I love you, I thought, you're built for speed. My Civic was doing me proud. I barely slowed at the 15-501 intersection as I shot in front of a school bus. At Trestle Road, I braked and turned. Past Magnolia Manor, the road became a washboard of ruts, but I didn't dare to slow.

As the road twisted and curved, the wheels of my car sprayed gravel, spinning to gain traction. The road was narrow and tall trees hugged its shoulders. At one point, as I was skidding around a sharp turn, my wheels hit a pothole and the loss of traction sent the car into the brush, the wheels spinning until they bit and pulled us back onto the road.

I didn't see Blue until the gravel road straightened and began a downward slope to the river. There he was. About a hundred yards ahead, wearing a red windbreaker and pedaling in the manner of one who rides a bike for transportation, not to train for the Tour de France. He had almost reached the long, single-lane bridge, the one with the uncertain wood railings, built in 1922 for horses and hay wagons to cross one at a time, a protocol that worked only when all parties were aware of it, paying attention, willing to be patient and wait. I felt a rush of relief that Blue was okay. He rode onto the wooden bridge as I coasted to my end and stopped, waiting for him to get across before I followed. The bridge was wide enough for a car and a bike abreast, but it would be a tight fit, and I didn't want to alarm him. The rain had settled into a steady downpour and the bridge roadway was probably slick.

Then I saw another car, a compact sedan, on the opposite side of the bridge, at the top of the rise leading down to the river. Uneasily I watched it roll forward.

Blue's red windbreaker was plastered against his body as he struggled across the bridge in the wind and the rain. He was almost halfway across when it became obvious that the oncoming car was picking up speed, not slowing, as it grew closer to the bridge and Blue on his bike. "Can't even wait to get your money back, can you," I muttered, and floored the accelerator.

My rear tires slipped on the gravel and the car fishtailed, smashing the wooden railing and for an instant it felt like one tire was over the edge, then it grabbed the bridge road surface and I centered the wheel, heading straight-on toward the oncoming car. Passing Blue, I caught a glimpse of his pale face half-hidden by the red hood, his expression of fear like a mirror.

About twenty feet past Blue, just at the halfway point on the bridge, I smashed into the oncoming car. At the very last, the other driver braked and swerved right. But I didn't pull right, and I didn't slow down, and as I hit the driver's side of that car at eighty feet per second, the energy of the collision sent both cars spinning, crashing through the wooden guard rails, into the river.

Instantly disoriented by the stunning force of the exploding airbag, for a moment I was unable to breathe, then the cold water pouring into the broken windows panicked me. The airbags were deflating and I struggled to undo my seatbelt as water flooded into the car, the car tilted onto the driver's side. . . . *don't panic don't panic* . . . and I squeezed my way past the airbag and through the passenger-side window up to the surface of the murky river as the car slowly sank toward the silty bottom. I swam to the other car, fast as I could, but I was hampered by my vest, my clothing, and the river was so murky with silt that I could hardly see the car. The driver's door was crumpled, and as I felt around in the mess of airbag, glass, and metal, a jagged edge sliced my arm, then I touched a face, and something different, and I began to need air, but I tugged until it gave and I needed air real bad so I burst to the surface, knowing it was too late for whoever had been driving.

I sucked in a great lungful of damp mist, and another, then turned and floated toward the riverbank. Cold rain fell onto my face and blood poured from my arm, mixing with river water, and running in rivulets over the prize I'd pulled from the neck of the dead driver.

A cervical collar.

# CHAPTER 23

*Tuesday Early Evening*

By the time I dragged myself to the river's bank, a precipitous slope of muddy rock, Blue was there to grab my hand. Together we scrambled up to the road. It was raining harder, now, and he was as wet as I was, but chilled from the wind. His teeth chattered as he shivered with cold, living up to his name.

"Get us some help," I said. "Hop on your bike and find someone with a car."

"Which way?" he asked.

"Whichever way's shorter."

He got on his bike and pedaled onto the bridge, up the hill toward the Rosscairn Castle. I examined my right arm. It was sliced open below the elbow, bleeding but not arterial, and starting to hurt. I decided to ignore it. Pain is in the brain and I had other problems. Gusty winds, cold rain, and a head-to-toe soaking had me shivering uncontrollably. Help would be a while in coming, and I was concerned about the effects of hypothermia. To generate some heat, I started jogging along the bridge after Blue. When I reached the splintered railings, I slowed and briefly glanced down, but the water was too murky to see Gregor McMahon's car. Or his body. I struggled on, miserably cold, until Wyatt's white minivan appeared and the doors opened and Blue jumped out with a blanket. Blue was turning out to be quite the little genius, though he had some explaining to do.

And in only moments, it seemed, we were at the Castle B&B, where Liesle performed first aid on my arm, and then let me root through a bag of items left by their B&B guests. I found a pair of too-big sweatpants, socks, a white tee-shirt, and a very nice black Merino wool cardigan sweater she said I could keep. She handed me shampoo and pushed me into a bathroom for a shower.

After all the river-stink had been washed from both of us, Blue and I cozily sipped hot chocolate in the parlor in front of a blazing fire. I ran my fingers through my hair to help it dry, feeling victorious and alive and warm in my new sweater, with Liesle's cocoa in my tummy, Jax under lock and key, and Justine's murderer in the drink. Or perhaps, by now, in the morgue.

"You saw McMahon in the barn, the morning of the wedding, didn't you?" I said.

Blue shrugged. "I knew he was a guest. I remembered that collar thing he wore. I was scared he'd see me."

"Because . . ."

He blushed, and pulled the blanket more closely around his shoulders. "I was messing with the water tank."

"Tell me more."

"I put a dead squirrel in it. You know, when I was . . ."

"That doesn't matter right now. What about McMahon?"

"Dude came into the barn, and like, scared me. I squeezed behind the tank to hide. He looked at all the chemicals. Finally he opened one and poured some into a plastic bag and left."

"So when you heard Justine had been poisoned with strychnine, you decided to blackmail him?"

Blue looked affronted. "No!"

I raised my eyebrows. "You contacted him?"

He stretched out his long legs toward the fire. "It sounds stupid."

"We all do stupid things. What?"

"I didn't want anyone to know I saw him because then they'd know what I was doing in the barn. But I thought he'd turn himself in if he knew someone saw him. So I got his name and phone number from his registration card and called him."

"He didn't turn himself in, obviously."

"He said she was a murderer, but it couldn't be proved in court. That she was a phony woman and he couldn't let his friend marry her. He didn't think she'd die, he said. Her dying was an accident."

"He gave you money?"

Confusion flickered across his face. I waited while he tried to work it out.

"He gave me five thousand dollars to be cool. He figured out I'd messed with the water tank. He said I was an accessory."

"Hush money."

"I spent some on a phone. But I knew it wasn't right."

"So when Fern asked you about it—"

"Fern?"

"My grandmother. Staying at your mom's B&B."

"Oh yeah. She's cool. I showed her some of my drawings and she wants me to join her painting class."

"Fern said you should give the money back?"

"Not exactly. She asked whether I earned it and did my mom know."

I nodded. How well I knew Fern's gentle oblique approach with teenagers, asking that one question you didn't want to answer.

"Who do I give it to now that the dude's dead?"

"I don't know." Maybe Blue deserved to keep the money, given that Gregor McMahon intended to kill him on the bridge. A survivor's reward.

★ ★ ★ ★ ★

My eyes were red and irritated from the river water, so I closed them. The next thing I knew, someone was gently waggling my blanket-covered foot. The fire had almost gone out, the rain had stopped, and through the big windows at the end of the room I could see the mid-afternoon sun hitting waterlogged air, creating a rainbow. Looked like its end was somewhere over Durham, parts of which could use a pot of gold.

"You okay?" Anselmo said. He stood at the foot of the couch, looking solicitous.

I sat up and stretched, aware of how disheveled I was, wearing secondhand clothes and blood-stained bandages, my hair an untamed tangle, my face still a mess of bruises. Someday, I thought, I'm going to clean up nice for this man, married or not. "I'm cold. Apparently Wyatt doesn't believe in central heating. What's up?"

"They pulled both cars out. One body."

"Uh, where's Blue? He was there."

"He just left, with his mother, in a cop car, to be interviewed."

"Geez, did Wyatt see them?" Wyatt would have been surprised to learn who Blue's mother was, and I missed that. "Oh, never mind. You want to know how McMahon ended up in the river. Have a seat." I pulled my legs up to give him room on the couch. "Wait, put more logs on the fire first."

He crouched in front of the fireplace, rearranging the logs and adding kindling, until flames blazed and the wood crackled. When he sat down on the couch, next to my blanket-wrapped toes, I wedged them against his solid warm hip. "My feet are really cold," I said. "Sorry."

He didn't seem to mind. "I talked with Blue," he said. "Based on what he saw in the barn, and what Gregor McMahon told him, we can close the case. McMahon said Justine Bradley caused his wife's death? I thought he barely knew Justine."

"That's right, he didn't know her. But his wife, Emma, did. You know, we were looking at Justine's murder from the wrong angle. We thought someone may have murdered her because she was transsexual, to stop the wedding. But she was murdered because she tried to keep her gender change a secret. So badly, in fact, that she allowed Emma McMahon to die at that picnic six months ago."

"She allowed her to die?"

"Imagine Justine's fright when Emma shows up at the picnic. Emma's a childhood friend, the only person for miles who knew her as John. They even went to a prom together. Justine hasn't informed her boyfriend Mike of her sex change, though Mike just slipped a giant rock on her finger. Now Emma is Allergy Queen, always has been, and Justine would have been well aware of that. Does she warn her—hey, there's cashew butter in that chili you're about to enjoy? She does not. How could she? She's Justine, not the old pal Johnny who knows what Emma's allergic to. Five-ten minutes later, as Emma's gasping for breath, why is Gregor McMahon's car locked? What happened to Gregor's keys? He can't get into the car fast enough and Emma dies. It's cold-blooded but it ends Justine's panic that someone would reveal her past, on that day of all days."

Anselmo half turned on the couch, and pulled my left foot onto his lap. He began to knead the arch of my foot. "Uh, is that appropriate?" I whispered. The sensations were religious. I closed my eyes to concentrate.

"Shut up. They're just feet." He began to gently squeeze each toe in turn. "Blue said McMahon looked through the chemicals in the barn and took some of the gopher bait. It's a reasonable inference that he poisoned Justine. Only . . . why then, right before the wedding?"

"Oh that feels good. Don't ever stop." I opened my eyes and uncrossed them. "The previous evening, Justine had given everyone at the dinner a copy of her cookbook. The chili recipe—the same chili she took to the picnic—lists cashew butter as an ingredient. Let's conjecture that Gregor notices the recipe, as he might have done, because her chili was a big hit at the picnic. Perhaps someone asks specifically about the recipe, and she talks about the unusual ingredients. Gregor hears 'cashew butter' and makes the connection—Emma was deathly allergic to it—and he realizes that Justine's chili might have caused Emma's reaction. Then, a few hours later, Ingrid delivers the bombshell news to Mike's parents that Justine is transsexual, and that she, Ingrid, knows this because she went to school with Johnny Bradley, now Justine Bradley. Someone in the inn was standing in the hall, and overheard that conversation. I'm pretty sure that it was Gregor."

"A recipe? Sex-reassignment surgery? How would he put them together?"

"He has all night to think it through. He knows that Emma, like Justine, was a friend of Ingrid's through high school. He realizes that Emma knew Justine when she was male. Justine would have recognized Emma at the picnic. He remembers Emma enjoying Justine's chili, with its fatal ingredient, cashew butter."

"Pure conjecture."

"It's logical. The next day, right before the wedding ceremony, Gregor visits Justine in her room. He brings the bracelet—perhaps to show her the caduceus symbol. Possibly he wants Justine to admit that she knowingly served Emma something that would kill her. Does Justine confess anything? Or not? Either way, he realizes that she will never, ever, be punished for his wife's death. Justice will not be served. Maybe she says something rash. The guy could bring out the worst in people, I tell you."

Anselmo slowly pulled the sock off my left foot. He pressed

his thumbs into the sole, working from the heel to the toes. His hands were warm, strong, tender, and my foot was happy. "It explains the bracelet being in Justine's room, gives McMahon a motive for Justine's murder and the attempt on Blue's life," he said. "And going back to the picnic, it explains why Justine allowed Emma to die. But we'll never know what happened in Justine's room that morning."

I imagined Justine in her bridal finery, admitting Gregor into her room. He holds out the bracelet and points to the caduceus symbol. He insists she knew about Emma's allergies, to insect stings and nuts and too much sun. Justine doesn't realize the danger she's in. She's preoccupied because she's going to be married in a few minutes. Does she ignore his accusation and turn to the mirror to admire the pearl strands in her beautifully coiled hair? Does the teapot whistle, and he offers to pour the boiling water over the tea bag for her? *"Sugar, Justine?"* he asks. *"A bit of soymilk?"* She smiles, admiring her reflection, her perfect nose and chin, her satin-covered curves. She takes the mug from him. *"Thank you so much, I am a bit thirsty."* She drinks. He watches for a few minutes, then leaves to join his friend Mike, Evan Ember, and Scoop Scott in front of the gathered guests, who wait patiently. I shivered, thinking of the agony of Justine's last minutes.

"You still cold?"

"Thank you. My feet are much warmer now."

He took the sock off my right foot and started that thing he did with his thumbs on the sole of my foot. I closed my eyes as his hands tenderly kneaded the arch, just firmly enough not to tickle. They're just feet. I was finally warm, suffused with an unusual feeling of relaxed contentment I decided must be happiness. I sank into it, as the fire snapped and crackled. Outside, gusts of wind blew spatters of rain against the windows.

# CHAPTER 24

*A Saturday Many Months Later, Mid-Afternoon*

Fern's farmhouse looks its very best in May, when, like well-applied makeup, Nature camouflages the property's many flaws. The ramshackle woods encircling her field are dotted with dogwoods, their floating white-petaled flowers distracting the eye from the rampant kudzu. In the field, lush grasses disguise the gopher holes and mole tunnels. Carolina jasmine winds around the crumbling wood of the trellis over the front door.

Fern had planted white impatiens among the blue iris clumping along the cinder-block foundation of the house, and the flowers almost succeeded in diverting any visitor's gaze from peeling paint and missing porch rail balusters. Earlier in the week, Mike Olmert had replaced a dozen rotted floorboards, so the porch was safe for the brides to stand on while they spoke their vows.

Perhaps others didn't notice the falling-down aspects of her house as much as I did. I guess it looked historic and charming, ideal for a small wedding. Er, commitment ceremony. Gay marriage is unconstitutional in North Carolina, so although family and friends would witness Ingrid and Kate's ceremonial vows, there would be no marriage license.

"You're in charge of flowers," Fern said. She slid another bobby pin into my hair to capture an errant curl that threatened to spoil the "do" she'd copied from a picture in a magazine.

I didn't mind; I was glad to be able to help out. I'd worked one summer for a florist and knew my way around foam, wire, aquapics, and tape. "There's two hours left. Where am I going to get flowers?" I asked, turning my head to catch her eye. "And more importantly, how come you don't have a tummy?"

"Good posture and sit-ups, darling. And I don't eat ice cream every night like you do. Kate went up to the farmer's market in Carrboro real early and bought buckets of flowers. Hold still." She aimed the spray can at my head and I closed my eyes while she misted me. "There. Go take a look."

I went into the bathroom. My hair was pulled up into a complicated twist that any mild breeze could dismantle. Fern peered over my shoulder, tucking in strands here and there. "Turn around," she said. "You should wear dresses more often. Shows off your—"

"My hot bod. I know. Point me to the flowers and tell me what's needed."

"They're in the kitchen. Here." She handed me a list.

I headed for the kitchen, where I had to look twice before I recognized Tricia Scott, counting silverware. Her hair had reverted to its natural silver, cut short and spiky, and her skin was a light golden tan. I told her she looked great.

She laughed. "My hair? Rinse and run. Half my life is on the beach, the rest is snorkeling."

"The tours for couples?"

"Yup. Going great. We go to resorts in Belize and Cancun. My speakers like it so much they work just for expenses. You should join us. Do you have a boyfriend?"

Did I? Hogan's relationship with Candy had foundered over her refusal to appear in public with him, but he'd wasted not a day in finding a replacement, a nice woman who read books for the blind. Even Fredricks had a girlfriend, a veterinarian's assistant he'd met when he took his boys' new puppy in for shots. The only other man in my life was the state trooper who flew me around in a helicopter to look for indoor pot farms with a thermal imager. Yesterday he'd put his moist and meaty hand on my thigh. Did that count?

"Not at the moment," I said. "Maybe if you had one for singles."

She looked at me searchingly. "I just might do that. In fact, it's a brilliant idea. I'm single myself, did you hear? My ex is in jail. All I can say is—thank the Lord Scoop didn't let me own any part of his quote unquote church or I'd have been an accessory."

The kitchen counters were covered with plastic-covered serving dishes—collard greens, Brunswick stew, cornbread, fried chicken, deviled eggs, succotash, pickles of every variety. On the stove, a big pan of barbeque was warming. "Smells good in here," I said.

"I can't take the credit," Trish said. "Most of it's catered off a Sunday-after-church menu."

Bemused by the old-timey meal and Tricia's transformation into a hip divorcée, I pulled the bucket of flowers over to the table. I scanned Fern's list and mentally matched it with the contents of the bucket—tulips, peonies, iris, forsythia and larkspur, with plenty of astilbe and ferns for filler. I clipped three pieces of larkspur, added a fern leaf, and taped them to a white tulip. Corsage number one, check. I started on the second one. "This is a good day for you, then?" I asked.

She nodded. "Kate's so happy. She really loves Ingrid. I'm almost jealous—I don't think I've ever had that in my whole life."

"You will, Tricia. Just get that singles retreat going."

After I finished the flower arrangements, I went outside to find Kate and Mike.

Mike and his fellow fireman had recently completed the

chicken house, a favor Fern had returned by painting a portrait of their retiring chief. The coop still smelled new, like pine boards and clean straw. A dozen bantam chickens—little red birds with feathery feet—cackled softly and hustled themselves out of the way when I stepped into their domain. In the outside run under a vine arbor, Kate twirled slowly in a white ruffled dress, an off-shoulder muumuu style. She beamed when I handed her the bouquet of pink tulips and white peonies. "Gorgeous," she said, "thank you."

Mike looked different—his head was shaved and he wore wire-rim glasses. I pinned his boutonnière, a white tulip, to his blue-flowered Hawaiian shirt, and he opened his arms for a hug. I obliged with trepidation—it was like cuddling with a refrigerator.

"Thank you," he said. "For too much. You almost lost your life. That was very brave."

"Firefighters are brave," I said. "I acted without thinking."

He looked grim. "Gregor wasn't who I thought he was."

"Obviously." Kate shuddered. "You chose him to be your best man."

"The boy who saw him in the barn—Blue? Said Gregor claimed it was an accident," I said. "If that helps."

"Maybe. Sorry I brought it up." He looked at his watch. "Five minutes to go. You ready, sis?"

Kate pumped her arms up in a victory salute, like she'd just trounced one of the Williams sisters in straight sets.

We sat in a semicircle of borrowed lawn chairs, cooled by the green shade of the big maple trees. Next to me, Bebe held her baby on her lap. A chunky drooling fellow, he cooed at me like the big flirt he already was as he chewed on a string of plastic beads. He and Oliver wore matching outfits—white shirts, navy blue pants, and red-and-white striped vests, unmistakably hand-knit. Fern had found a new outlet for her knitting needles.

Bebe had gained some weight and lost that haggard look. She smiled, and I saw that her teeth had been repaired—they were straight, white, and all present-and-accounted-for. "Your grandma took me to this dentist friend of hers and I got veneers, nearly free. Though I have to cut his hair for, like, five years." She barked a laugh. "I'm getting my license again, did she tell you?"

"Good for you," I said, just as the musicians began to play a haunting jig tapped out on a hammered dulcimer and guitar. From the chicken house, Kate and Mike emerged arm-in-arm, and walked to stand in the center of the half-circle. The only hint of Kate's usual tension was a flexing of her fingers and a half-manic grin on her face as she waited.

We all waited. Minutes passed. I felt a small pang of apprehension, completely irrational, just a smidge of déjà vu all over again. Finally, the front door opened and Ingrid appeared between her parents. She was no longer rectangular. Her cheeks were plump and her breasts swelled up from her dress, a ruffled white muumuu like Kate's. The folds of the dress only partly disguised her curving belly.

"Baby's due in three months," Fern whispered to me.

Ingrid took Kate's hand and began to speak her vow of simple love, partnership, shared dreams of family. Then it was Kate's turn to speak, her voice strong and clear. Ingrid's mother sniffled; Tricia sighed. Mike blinked and swallowed. The two women kissed gently, and then it was over. The dulcimer and guitar duo began winkling happy chords in a major key.

Fern was smiling mysteriously.

"What are you thinking?" I asked.

Her sea-blue eyes scanned my face. "What I am thinking is . . . I think they look happy." A strand of my hair had escaped from the up-do and dangled over my nose. She tucked it back into place and patted my cheek. "There. Now you're perfect."

# JUSTINE BRADLEY'S CHILI RECIPE FROM *ENCHANTED FOOD*

1/4 c. olive oil
1 med. onion, chopped
1–2 cloves garlic, minced
2–3 large carrots, chopped
1 6-oz can tomato paste
1 red or green bell pepper diced (optional)
2 c. veggie stock or water
1 15-oz can black beans
1 15-oz can garbanzo beans
2 15-oz cans dark red kidney beans
2 T. red curry paste
1/4 cup cashew butter
2 T. bourbon
1 1/2 oz. dark chocolate bar
1/2 tsp each: ground cumin, chili powder, cayenne pepper, black
    pepper, salt, dried ground basil, garlic powder.

Sauté onions in olive oil five minutes, add garlic and cook
another minute. Add remaining ingredients and stir until mixed.
Cook 30–45 minutes over low heat. Serves 6.

# ABOUT THE AUTHOR

**Karen Pullen**'s short stories have appeared in *Ellery Queen Mystery Magazine, Spinetingler, Crime Scene Scotland,* and the anthology *Fish Tales.* She earned an MFA in Popular Fiction from Stonecoast at the University of Southern Maine. She lives in Pittsboro, North Carolina, where she teaches memoir writing and fiction workshops. *Cold Feet* is her first novel. Updates on Karen and her writing may be seen at www.karenpullen.com.